Faces in the Pool

Faces in the Pool

JONATHAN GASH

First published in Great Britain in 2008 by
Allison & Busby Limited
13 Charlotte Mews
London W1T 4EJ
www.allisonandbusby.com

A CIP catalogue record for this book is available from
the British Library.

10 9 8 7 6 5 4 3 2 1

13-ISBN 978-0-7490-7905-5

Typeset in 13/16 pt Garamond by
Allison & Busby Ltd

The paper used for this Allison & Busby publication
has been produced from trees that have been legally sourced
from well-managed and credibly certified forests.

PEFC
PEFC/16-33-111
CATG-PEFC-052
www.pefc.org

Printed and bound in Great Britain by
MPG Books Ltd, Bodmin, Cornwall

JONATHAN GASH is an award-winning author who has been writing for thirty-five years. A retired doctor, he worked for many years in the Middle and Far East.

AVAILABLE FROM
ALLISON & BUSBY

The Lovejoy Series
The Ten Word Game ● *Faces in the Pool*

The Dr Clare Burtonall series
Bone Dancing ● *Blood Dancing*

Other Crime Fiction
The Year of the Woman ● *Finding Davey*
Bad Girl Magdalene

ALSO BY JONATHAN GASH

The Lovejoy Series

The Judas Pair ● *Gold From Gemini* ● *The Grail Tree*
Spend Game ● *The Vatican Rip* ● *Firefly Gadroon*
The Sleepers of Erin ● *The Gondola Scam* ● *Pearlhanger*
The Tartan Ringers ● *Moonspender* ● *Jade Woman*
The Very Last Gambado ● *The Great California Game*
The Lies of Fair Ladies ● *Paid and Loving Eyes*
The Sin Within Her Smile ● *The Grace in Older Women*
The Possessions of a Lady ● *The Rich and the Profane*
A Rag, A Bone and a Hank of Hair ● *Every Last Cent*

The Dr Clare Burtonall series

Different Women Dancing ● *Prey Dancing*
Die Dancing

AS JONATHAN GRANT
The Shores of Sealandings ● *Storms at Sealandings*
Mehala, Lady of Sealandings

AS GRAHAM GAUNT
The Incomer

*For Matthew, Jack, Sarah
and Charlotte*

*Thanks,
Susan and the Lost Tribes*

Chi disprezza compra
(It. 'Who criticises, buys')
LOVEJOY

'Nature takes revenge on those who want to perform
miracles...and forces them into poverty'
LEONARDO DA VINCI

Chapter One

**wallet: one who finances an antiques scam
(trade slang)**

Women and antiques are out there. They mean trouble.
The reason is greed, everybody's greed.

A lady visited me in prison.

She eyed me. 'I'm Ellen Jaynor. You're not much to look
at.'

'You've got the wrong prisoner, missus.'

Her eyes scored points. 'Do you have trouble with
religion?'

Huguenot? No meat on Fridays? Jewish? One lot had
prayer shawls, but was it her team?

'Diwali? Ramadan?'

Her lip curled in contempt. It cheered me up. Right
bloke after all.

I'm nothing to look at, average everything in a worn
jacket. My hair's a thatch. I'd cut the fraying edges of my
shirt cuffs, and my shoes are soled courtesy of Kellogg's
cardboard.

She was bonny. Thirtyish, dressed in blue with an

antique necklace of tourmalines with one showy diamond. I guessed 2.4 carats. No wedding ring, just a hen's egg of a ruby (Sri Lankan, not that Madagascan muddy red people praise these days). Victorian jewellers were class.

The screws and passing gaolbirds were lusting Force Five. I felt proud of my classy lass, but mistakes don't last. Who exactly was Ellen Jaynor, down among us lowlifes?

'I'm offering you a job and a release permit.'

Two months early? Permit is a filthy word. It always sounds its opposite, like licence. 'Er, job?' I didn't want to do another robbery just yet.

'Speed-dating. Merely speaking to women.'

'I do it all the time.'

'The Anglers Manglers Speed-Datery pays a flat rate.'

She gave me a smile like sleet. Women lack trust, I find. 'Balaclava Street drill hall in an hour.'

The screw smiled and let her out. Back in my cell I collected my stuff. I'm not so daft I can't recognise a scam. It had to be antiques because I'm good at nothing else.

One odd thing happened. I went to write my so-longs on the library blackboard, our tradition. There sat Rocco. He was reading. He saw me, and his giant builder's hands flicked the tome under his chair. Hiding something? Rocco can't read. He said good luck. I forgot the incident. You can't explain what happens in gaol.

The nick faces the old Odeon in Crouch Street. I signed out on police bail – a legal shackle to allow lawyers more golf time. The desk screw grinned.

'I've bet you'll be back in five weeks, son.'

'You've lost, George.'

With a flourish I signed *Lovejoy, 1 Hyde Park Gate, London,* and departed. Wellington's old address would irritate them.

Our town's morning rush was in full flow, two buses, one car, a donkey cart and a crocodile of school children going to the Headgate Theatre. Hepsibah Smith their teacher ignored me.

She carolled, 'Hurry, children! We mustn't be late!'

Elizabeth is seven years old and lives in my lane. 'Miss Smith isn't speaking, Lovejoy,' she announced in a voice of thunder. 'You're in prison.'

Hepsibah's lessons in tact had failed. I said, 'Shut your teeth, you little sod.'

'Lovejoy sleeps on his new auntie,' Elizabeth shrilled, 'with her legs—'

'*Elizabeth!*' Hepsibah said, schoolmistress fashion: Eliz-a-*beth*. 'We are ambassadors for our village!'

'I seen him through his window…' Elizabeth's bandsaw voice faded.

Guiltily avoiding stares, I eeled through St Mary's churchyard. So much for the sacking I nail across my cottage window for privacy.

Puzzled by Rocco's concealment, I called in the town's naff bookshop. I recognised the olive-green dust jacket – ugh – and gaped. *Ancient Rock Paintings of North Africa.* Jesus. Well, lots of pretence in the nick.

The drill hall in Balaclava Street looked derelict. I knocked and pushed. 'Hello?'

'About time.' Ellen Jaynor was inside.

She lit a fag, pluming cancer-producing pollutants. The

floor was unswept, a flag drooping from a broken pole.

'Space those tables. Female clients sit against the walls.'

'Eh?' A dance seated on chairs?

'Watch it once round, then join in. Do the tea urn.'

In the anteroom stood a begrimed tea thing, plastic cups and a box of biscuits. Not quite Disney World. I lit the gas burner.

A fat girl came in and sat. Without a word she passed me a tea. Foul, but the best I'd had in weeks.

'I'm Trina. Are you the thief?'

I went red. 'Er, yes.'

'I take the money. Jaynor dongs the bell, stingy old bitch.'

Ellen Jaynor could hear but made no sign. I felt better for an ally.

'Twenty-four today.' Trina showed me her list. I gasped at the fee. For a chat? What happened to saying hello at the bus stop? 'Here. You're not that mare's friend, are you?'

'Never saw her before.'

In case you've never heard of the Anglers Manglers Speed-Datery, I report that it is degradation. No courtship, no sweet glances in Sunday church. In short, we're barbaric.

In speed-dating you're shoved at strangers. It's gab, grab, run to the fun, for now romance begins in a shoddy drill hall, at wonky card tables. Females – any age, any shape – face males – any age, any shape. On the tocsin the sweating males move to the next bird.

Some daters were nervy, others brash. A swig of tea, a dry biscuit and a three-minute natter didn't seem much for paying a fortune, but this was progress. Some women were

young, others middle-aged, one frankly old, most in the
grip of silent hysteria.

Sessions ended on a double bell. Trina ushered them
into the anteroom. Most women clustered, though one or
two mingled. Embarrassment always makes my knees itch.
I stood there filling cups. Eventually Trina beckoned me
in. The bell sounded, and I sat.

'Wotcher,' I said, my chat-up line.

'Maureen,' the girl said irritably. 'Got a car?'

'Where do you want to go?' Her glance withered me.
'Er, no.'

'How much do you get?' And explained, 'Money. Your
job.'

'Er, I'm between jobs.'

Her eyebrows were question-marks one hair thick. I
tried to smile but my smile often has bad days.

'Have you got property? Email?' And when I stuttered
she added, 'Where d'you live?'

'In a rented cottage.' I'd stolen it by means of three
fraudulent mortgages.

She stared as if I'd mentioned leprosy, and called, 'I'm
wasting my frigging time here.'

The merciful bell rang. I moved on. The lady there was
about forty, determined to put a bright face on this brawl.

'Hello.' She gripped her handbag. 'I'm Joanna.'

We spoke in staccato phrases. Joanna worked in a shop,
and had been divorced for seven years. She told me this
in a don't-blame-me rush. I liked her. The bell came too
soon. She looked back. I was a disappointment again.

The kaleidoscope of faces came and went. Tracy was
voluptuous but sneered. Seena had the shakes, craving

doses only a pharmacist would know. The fifth made white-hot demands to prove I wasn't married. Can you disprove a negative? Her final words were, 'I need a fucking drink here.' Romance was in the air, but not in Balaclava Street drill hall.

The sixth was an enemy. I missed the signs.

'Laura,' she said without preamble. 'I'm forty-three. Well?'

Bossy and attractive. Smart suit, with a brooch that caught my eye. 'I only do antiques.' I shrugged.

She cut to the chase. 'What antique is in this bag?'

Laura must be the reason I'd been sprung. When all else fails I go for honesty.

'Show me and I'll have a go.'

Her expression became a snarl. 'I've driven three hundred miles to waste my time. You'll suffer for this, Lovejoy.'

My name? I hadn't told her my name.

'Nice brooch, Laura.'

She was about to sweep out but paused. She peered at her lapel. A rose, four buds, diamonds in silver. 'It's off a street barrow.'

'Lucky you.' I delved into her shopping bag and found a teddy bear, long of snout and hump-naped. 'I thought you said antique.'

'It is a Steiff. It's genuine, unlike you.'

'Worth a lot,' I agreed. 'But 1903 isn't old.'

Uncertainty crept in. 'Made a century ago, and not old?'

'Has to be 150 years before I get the feel.' She went silent. I tried to help. 'Work it out. Its stud is plain, so it's early. Steiffs had an elephant emblem, then this domed blob. Those eyes are only shoe buttons.' I stood to leave.

The bell double-donged. Clients drifted into the anteroom and the next lot filed in. Laura just looked.

'You said about my brooch?'

'*Pavé*-set. Gems laid like paving, each stone held in place by a dot of metal.' I found myself smiling. 'It's genuine 1795, Belgian or French.'

Her eyes narrowed. 'Genuine, without a hallmark?'

'Continental antiques often lack marks. Junk shops mistake genuine jewellery for scrap 1960 lookalikes. So-long, missus.'

'Wait!' Ellen Jaynor grabbed my arm. 'Wait, or I'll not pay you!'

I'd had enough. 'Being bonny doesn't mean you can cheat. Ta-ra.'

Trina fisted the air in silent applause. The Joanna woman was in the foyer. Her expression brightened. 'Oh, Lovejoy. I'm so glad to catch you—'

'Sorry, love.' I pushed past.

The door swung shut. Free! So I thought.

Chapter Two

merk: to face down, disconcert (Lond. slang)

Badly needing to know why I'd been sprung from the nick, I headed for the Sloven Oven, nosh bar and gossip mart. I saw Paltry.

He crossed over. 'You got out, then?'

Paltry wants to change his sex, and hopes gambling will pay for the surgery. Local dealers run a charity so Miami surgeons will make him female. He wears high heels and a flowered skirt, his face a crazy mosaic of cosmetics.

'Look, Paltry, who's been asking about me?'

His painted features went shifty. 'Any chance of a loan? Three-thirty at Doncaster.'

'I'm skint, Palt.'

He teetered on. If you don't contribute, Paltry ignores you. The Sloven Oven Caff is where Woody, a symphony of cellulite, sells cups of outfall and congealing cholesterol fried in gunge. I sat hoping for somebody to buy me some grub, my belly rumbling.

'Lovejoy?' Chloe lodged her white stick on my chair. I think she identifies me by scent. 'Starving?' She signalled to Woody to bring me a special, and half a lentil for her.

She's always on diets. 'Did she find you?'

'Mrs Jaynor? She hired me as a speed-dater.'

Chloe laughed. A star-spangled witch in a vermilion cape covered with zodiac signs, she wears enough bangles to sink a ship. She also has King Lear for a spirit guide. She asked a vacant chair if it wanted anything.

'Does he?' Woody called.

Who believes in this psychic malarkey? Lear, incidentally, was an ancient British king before the Romans landed. You see my difficulty. Ancient kings shouldn't be having tea in Woody's.

Chloe said, 'Lear'll have chips with his usual, please.'

How come King Lear liked spuds, which hadn't reached ancient Britain from America back then?

'Lear says they're an acquired taste,' Chloe told me.

Quickly I stopped thinking. Her pre-emptive rejoinders are weird. I like people to hear what I say before expecting a reply.

'That Laura's a funny woman, Lovejoy,' she said. Other dealers leant to overhear. 'She bribed Paltry. Lear hated her. All fur coat and no knickers.'

Woody brought plates of decent grub – chips, pasties, beans, peas, bread, and tea thick enough to plough. We dined. From politeness, I tried not to watch Lear's plate, but hunger makes things difficult. Chloe says he only eats the essence.

'Chlo,' I said, 'how come you're kind? I'm broke.'

'You sympathised over Cordelia.'

After a séance with Sandy and Mel, exotic partners in the Antiques Arcade, Chloe became an antiques dealer, refugee from some marital uproar. Sandy and Mel thought it 'perfectly sweet'. Local dealers guessed Chloe was off her trolley. I just like her.

'Did I?'

Finishing my repast, I eyed Lear's grub. It seemed a waste of good, wholesome saturated fat.

'She wants you for an antiques hunt.'

That shook me. 'Cordelia?'

'No. That Laura.'

My headaches start at my right temple. I felt the first twinge and thought, Here we go.

An antiques hunt needs a team. I labour alone in my bare-flagged thatched cottage, aka Lovejoy Antiques, Inc., except for a drunken bum called Tinker. My barker is a dosser of low repute who sleeps in St Peter's churchyard.

'Here, Lovejoy.' Paltry would have slid into Lear's chair but I shoved him away. 'Oh, sorry, Chlo, Lear. Didn't think.' He dragged a chair over.

'What?' Paltry had betrayed me.

'Sorry, mate. Not mad, are you? Darrow said her teddy and pin were worth big money.'

I stood to go, when Gentry and Lois, two dealers, came across.

'Settle this argument, Lovejoy.'

Minutes later I was embroiled in a familiar row. Name the greatest ever silver thief.

Lois was giving it, 'The greatest ever is Noddo.'

'Balderdash,' said Gentry, who hated America. 'He's a Yank.'

'Noddo can't help being born in Wisconsin.'

Talk shifted to where Wisconsin actually was. Some dealers guessed it was near Las Vegas.

'Noddo,' I said. 'No question.' Lois applauded.

'Why?' Gentry demanded, moustache quivering.

At that moment I suspected Gentry had engineered the argument. I should have heard warning bells.

Gentry was a real gentleman, gold-headed cane, leather shoes from London's Jermyn Street. He does nothing for a year, then spends a neap tide of money buying up old colonial artefacts from Africa or India.

'Noddo's a loner.' I ticked points off. 'Obsessively tidy, stacks window beading when breaking in. Expert on antique silver. Shuns drugs, drink, smoking.'

Gentry shrugged. 'So he's a pro.'

'Gent, he's formulated his own burglary rules. Sound as a bell.'

'A *silver* bell.' Lois laughed. 'Get it?'

'He depends on lucky breaks.' Gentry loved condemning Americans.

'Like what? Napoleon promoted Marshal Ney *because he was a lucky general.*' I became interested in winning. 'OK, Noddo's only five feet four inches. He's a real cat burglar. He doesn't sweat, eels past any guard dog. He's even burgled mansions staked out by police. He keeps fit, diets.'

'Like you, Lovejoy?' Gentry smiled.

The place erupted. Even the caff cat laughed.

'He's nicked umpteen millions,' I said over the riot.

The assembled dealers moaned in envy, sounding like the onshore winds at Goldhanger.

Gentry played his trump card. 'Then why is he always in gaol?'

'Because neurotic detectives wouldn't give up.'

Amusement died. I'm not taking sides here, just telling how it is.

'Or he wants to be caught.'

'Don't be daft, Lois. Nobody wants to get caught.'

'You're wrong, Lovejoy,' she said seriously.

'Well, I don't.'

Gentry said quietly, 'Then do a job for a friend of mine, eh, Lovejoy? She'll pay well.'

Best offer I'd had all day. He rose and left, touching his hat twice, meaning in two days. I could manage that, unless I died of starvation in the meantime.

The cowbell over the door clonked. Laura no less. 'You can go,' she told Paltry with distaste.

This narked me. We keep Woody's caff secret from punters. Paltry's treachery was a dead liberty. Now even the Sloven Oven was unsafe. She made to sit in Lear's chair. I stopped her.

'That's for friends.'

She appraised Chloe. 'What are you staring at?'

'Nothing.' Chloe has superb logic. 'I'm blind.'

Laura didn't even blink. 'Tough.' She turned to me, suddenly a hell of a lot harder. 'Well, Lovejoy? Prison or money?'

The Sloven Oven's clientele held its collective breath at the world's most sacred word, money.

'You must do a test first.'

'Headache, Lovejoy?' Chloe said, rummaging in her handbag. 'Lear said you've a zinger coming on. Paracetamol?'

'I'll be OK, love.' I stood and told Chloe and Lear so-long and ta for the nosh. Laura looked puzzled at my double farewell but followed me out.

'My limo will be along in a moment, Lovejoy.'

'Cars can't come down this alley.' It was no-entry.

'Rules do not apply to money.'

A saloon motor the size of an Alp glided up and parked, Ellen Jaynor at the wheel. A smirking traffic warden touched his cap.

Laura saw my hesitation. 'In, Lovejoy. You've no choice.'

I got in, leant back and closed my eyes. Julius Caesar, no less, invented the world's first off-street parking laws, but not for the moneyed, I supposed.

chapter Three

honest: genuine (of an antique, trade slang)

Sitting on a newspaper stops travel sickness, but no luck in the limo.

'Do a successful test, we'll pay you well.'

'And if I fail?'

She smiled. Ellen smiled. I distrust smiles. A university recently tested women's intuition. Men spotted false smiles better by a whopping seventy-two per cent.

'Then it's back to prison, Lovejoy.' They laughed. Laughs can't be trusted either.

We floated to the Donkey & Buskin, a quiet tavern near the estuary. We went to an upstairs room. Old Mr Smethirst was there.

'Wotcher, Lovejoy,' he said. 'I guessed it might be you.' He gestured to the table. 'Best I could get, son. Will they do?'

'Dunno yet, Smethie.'

'Seven items, as you instructed, lady.' Smethie was all anxious.

'Get out,' Laura commanded. He obeyed.

So Laura must be new money. People who get a massive windfall cloak uncertainty with bullying. The most obvious giveaway, though, is they are deliberately rude.

Remember a certain prime minister? His millionairess wife was 'a true socialist', her phrase, who sat down before the Queen at a banquet. The PM was worse, and plonked himself into the Queen's place. Her Maj smilingly showed no umbrage, and the festival went swimmingly. Except the entire nation squirmed. My knees itched. For the first time, suspicions surfaced that the 'golden couple' might actually be prats. I'm not being political here, just felt the same when Smethie got the heave-ho. As old as my dad, so why treat him like dirt?

Laura inspected the antiques. I seriously didn't like her. Two wrongs don't make a right, three wrongs make a blight, four make a fright. And it wasn't even teatime.

She told me to get started. A kulak from the bar below brought tea and biscuits. The two women poured for themselves. I felt I'd seen them before. I'm good with faces.

'They are from Gimbert's auction, Lovejoy. Identify each one.'

The collection needed only a glance before I hopped it, downstairs and out. Once there, I didn't know what to do. Old Smethie had gone. I sat on the wall. Feet sounded on the gravel. Ellen and Laura appeared, spitting feathers.

'What the hell do you think you're doing?'

'Laura. I can stand anything except bad manners and dirty forks. And you.'

'I'll have you in gaol.'

'Then get on with it, missus. I'm sick of the sight of you.'

Silence for a second. Ellen Jaynor asked, 'Do you want a drink, Lovejoy?'

'Sod off, missus. I'm well narked.'

A motor arrived and students raced shouting into the pub.

'Are the antiques worthless, then?'

I said, 'The poster's not worth much, say a week's holiday.'

It had been an old music-hall bill. You still see some on forgotten hoardings. It showed a stout Victorian lady entertainer.

'Is that all?'

'A tip, missus: fame isn't value. It's public whim.' Or was whim the same as fame? I felt so tired. 'The poster lady. She was a fat, drunken tart. All London laughed at her. She is the most talked-about corpse on earth.'

They were all attention. 'Dr Crippen is the most visited effigy in Madame Tussaud's Waxworks. Cora Crippen's posters aren't worth much.'

'Would you have bid for it?' Ellen asked.

'I'm broke,' I said with bitterness. 'A six-sheet sized poster of Jane Russell's 1943 film *The Outlaw* would be worth something. Christie's sold the only surviving one for the price of a house.'

They glanced at each other, Laura making notes.

'Look, missus. Those priceless antiques were dross.' I wanted to go. I had a life to lead.

'And the wall mask?'

'It isn't antique. And any forger can do Clarice Cliff.'

'What's wrong with it?' Laura asked quietly. She was learning.

'The orange colour's too thin, and Clarice Cliff's glaze is honey-coloured, not grey. She painted with a loaded brush. Some idiot will still buy it.'

'Examine the rest, Lovejoy.'

'No.' Not one had made me feel strange, so they were all modern or forgeries. 'I'd rather have gaol than you.'

I started walking. Laura spoke loudly after me. 'Would you marry again, Lovejoy?'

A couple at one of the trestles had been bored. Now they focused.

'I have a proposal.'

Did she mean a proposition? 'Are you going to kneel?'

Laura linked her arm through mine and walked me to an arbour overhung with Lancelot floribundas. Out of earshot of the couple, I noticed. I watched the two women warily, like I concentrate on stage magicians when I try to spot dwarves and mirrors.

'What if marriage was necessary for you to carry out the perfect antiques scam?' Laura was polite now. Money makes saints of us all.

Wearily I shook my headache. 'You've had your laugh, missus. I'm going home.'

'Don't you want to own millions, Lovejoy?' Women are cunning. They use logic just when you think you've got them. 'Whatever we make on the antiques, you keep.'

'Marriage?' I wondered if I'd heard wrong. 'Me?'

'Once the robbery is done, the marriage will be dissolved instantly.'

Marriage *and* robbery? 'It's against the law.'

'Lawyers can do anything.'

A man has only one marriage in him, but a woman can use marriages as stepping-stones across life's river.

'Who to?'

Laura's colour heightened. 'Me. Divorce follows the very next day.'

'There's no such thing as a false wedding.'

'Never heard of a marriage of convenience, Lovejoy? There is no risk.'

'Who says?'

'Money does.' Laura was all confidence. 'It will bring my ex out from hiding. He's gone to ground, but will emerge if he learns I'm to marry a divvy. That means you.'

Ellen chipped in. 'Still unsure? Railways use the law to ban innocent trainspotters. Parliament legally arrested a poet for reading a few names. People are suing the TV weather girl for predicting rain last Good Friday. Law,' said this paragon of social order, 'does what money tells it.'

Money was a big plus. I know I'm pathetic. I still couldn't see honesty in those smiles.

I found myself being walked to the car past the staring couple. Life was safer in gaol than outside. I've often found that.

A point here: I live for antiques. The world to me has only three groups. First – and most hated – are auctioneers. They are rich because they charge us Value Added Tax, and commission which *they* decide. Second – and poorest – are dealers, who scrape a living hunting old tat and dream of finding a Gainsborough for ten pence. Every year, half of us go bankrupt or get gaoled. But all dealers know, or know of, each other. Third come the millions known as the 'honest old public', though there's no such thing. Money and greed banish truth and trust.

I'm one of the second lot – broke, a scrounger, but always full of dazzling dreams.

Chapter Four

bobbins: rubbish, worthless (Cockney slang)

The limo dropped me in the lane. I called ta, glad to see the back of them.

A *For Sale* notice? My cottage was boarded up.

The place is ramshackle pargeted walls and a rusty gate. My Austin Ruby corrodes in undergrowth with sublime indignity.

'Lovejoy, you are despicable!' a lovely voice said.

It could only be Lydia, my apprentice. I don't know what mellifluous means, but her voice is.

'Sorry, love.' I, an innocent, get imprisoned, abducted by marriage-crazed madwomen, and I tell Lydia sorry. Have you ever noticed how often we blokes say sorry? I blame TV soaps.

'I resign, Lovejoy! Do you hear?'

'Got an aspirin?'

'You have no consideration!' she blazed. I sat on my half-built wall. Then, quieter, 'Is your head bad? What have you been up to?'

See? I'm at Death's door, so she demands what have *I* done wrong. It's their minds.

She marched off. Pause. Her footfalls dopplered back and a flask unscrewed. A hand came in sight with a Royal Doulton cup. Standards don't fall where Lydia lightly trippeth, that's for sure. Two tablets felt my palm.

'Ta, love. You're a saint.'

'Have you been divvying? Lovejoy, you are your own worst enemy!'

'The women made me.' Adam's defence hasn't had much success since that apple business in Eden, but there you go.

'What women?' Even Lydia's snarls are delectable.

To Lydia, all females are rivals – why, nobody knows, but they're out there.

'Ask Mr Smethirst. You know him, that Spurgeon Baptist.'

'Those two old women in the motor?'

My spirits flickered optimistically. Laura and Ellen weren't old, but Lydia was on a roll.

'The one who proposed to me.'

'Who *what*?' in a shriek.

Whimpering, I tried to shut out her noise. She moved into view. Glorious figure, hair drawn into a bun, spectacles, Coggeshall lace blouse, elegant suit, high heels, good enough to eat without a spoon. Her syntax is meticulous, her punctuation precise, and her antiques work unfailing. Morals of a nun, beauty of a tart and bright as a diamond. I'd marry her if I wasn't a bum.

'Gawd, Lyd,' I whined. 'Shut your frigging noise.'

'Lydia, please,' she said, frosty. 'And mind your language in public.'

In a remote garden among non-existent crowds? 'Sorry.' (Another sorry, note.)

My cottage door opened and out stepped Mortimer. 'Good day, Miss Lydia.' Like the bishop was in for sherry.

'Good day, Mortimer.'

They're a right pair, not that they are. He's my illegitimate son. She helped me inside. Mortimer hauled the divan down and I collapsed.

'How long has Lovejoy been poorly, Miss Lydia?'

'He divvied for some women. One proposed.'

They talked over me like I wasn't there. Edible Lydia and a teenage Beau Brummel. How had he opened the door if the bailiffs nailed it shut?

'Could you both please go away?'

Somebody took my shoes off. Lydia held my face and trickled tea into me. The world closed.

Twenty past eight, I woke into a one-candlepower gloaming. Mortimer sat reading by the light of a Norfolk lantern – a stub burning in a perforated cup, our version of the Roman oil domestic lamp. I moved inchwise and was astonished. My head felt OK.

'Better, Lovejoy? Ramps tea, with hindberry leaves and sage. Don't worry. I didn't include feverfew.' I vaguely remembered my gran stuffing a chicken with sage. Mortimer knows birds and folklore, so is easily ignored. 'You have no right to make yourself ill.'

Mortimer riles me as much as Lydia. 'Everybody tells me off, yet I'm the one who suffers. Is there anything to eat?'

'Miss Lydia says no food until tomorrow.'

'Why are women against eating?' I felt something on my head and pulled off a circlet of leaves.

'It's rue, for headache. You may know it as herb-of-grace.'

Never heard of either. I swung my legs off the divan and stood experimentally. 'Ta for the, er, fronds, Mortimer.'

He indicated a chipped mug. I swigged. Bitter. I looked at him. He looked back, this monosyllabic in-control lad.

Mortimer Goldhorn's mother Colette and me made *multo* smiles, then Mortimer was born. Arthur Goldhorn, his mum's husband, was Lord of the Manor of Saffron Fields, large estates with a river, canal, some hamlets and a mansion. The title is Mortimer's now. It's one of those monikers everybody says they ignore, but in the Eastern Hundreds people still give way to him. An agent leases his lands, while Mortimer lives alone in a hut among dense foliage. You'd not find it with a bloodhound. He is also the world's only other divvy except me – a triumph of heredity over environment, I suppose. Colette frolics in Monte Carlo among gilded youths. She never visits.

How to cope with offspring you never knew you had?

'Laura', Mortimer said, 'lately won the National Lottery and became a multi-millionairess. She did law for an antiques complex in Wolverhampton. Droz told Laura about you, Lovejoy.'

Droz, a con artist, sells titles – Princess This or That – to Dutch ladies off the Hook of Holland ferry. He sold the zoo's zedonk, a zebra-donkey cross (ze...donk, get it?). Why the blazes zoos don't lock their animals up at night instead of letting them make illicit smiles in the lantern-lit hay I'll never know. The poor striped donkey always looks miserable, but it's the only one of its kind. Droz also sold St Edmundsbury's town hall bronze gates. I admire Droz. Nothing he sells ever changes hands, the hallmark of a classic con artist. Like, the princesses never get their parchment scrolls, the zedonk's still in the zoo, and the bronze gates never existed in the first place. See? It's genius.

Point here: I'm not praising crooks. Droz only does what you, me, and the Government do. A lovely woman once told me, 'Women do what they can get away with.' It shook me, because I'd sort of hoped women were almost nearly partly possibly trustworthy. *But it's everybody's nature to get away with whatever they can.* Look at Lichtenstein. In March 2003, their Prince Hans Adam (we crooks still admire him for antiques trader frauds) insisted he become an absolute monarch. Check the date. *And unbelievably he did.* Even George the Third wasn't that. Put not your trust in princes, someone once said, but he was on the scaffold.

Facts, except in antiques, are always mad. Example: the universe consists 'precisely of four per cent atoms, plus ninety-six per cent unknown entities.' And physics is a 'precision science'. Ever heard such twaddle? If you *know* four per cent of your way to our village shop and *don't know* the remaining ninety-six per cent, then I reckon you're lost – or have I missed something here? And the longest-running court drama in Los Angeles concerns AA Milne's Winnie the Pooh. Learned lawyers grapple over this non-existent, non-toy non-sense while Planet Earth rots. There's one glim of light.

It's antiques.

Antiques are the only known synonym for love. The

proof? Leonardo da Vinci was illegitimate, couldn't draw feet for toffee (check those terrible feet), never finished a single sculpture, wrote backwards, and left his mere fifteen paintings half-done, but we're still daft about him. See? Antiques are simply love. I think people should ignore the news, and think of antiques.

'What are you talking about?' Mortimer said.

'Sorry.' I must have been thinking aloud.

The antiques trade isn't Boolean astromathematics, but it's preferable to real life.

'What's Droz got to do with us?'

'He told Mrs Ellen Jaynor that a divvy wasn't just in fairy tales. He brought her to me.' He looked embarrassed. 'She was disappointed at my age.'

Looking for a marriageable divvy for Laura? 'I'll kill them.'

'Mrs Jaynor knew Dad.'

Arthur respected Mortimer and let him live wild. I'd still fix the Jaynor bitch. I felt responsible for this newly legitimised offspring.

'The rotten cow is up to something.'

'Please do not speak in those terms, Lovejoy.' Lydia entered. 'I have Mr Droz.'

We'd get on faster if we cut a few corners. Like, I always wonder why the Italians don't knock off their terminal vowels and save on printers' bills. Same as Lydia, to whom everybody has to be Mister This, Missus That. She drives her motor like she talks, ten miles an hour with tyres squeaking on every kerbstone.

'Wotcher, Lovejoy.'

He's a Mockney, as folk call a sham Cockney. Tall and

languid, elegantly suited, hair permed – *permed*, and him an ex-footballer, can you imagine? He lusted after Lydia.

For some reason I scare Drozzie. It was to do with his friend's death. Accidents happen, and I mean that most sincerely.

'About that Laura.' I thought, God, am I engaged?

His eyes flicked to Mortimer, but the lad had gone like a frigging ghost.

'I worked for Laura's husband, Ted Moon, in Brum. I did it to lie low.' He snickered. 'Get it? *Lie* low?'

'Forget cheating. Who're we dealing with, Droz?'

'Not cheating, Lovejoy!' Con men get really barbary if you tell it as it is. 'I don't *cheat*. I *educate*.'

'So everybody is Saint Alban? Aye, right.'

'Ted Moon worked in thirdies,' Droz said gloomily. Confidence tricksters, like antiques dealers, deal in thirds, meaning they buy at one-third of an antique's value. So (important tip, this) divide any dealer's price by three, and that's the most he paid for the antique he's trying to flog you.

'So you've a load of gelt, right, Droz?'

'Here!' he exclaimed, outraged. 'How much d'you think I make?'

'Sorry.' Another sorry? 'Why did this Ted bloke leave Laura?'

'Fell for some tart. Laura's hunting him.'

Nothing new there, just human affairs. Social scientists calculate that two-thirds of married men, and one-fifth of married women, 'cheat' on their respective spouses with only one other married lover. Don't these figures simply mean that one-third is lying? I gave Droz the bent eye.

'Who's Ted Moon's new woman?'

'Laura Moon never said, and Ted's gone.'

At last a clue even I could understand. 'So it's simply vengeance? Why all this marrying stuff?'

'Dunno, Lovejoy. Ted's a dealer, and a ladies' man.'

'Where are you these days, Droz?'

'I'm janitor at the Red Lion.'

Few would find him there. Nobody ever goes, stays, dines or kips in the Red Lion, though once Good Queen Bess did. It's haunted, of course.

'That Laura's phoney. I want to know what her scam is, Droz.'

He rose to go, thankful. I let him get to the door then called his name. 'Droz, there's more at stake here than just me. Or even you.'

'Honest, Lovejoy.' He said it in a tremble. The door wobbled to.

The herb tea had gone cold. I found some Gunton's sandwiches in waxed paper with a pencilled note:

Lovejoy,

I should be greatly obliged were you not to reveal to Miss Lydia that I left this food. It is vegetarian. Please remember that Mrs Ellen Jaynor was once kind to Dad, and may possibly deserve your assistance.

Yours sincerely,

Mortimer.

Post scriptum: A lady called Mrs Penelope Castell of Saxmundham seeks your assistance on the recommendation of Mr Gentry. Her motor will call for you tomorrow at three-fifteen post meridiem.

Only Mortimer and Lydia write abbreviations in full. Mortimer asked me to help Ellen Jaynor, but not Laura? Rum, that. I felt better.

He'd left me two candles, matches, a razor, soap and a towel. Hint. I must pong like a drain. I sighed at Mortimer's sombre style. Everybody now talks like the United Nations. Mortimer called Arthur 'Dad', me being a superfluous prat. I dined in elegance, and slept like a babe.

Chapter Five

sexton: fake, forgery (Cockney rh. slang, Sexton Blake)

Sometimes misfortune is disguised as luck. I boarded the car that came and was whisked to Saxmundham. Daft as ever, I forgot the trillion fashionable antiques dealers Mrs Penelope Castell could have hired instead. Pride makes you think you matter.

She met me at the door, smiling and attractive.

'Dr Castell was a Cambridge University academic,' she explained. 'I'll make tea. You two get acquainted.'

The big deal looked a dusty fifty-year-old bookworm. All he needed was a Squire John Aubrey pillbox hat. He wittered a while about archæology, drinking stiff whiskies and making me fidgety.

'Come on, Doc,' I said at last. 'Where's the antique?'

The mansion was luxurious, but disappointingly modern. I couldn't feel any antique tremors.

Mrs Castell bit the bullet. 'Giles is to be elevated, Lovejoy.' I looked from one to the other. Levitation? 'To the peerage.'

'Made a lord? Congrats.'

Maybe they wanted me to buy an antique for a crooked

politician? Buying antiques on commission is easy because you can't be blamed for guesswork. Money for jam.

'In my youth I was a scamp, Lovejoy. Endless japes.'

His dated slang was like listening to an Edwardian schoolboy read the *Boy's Own*.

'A bounder!' His missus trilled a merry laugh, the visit going with a swing.

'And the relevance of your scamphood?'

He cleared his throat. 'Could you steal something, Lovejoy?'

'Look. Everybody on earth dreams of the perfect antiques theft, scam, con, forgery. Stay out of it. There are crooks out there who leave the police standing. You want to make money? Then hunt down Commodore EJ Smith's last letter – he captained the *Titanic*. It'd be worth a million. Scrotch in Walberswick will knock you up a gold fake Roman brooch of the Second Legion from Vindolanda in Northumberland, AD 125. He stores the centurions' names.'

Mrs Castell smiled. 'Our robbery is perfectly above board, Lovejoy.'

'An *honest* theft?'

Dr Castell said quietly. 'Yes. The object is already mine, you see.' Their warm, comfortable drawing room, views of a river with ducks, suddenly seemed colder. 'One of my youthful pranks involved faking an antique. It's in Eastwold College, where I met Penny.'

'And you want me to borrow it back?'

Penny was quietly determined. 'British Museum experts are due soon. Giles's spiffing larks are problematic now.'

'Look. I honestly don't think—'

Penny patted Giles. She would handle it from now on. 'We shall pay *whatever* it takes, Lovejoy.'

She was all curves. Women have no such thing as age, only what they do or don't do. I dragged my gaze away. Giles ignored his wife's vamping of a visiting scruff. I recognised the power of snobbery.

'The theft will save my reputation.' He looked at Penny with worship, and I understood how hard, how very hard, she had worked to advance his career.

He began to tell me about the Xipe Totec masks.

Archæological finds from the ancient world are ultra-famous. Ask any museum curator about the Xipe Totec masks, he'll take a fortnight to explain. Simply, think Aztec gods.

Xipe Totec was a deity. To celebrate him, priests flayed some humans, then wore the poor victims' skin for the ceremonies. Skin includes the face, so they made stone masks, always with a gaping mouth and eyes tight shut. They are seriously sickening. What religion isn't? The British Museum has Xipe Totec stone masks. Controversy rages. Are they genuine Meso-American, or fake? Nobody knows. Ignorance makes us all experts.

'I was very skilful, Lovejoy.' And as Penny smiled with fond pride, 'Researchers are re-opening the issue, and want Eastwold's relic.'

'Can't you say you've just forgotten?'

'Hardly, Lovejoy. Remember Piltdown Man? Imagine if that fraudulent priest Teilhard de Chardin attempted that deception nowadays. With modern technology they'd not last a week.'

Penny showed where her values lay by moaning softly.

'Think of me, laughed out of society. The mask is in the college museum, labelled *On loan from Giles Castell, Cambridge University.* There is little security.'

'How do you know?'

'I visited lately. A child could take it.'

She was cool, but I was taking the risk and she wasn't. If anything, she was amused by the obvious effect she was having on me. It was an odd do. Still, money is money, and I was skint.

'I'll need a motor, please, and a college plan.'

'Thank you, Lovejoy.' Giles was so grateful.

'I'll drive you, Lovejoy.' She handed him another whisky. 'Tonight will be fine, don't you think?'

The remark of a woman about to betray, of course.

'I'll phone a bloke who knows security systems, missus.'

'You won't reveal the...heist, Lovejoy?' She sounded excited. 'It will be quite a dashing escapade.' We were starting to sound like Dan Dare plus Bulldog Drummond.

Hours later I entered the Dog & Duck near Long Melford and collected a thick envelope from Quemoy in the vestibule while Penny waited. Ready, steady.

After driving for yonks in the darkness, Penny gave me instructions.

'Nine inches across. That's two hundred millimetres. Not heavy.'

'Right.' Quemoy had given me all the facts about Eastwold.

'It's in a glass case, first on the right from the main hall.'

'Left,' I corrected, fed up with her.

She was surprised. 'Is it? How do you know?'

'Go down this cart track. There's a lay-by two furlongs along. Stop there.' My certainty worried her. Quemoy costs the earth, but he is never, never ever, wrong. The lay-by abutted on a pea-field, its peas just about to burgeon.

'Have you been here before, Lovejoy?'

'Never.'

She switched the engine off. 'The school is across that field. The display case has one lock.'

I'd had enough.

'There are two locks,' I said. 'One's a reinforced Chubb, the second a modified Bramah. The display case is restored Indonesian mahogany. The glass is reinforced fibre-mesh Pilkington from St Helens. Three cameras, one presently inactive from spiders. The Xipe Totec mask is actually third along, if you count the Roman silver display. The green baize hasn't been cleaned since the Great Civil War ended in 1648. The security guard is seventy-two years old, and will be watching Manchester United re-runs on BSkyB TV at eleven o'clock.'

'How do you know all that?' She was visibly shaken.

'I do my homework. Saves getting nicked.'

Her tongue touched her lips, retreated slowly. 'What will you do if you get caught?' She took a breath. 'Fight?'

'Run, missus.'

'Penny.' Her voice went husky. 'I've heard about you, Lovejoy. You're not innocent, are you? Somebody said—'

'Gossipy Mrs Somebody again? Rumour is a tumour feeding on itself. Be here, please.'

'Nobody's about.' She looked mischievous in the dashboard glow. 'I thought you might want to—'

'Two hours.'

She giggled. 'I used to sneak out through the chapel gate and meet the village boys. Now the little bitches simply invite them in. Stealing like this is far more exciting.'

For a blank moment I sat back wondering. 'You silly cow.'

She gaped. 'What?'

'You've no idea, have you? Listen. Once upon a time, thieves nicked a Leonardo da Vinci painting. Worth about 50 million zlotniks. Owners wrung their hands, then they offered a 165,000 zlotniks reward. Mathematics aren't my thing, but is the reward *less* than 0.0033 of the painting's value?'

'But this is nothing to do—'

'You don't think so? Back in 1989, a small oil-painting was valued at 6000 zlotniks. Then rumour hinted it was by Raphael. November 2002, the Duke of Northumberland sold this *The Madonna of the Pinks*, quite legal, to the Getty outfit in LA. The baby Christ holds some pink flowers. Price: $US 57.4 million, plus change. London's National Gallery came unglued, then offered $34 million. Work it out, Penny. The difference was the Duke's tax bill. *We* would pay to cover the Duke's tax bill. Get the trick?'

'No.'

'The Inland Revenue came out smelling of roses, saving the Raphael for the nation, hip-hip-hooray, by screwing us all out of *their* Value Added Tax, at 17.5 per cent of every groat. Penny, love, if the Inland Revenue got proper jobs they'd starve. They make the rules. *That's* the trade you're frigging about with here.'

'Is hatred why you do it?' Her eyes were hard.

'You're not thinking, silly cow. *The Madonna of the*

Pinks never was by Raphael, being only one of forty or so replicates of a fake of a copy of a sham…*So didn't the Inland Revenue do a good deal for His Grace the Duke?* I want to know who paid what for what and to whom for a fake, but the Government won't tell me.'

'So everyone is unfair to you, Lovejoy,' she taunted. Narked, I got out, and she said something that made me look back.

'I'm wearing stockings, Lovejoy,' she said, smiling. 'And I've brought enough hankies. Hurry back.'

I thought, Did I hear right? I followed the badger path across the pea field. There was just enough sky-gloaming to see by.

Quemoy is a Taiwanese bloke, and had done his usual sound job. You get enough details to invade Cambridgeshire. He's one of these computer blokes who can't stop himself. In that instant, I suppressed my unease, but I'm thick where women are concerned.

I'm useless in countryside. I sound like a bag of popcorn however quiet I try to be.

Eastwold College was a black shadow, with a few lights showing. Dormitories? I did the fifth window from the end, as Quemoy advised. It took me half an hour. Some blokes I know would have gone through without breaking step.

Using Quemoy's pencil torch, batteries provided, I found the museum next to the library. I did both locks on the case and took out the fake mask. No strange quivering in my chest. I paused for a serious think.

Penny Castell all but promised to ravish me. I'm no

Handsome Jack. OK, she was desperate for Giles to get lorded, but her lust didn't quite ring true. I can understand a married woman getting bored, but posh Penny actually sought me out – me, a gaolbird without a bean. Why? To set me up.

Risking my pencil flashlight, I checked the label: *On Loan from Giles Castell, Cambridge University*, and pondered these new worries. I took a discus from a sports collage, and slipped it in the cloth bag Penny had given me. Going through to the library, I paused in Reference, and used the library steps to slip Giles's mask, the crowbar and washing-up gloves, behind the dustiest tomes on the highest shelf I could reach, before eeling into the night.

She was in the motor, breathless with expectation. 'Did you get it?'

'Yes.' I showed her the heavy bag. 'Click open the boot. I'll put it in.'

'No need. I'll—'

Quickly I went round to the boot. In the darkness, I removed the discus and flung it into the pea field, slammed the boot shut and joined her.

She gave a whimper of delight. 'All done? Payment time.' She spoke in a thick voice. 'I want your hands first, lover, then…'

Some things don't make me proud. I don't have to be. Pride is OK if you're rich, but it's grubby stuff down among us bottom feeders (sorry for the pun). Of seven hundred East Anglian antiques dealers, only three can afford a holiday. The rest fiddle expenses and hope for the Big Break.

Penny fell on me like a mad thing. I was relieved I'd

misjudged her. We made tumultuous smiles, the windows steaming up. A new car park is planned in Vinci, Tuscany – where else? – for snoggers. In that new love zone, police are not to arrest lovers who are hard at it. Essentials, if you follow, are on hand in slot machines. The only concession Penny made to propriety was to gasp, 'Don't mark me!' If I'm on Planet Mongo how could I control events in her car?

Afterwards, she dozed, a novelty, because after making smiles women always want to talk. They'd be loved for ever if they let their bloke's soul marinate for a minute afterwards. She got me to hook her brassiere. She got mad when her blouse tore, but whose fault was that?

The crunch came just outside St Edmundsbury. She stopped for petrol and went to pay in the well-lit garage shop. Dopey from galactic pleasure, I nodded off. A bobby tapped the window and arrested me, while she watched smiling from the window among other customers. The motor was searched, and thirty minutes later I was back in the pokey.

Ten o'clock next morning, Penny came in dazzling yellow and sat with glittering knees to vamp the beaks. She testified I'd simply appeared while she stopped to adjust her driving mirror. Cruel, vicious, animal Lovejoy ravished her ('with an angry snarl,' she perjured sweetly), and took her hostage.

She outwitted me, she testified, by phoning the police. Put not your trust in…or have I already said that, Titus Oates on the scaffold? I conducted my own defence, as lawyers can't be trusted, law being so fragile. She said I'd told her that I'd just done a robbery nearby and stowed the loot in her car boot. She couldn't mention the truth without giving her game away.

The court remanded me in custody, to decide random guilt later.

In the nick I grumbled as usual about police starvation, and slept the peace of innocence while East Anglia's finest watched football re-runs. Manchester United, I can report, won 2-0, but the referee was clearly bribed. I guessed he was also a lawyer.

Chapter Six

butty: an inexperienced lawyer (crim. slang)

They fed me a runny egg, truly vile. I could have made furniture out of the bread.

'I'm starving, Mr Kine,' I told the plod.

'Then don't keep coming back, Lovejoy.'

Kine is skeletal and affects a bowler hat and pinstripes. All ploddites pretend to be respectable.

'Spoken to anyone?' My hopes lay in Laura Moon. And Lydia, always assuming she wasn't livid. 'Who's that lady?'

A super-elegant lady was seated on a chair. Fiftyish, dark complexion, guinea-an-inch, as East Enders say down Brick Lane. A huge driver waited with two besuited butties.

'Do you know her, Lovejoy?'

'No.' He frowned. 'Honest. Whose are the butties?'

A butty is an inexpert lawyer named from living on sandwiches.

'Yours, Lovejoy.' I cheered up. Sad ploddites are good. 'First see the Castells.'

'No, ta, Mr Kine. I've done insanity this week.'

Kine has this cadaverous smile. Everything is recorded

in the cop shop, even in the loos, so never say anything. In came Dr Giles and Penny, looking less than their usual exalted selves.

Kine doffed his bowler. 'Lovejoy, vital evidence is missing.' A plod fiddled with a tape deck, yet more pretence. 'Namely, the mask you stole.'

'Good gracious,' I said mildly. 'What mask?'

'We have no evidence. We searched your cottage,' he added casually. 'Your henchman, Tinker Dill, allowed us.'

'Tinker's out of remand, then?' More jubilation.

'A college window had been forced.'

'Tut tut. Maybe those girls slip out to meet village lads in the lantern hours, eh?' I looked at Penny.

Silence spread. The policeman's machine whirred.

Shadows fascinate me. We've lost the Victorian art of watching shadows. They reveal so much. Shadows can recapture memories when we are alone and sorrowing. This accounts for our modern lack of insight, and shows how barbarous we really are. Nowadays we want instant everything. We want diplomas without study, money without work. We want the woman to undress, not even knowing who the hell she is. It doesn't do.

Sometimes when I'm melancholy, I light a candle and look at shadows. They are a gift. Reminiscences bring light to the recesses of the heart where forgotten things live – people, children, memories welcoming you back. Shadows gladden in bad times.

Look at Leonardo da Vinci's portrait of Lady Ginevra de' Benci. Not a shadow on her lovely face? Oh, but there *is*, so fleetingly slight you don't see it at first. Incidentally (I'm not one to spread gossip) I don't believe the great L da V really did use that rent boy Jacopo from the goldsmith's shop in the Vacchereccia, Florence, though it landed Leonardo in the pokey…

'Eh?' Kline was speaking.

'Your chat will not be recorded.'

The ploddites left. No shadows here. It's odd, meeting some woman you've ravished. Penny was enjoying herself. I felt in a tableau.

'Lovejoy,' Giles pronounced in his superb timbre. 'Where is the Xipe Totec mask, please?'

'Dunno. I did as you said, Giles. Penny told me to burgle Eastwold College. I got scared by a guard dog so I returned to Penny. We drove off.' I spoke clearly, police recording machines being naff. 'Penny stopped at a garage. The plod collared me.'

Keeping a straight face took effort. Quemoy's note on this life-threatening wolfhound read: *The patrol-man's dog is called Daffodil. An English Lurcher aged eleven months, it responds to bribes of Peak Frean biscuits. Two are included in this envelope. Further supplies are obtainable from Gunton's, address in Appendix 2A*…Quemoy is class.

'Look.' I was arguing for freedom, and I had a marriage to avoid. 'I can't find things that aren't there, can I?'

'Is there a possibility the mask was stolen by someone else?'

This was new. 'Who?'

'A group of overseas visitors is in East Anglia. They made me an investment proposition.'

'You have criminal contacts?'

Penny chipped in. 'Lovejoy, they might blackmail Giles. He was once in the diplomatic service. Please help us.'

'I don't get it. You're in the clear. Get yourself lorded.'

She crossed her legs at me, though she already had my complete attention. I ached with anatomical proof.

'The overseas people do not brook failure. Come round this evening to settle your fee.'

'I can't. I'm in this dump.'

'That is already settled, Lovejoy.' She gathered her handbag, smiling as they left. Moments later, Kine beckoned me out.

'Lovejoy,' he said, 'things don't add up. You are a toad. Shagging Mrs Castell in Suffolk's leafy lanes seems about right. But forcible abduction and rape of a society lady? You wouldn't know how.' He chuckled, hoof-hoof-hoof, a laryngitic owl trying to announce its vigilance. He knocked out his pipe on a radiator. A passing policeman said, 'Excuse, sir, but—'

Kine said testily, 'I know, Mason. Bloody rules.' We walked outside while he filled and lit his pipe, pop-pop. 'The Castells withdrew the charges, Lovejoy.'

'I'm free?'

'As air. Just one thing. What's this marriage business?'

'Rumour's wrong,' I said sharply. Free as air? That'd be the day.

By six o'clock, I was up. Cracking an egg scares me in case I find a chick staring up in reproach. This time I was lucky, and fried them in a pan over a petrol-filled hole in the garden. Defying Lydia, I ate all the bread. My tea is horrible. I don't drink coffee, because only Yanks can brew it. I decided to find Colleen, a daft bat with visions, so I got a lift into town from Eleison, a priest defrocked for giving the parish of Underlanes, Norfolk, to the poor, so of course he had to suffer. He now trundles manure to farms.

'Wotcher, Lovejoy,' he said, snickering. 'Orf on your honeymoon? All the booys be larffin'. That bitch Laura scrubs up well.'

'Thank you, Sir Galahad.' Morosely I clung on near the garbage.

'Her husband Ted Moon were a pleasant bugger, though. He'm estuary folk.' Eleison shivered. 'He killt and yirded some lass.'

God Almighty. I felt like going back to bed. 'Laura's husband Ted killed and buried a girl?' And I'd just been imprisoned for being innocent. 'I hadn't heard that, Eleison.'

He gave me a wizened eye. 'You hear everything, booy, and know nothing. Want to sing the 'Kyrie eleison' wi' me?'

I declined, but he sang it anyway (read *any* way) and dropped me off at the War Memorial. I gave a nod to the poor dead blokes and went to the Antiques Arcade where Colleen sits.

Life in antiques is war and has the same three ignorances. One is what you *assume*, like the date of the Battle of Hastings. Second is what you *believe*. Third is what you *guess*. Last week I saw two ninety-year-old historians brawl, actually try to knock each other's block off. Their students had to drag the silly old sods apart. The big dispute? The Battle of Lepanto, 1571, and if Admiral Andrea Doria was a coward. (He was, incidentally.) Is that rational? Eliminate the three ignorances to make a fortune in antiques, then concentrate on bits that matter. Colleen for instance.

She sells wishes in the Arcade. Meaning she charges for each mystic wish, closing her eyes and swaying. People really believe Colleen. A rotund lady in a giant flowery skirt, hair in a Carolean mound, a vast bosom glittering with cubic zirconia, and there she is. She smokes black malodorous French cigarettes.

She was seated on her stool, knees a-splay so you have to look away. The Arcade's stalls are merely three sheets of sacking on poles, a plank between two wooden beer crates and bring your own stool. Sandy and Mel, Arcade owners, charge the earth for each nook. Betsy runs the tea stall. I paint pictures of garden ghosts for Colleen. Truth is, I never see any ghosts, but my Ghosts Among Flowers paintings sell. I invent the ghosts. Dealers saw me enter and bawled abuse, mostly to do with parentage and my famed IOUs.

'Morning, Lovejoy. That woman's a whore.'

'Could you be specific?'

'The horrid bitch loved Sandy's camp-gay-queer-trolling act.'

Sandy goes mad for an audience. 'Did you know either of them?'

'The lawyer woman's had a facelift, cow collagen and that botox poison. I can smell a lawyer at seven furlongs, love. She's as rich as that Greek king who became a donkey. Her lottery win was in the paper. Her husband, Ted, did a flit over some tart who got topped.' She smiled a wintry smile. 'Safe from her, I'd say.'

'Tell me about Ted Moon.'

'Information will cost you, Lovejoy.' She belched and lit a fag one-handed. 'Two ghost paintings. And not acrylic.'

Colleen and I once made smiles when she was glamorous Miss Eastern Hundreds. She gave me the elbow for saying her mysticism was rubbish, accusing me of unfaith. I hope I'm not making her out to be ugly, because she's lovely, just different. I like Colleen.

Laconically, I kept smiling. I do Colleen two ghost paintings a month. She hates acrylic and underpays me, the rotten bitch. Oils sell for ten times as much and are easily antiqued.

'Very well.' A lie always helps so I said, 'I like doing those.'

'By Sunday? And no more magnolias.'

'Can I help it?' I demanded, indignant. 'If a ghost appears beside my magnolia what can I do? Lend me money for the canvases, love?'

'Sod off.' She yawned, a wondrous sight. 'See Fibber Hollohan about marrying that bitch. He's our best marriage lawyer.'

As she turned back to her astrological chart, I asked, 'What about her husband?'

'Him? Had two homes down on the water and a naff antiques collection. Some woman met him, and off he went to Derby. That's men for you.'

'Won't he come back? Laura's rich.'

'Not for a gold clock. Hated Laura.'

'God Almighty. The seductress must be dynamite, when his ex-wife Laura had zillions.'

'Sandy knew him. Ted Moon never killed that girl.'

Sandy was by the door in a booth, with mercury-vapour lamps showing off his magenta hair. He was talking to Veronica from Bromley Cross.

It's hard to know what to make of Sandy. He has tantrums and wears anything that glitters, radiates, reflects. His hair changes colour faster than traffic lights. He wears enough make-up to keep the Old Vic going in high season and loves himself, money and Mel, in that order.

Sandy admired himself in his cheval mirror. 'Mel, dear. Have we had our wedding invite?'

Mel glowered. He glowers a lot. Their lack of scruple is legendary, and they only pay under torture.

Veronica is a nervous, rather plain lass I rather like. Her husband makes ends meet teaching handicapped children while she combs the Home Counties for antiques. In any pantomime she'd be Mistress Poverty. She was in tears.

'I'll miss the Hook of Holland tourists!'

'If you can't pay, dearie, you're out. Life is tragic.' Sandy swished his silver lamé cape.

Desperation scares me. I do a lot of it. 'Sandy, I'll pay Veronica's rent.'

He pivoted, his eyes large. 'But you're pig, Lovejoy.'

Pig in a poke, broke, Cockney rhyming slang. 'I've just sold Colleen two ghost paintings.'

'Oh, all right.' He recoiled as she tried to buss him. 'No! I don't *do* ugly. And for God's sake rescue that mare's nest on your head.'

'Look, Sandy. Was Laura really after your tatty miniatures?'

'Tat?' he screeched. Every head turned. 'My ceramics are exquisite, you swine!' He simpered roguishly.

'Don't trust her, Lovejoy,' from Mel.

'Oh, that's *nice!*' Sandy spat, viperish. 'Lovejoy sells himself, and *I'm* untrustworthy?'

'Then what did she want?'

'*Moi*, dwahhling!' he crooned, eyelashes fluttering.

I'd been his audience long enough. 'Ta-ra, mate. I'll send Veronica's rent.'

Sandy's ceramics drew me. These so-called apprentice-piece porcelains are collectors' items. Craftsmen made diminutive wares for Minton or Royal Worcester travelling salesmen. Astonishingly you can still pick up miniature Spode blue-and-white tureens, genuine 1820s, for a quarter of a week's average wage. Sandy had a Limoges miniature early 1900s gilt-edged tea set. Victorian families bought them for doll's houses, with which mothers taught their daughters domestic duties. (Tip: hunt miniature ceramics at boot fairs and junk stalls, because they'll have soared by the time this ink's dry. Named decorators, like Roberts of Royal Worcester, are highly favoured. Quick sticks, off you go.)

'Overpriced, Sandy,' I said to nark him. 'And your mascara's running.'

He started to wail. Mel shouted, 'Bully!' I felt a wart.

'Thank you, Lovejoy,' Veronica called. 'You're sweet.'

In my mind was the germ of a plot. Could I stay out of prison long enough to make something of it? It would be lovely to start eating again.

Chapter Seven

herd (n): latest street gossip (fr. herd word, slang)

A proposal, and it wasn't even a Leap Year? Barmy. I trudged into town to find Tinker at the Welcome Sailor, a dingy East Gates pub. My barker, Tinker, susses antiques out by osmosis. The barmaid, Dodie from Watford, sent him out.

He came, coughing, and stood blearily in the postern doorway. 'Lovejoy?' he bawled. Secret as Radio One.

As always, he wore his tatty greatcoat from God-knows-what-war, mittens encrusted with food, and has corrugated teeth like a derelict graveyard. My one loyal helper – Lydia excepted. Beggars can't, can they?

He cackled a laugh. 'Getting wed, eh? Want the herd word?' He swigged with relish from a bottle of unspeakable liquid. 'They say Ted Moon killt some lass. Habby corpy got him off.' *Habeas corpus.* 'His wife Laura got the lottery and a Lincoln hint owffed him from Stanstead on the great white bird.'

'I heard he's in Derby. Did Laura and Ted live near here?'

'Fellinsham, down Salcott-cum-Varley. Horrible estuaries,

lazy winds.' His rheumy eyes leaked despair. 'We don't
have to go there, do we? I got rheumatics.'

A lazy wind is one that goes through you instead of
going round. 'Tinker, get me some money. Borrow. I'll
wait out here.'

Lately, I've found I lie a lot. Well, Marilyn Monroe once
said that if she'd behaved, she'd never have got anywhere.
He finally emerged with a couple of notes.

'I sold Griff from Aston three silver Saxon coins found
in Manningtree. OK?'

'Gawd, Tinker. Hammered silvers, 1200 years old?'
Since the discovery of massive coin hoards in Holland and
England, the price had tumbled.

By two o'clock I was in Fellinsham Post Office asking
for directions to the Moons' house.

The postmistress's face clouded. 'I'm sorry, but the
Moons no longer live here. There was…difficulty.'

Going for lies in the interests of efficiency, I explained,
'I'm an artist. I was told to paint their, erm, cottage for
charity.'

She eyed me. The god of fibs revealed my sensitive soul.
'I'll brew up. I can listen for the shop bell.'

Peggy did good Eccles cakes, but her raspberry jam was
a bit runny.

'I can't really let Ted down,' I said, woeful.

'Everybody liked Ted. Supported the babies' school, too,
despite his wife's, well, it's a weakness, isn't it?'

'Definitely.' Weakness? Laura didn't look weak.

'The TV said there's treatment for it,' she went on. 'Do
you think so? Ted was a saint. That missing girl almost
ruined the village.'

'Well, it would.' I was quite lost.

'My husband Vic backs a horse in the Derby, but everybody does that. We pick nice names.'

Aha. Gambling was Laura's affliction? I agreed with Peggy about everything. 'Thanks, Peggy. I'll make a start. Light, you see.'

I made our farewell meaningful, holding her hand until she went red. Forty minutes later I was painting by the Moons' overgrown gazebo, when an elderly couple came out.

'Have you got permission?' the old man demanded.

'Yes,' I told them. 'A definite order.'

That took them aback. 'Who from?'

'The owner wanted a memento.'

'When?' Tweedledum and Tweedledee as one. 'He said nothing about it to us,' said the lady.

'He didn't answer my letters either, missus.'

It was then I recognised the elderly lady. Simultaneously she clocked me, and her face clouded with suspicion. She was Mrs Caulfield, who gave talks on embroidery. I'd heard her. She'd claimed the Tricot Stitch was easily adapted to complex crochet, when I knew – ta, Gran – it used to be called Railway Stitch because it was 'only for straight work and lazy fingers'. Gran called it the Idiot Stitch.

'Look,' I said as if giving in. 'I can see I'm worrying you. But if Ted phones, tell him you sent me away, OK? You know what Laura's like. Tell Ted I came. Still in Leicester, is he?'

'Lancashire now,' the lady said, quickly realising her gaffe and adding, 'If he contacts us, that is.'

Might as well have consciences hanging out of their

pockets. It finished my sleuthing in Fellinsham. I got the village bus. In olden days a river barge plied through, but that was before potholed roads and hopeless trains. The point was, Laura was a creature of heavy addictions. Who was the vanished girl?

Carrying my stuff, I reached home on the 66. I hardly had time to go to the loo before Laura barged in. Mrs Ellen Speed-Dater Jaynor glared from the motor as if sighting a field gun.

'You shall meet my contract lawyer, Lovejoy,' Laura said briskly. 'You receive a week's salary immediately.'

'What for?' I hadn't said come in, but she plonked herself down, wrinkling her nose. 'You mean your fraud?'

That smile again. 'Not fraud, *manoeuvre*. Here is his card.'

'Funny thing, Laura. One of the villagers thought she recognised you.'

'No more independent thinking, Lovejoy. I shan't warn you again.'

I didn't wave them off. I'd done enough serfing for her and Ellen Jaynor. For light relief from those two phoneys, and to find out more, I went to Whorwood's tea auction, where rules must never be broken.

Chapter Eight

tea auction: illegal clandestine sale of antiques among bidders

Profit needs three things: decision, a willingness to ignore the law, and money. One extra: bidders break your legs if you baulk the system. I hurried. You don't come late.

You'd assume it was as docile as its name suggests. Except your word is your bond. So you *must* keep your word. Excuses do not wash. The benefit? You put your Auntie Jane's superb Bonnington watercolour up for auction at three o'clock, you get your money at teatime. Buy, you slap ready money down in full.

More horrendous still, honesty reigns. Unbelievable. Bidders call bids out, whereas in Continental and London auctions they can wink, signal or wave a numbered paddle. You can see why tea auctions differ from the malfunctioning 'reality' of New York or London's Bond Street. Dealers joke, 'Never mind, mate. Paris and Austria are worse.' The quotation has entered folklore.

'Wotcher, Lovejoy,' Eunice Whorwood said as I came in.

'Tyling today, Eunice?' Tyler is the door guard.

'Yes. Easy peasy. I just count them in.'

'I'll have a look.'

I went for a cuppa, the tea auction's concession to gentility. Eunice is the size of a malnourished shrimp, but that hardly matters. A tyler simply reports defaulters and they suffer.

'Brought the wife, Lovejoy?' Eunice jibed.

By tradition, the eldest Whorwood girl is always named Jane, the younger girl Eunice. Historians will spot the reason: King Charles the First, imprisoned on the Isle of Wight before his execution in 1649, was minded by one Mrs Jane Whorwood. She gave the 'martyr king' provisions and, rumour has it, certain extra comforts. Royal letters survive in Eunice's family, 'tis said. Romantics speculate. I say let them be. If Eunice's great-great-whatever grannie gave Charles One passionate solace, good for her.

'Ha ha. What's worth nicking, Eunice?'

She's a bonny lass with flaming red hair (another clue: *red* hair). Seats all faced the organiser, Eunice's dad, Charles (nudge-nudge). A couple of antiques vibrated at me with such intensity I had to sit down, Eunice shoving me quickly into a seat and tutting the way women show exasperation, like I go whoozy just to annoy.

The little statue of Minerva was prominent on a plant stand. This Roman Goddess of Crafts and Arts eventually made the top-of-the-pop charts of Rome's soldiery. She became Goddess of War. Her statuette stood no taller than a hand. It was muddy grey, owing to its excavation on North Hill, only three hundred yards from where we were. Archæologists bragged about finding it to TV cameras. Local forgers were soon turning out fakes like Ford cars, claiming cast-iron authenticity for them all.

'Exquisite, love. Isn't that the original?' (Me, playing dim.)

'The one and only. It'll go for a fortune.'

'Always to the undeserving, love.'

She laughed. I scanned about for the other antique that made me feel queasy. The tea auction is virtually ye olde open-skies market auction. Buy something in 'market overt' and pay on the nail, then it stays yours *wherever it came from*. Even if nicked. By market overt rules original owners have no claim. Think of Statute of Limitations joyously reduced to zero, and that's it. So, sell an antique in a street market that you nicked the night before, and you're in the clear.

The tea auction perpetuates the ancient market overt. Tea auctions are nowadays highly illegal. But has anyone ever heard of attenders, auctioneers, organisers, vendors at *any* tea auction being arrested, tried, charged, found guilty? Neither have I. Once you've bought your stolen ancient British gold torc from 100 BC found last week in a farmer's field on the north bank of the River Deben (and I'm not making these up) you're the legit owner. Is that what the High Court says? Not exactly. Law says it's illegal and practised by utter cads. But the tea auctions of Merrie England believe honesty only operates down among us scavengers where old rules apply. The law doesn't understand.

There are risks, sure. The vendor must bring his antique to the tea auction, or describe it accurately. You may get arrested while carrying your stolen Rembrandt down Norfolk's leafy lanes. Priceless items from Baghdad's stunning museums turn up in Home Counties' tea auctions, and they were looted to the floorboards in April, 2003. Only the Kingdom of Jordan behaved honourably – their vigilant Customs and Excise men traced forty-three looted paintings from that shambles. The rest of the world's antiques hunters simply raked the money in.

Heaven knows why police antiques squads don't just visit tea auctions. *Unless, of course, they know all about tea auctions anyway and quietly ignore what really goes on.* Though I do believe in the total honesty of our police. I mean that most sincerely.

My divvy gift lacks direction so I had to look. The second antique was silently pulsing away on a small footstool – odd choice – by the auctioneer's chair. A genuine early decanter.

Eunice gave me an anxious look. 'It really is genuine, isn't it?'

'Genuine, yes.' I put my tea down.

Decanters came in during the end of the seventeenth century. Early American ones are lovely, but you hardly ever see them. English and Irish are hunted most. This poor thing was tapered, like trying to resemble a lady in a crinoline dress. It was about 1820, English, with the sort of milled neck rings crystal collectors lust after. Its original stopper quadrupled the price.

'It's described as mint,' Eunice told me, nervous. 'Is it?'

Stooping to glance obliquely at the metal – as dealers call glass – I tilted the decanter. A vague flicker of light showed. Somebody, worried by a corroded rim round the interior, had cleaned it with hydrofluoric acid. This dangerous stuff completely removes corrosion. Trouble is, it leaves a strange effect French crystal experts call the *peau d'orange*, 'orange-peel skin'.

My rule is this: *hydrofluoric acid ruins antique glass.* Walk away and go for a quiet drink instead.

'Price now? Getting on for nil.'

Quietly I explained to her stricken look, 'The white deposit is the giveaway, a snowy rust. Who was so desperate?'

She looked stricken. 'Sandy.'

Normally I wouldn't bother if they got in trouble. Now, I began to wish I hadn't come.

'What should I do, Lovejoy?'

'God knows. Call him?'

Eunice clicked at her mobile and returned, pale. 'No answer.'

No chance then, unless Sandy regretted his deception and came hotfoot to withdraw it.

'Any collections in, Eunice?'

'Everybody's asking that. What're you after?'

'That Laura's husband Ted is a collection nutter.'

'No. Dealers are squirreling cash away ready for some big spend. They're all at it. We start now.'

Geraldo, the auctioneer, arrived on cue. He carries an empty brief case of Italian leather, pretending he's about to unload vital documents. Then he scrutinises his watch, speaks to the tyler, counts the antiques. Then gets down to the serious business of polishing his spectacles.

He's a prematurely wizened, dapper gent so diminutive he would be lost in a school play. He closes his eyes and waits for the town clock to strike, then the game's afoot.

It crossed my mind that I could bid for the decanter

and save Sandy's skin, except I would abet Sandy's deceit and incur his punishment. Sorry, pal, I thought, friendship ends here.

The clock struck. Geraldo roused and began.

'Good afternoon, ladies and gentlemen. Item One is a blue glass pendant of triangular shape just smaller than six centimetres, two-point-four inches. An Art Deco fish, but no letter R in the *Lalique, France* signature…'

That showed it was after 1945, when the great designer died, so not antique. Those factories made over eight million pieces. Blue-Lalique anything is always more highly favoured – though a little of what you fancy does your wallet untold good. I listened as the lots were sold on a curt rap of Geraldo's gavel. All twelve antiques were quickly sold. A portly bloke I didn't know bought Sandy's decanter for a giddy sum. His obvious delight made me cringe. Big Frank from Suffolk won a silver tray inscribed with golf engravings. He's mad on silver, so he'd be the one to ask about collectors in that field. Big Frank also collects wives, and was soon to be married to his umpteenth. I hated being his best man, and helping bigamous unions becomes boring. He always says, 'You're always my best man, Lovejoy! It won't seem a proper wedding…' and so on. We were due to arrange it at the Welcome Sailor.

The rest were big-gelt visitors from the north. The man who bought Sandy's decanter asked after me, but Eunice said she'd not seen me.

'Do you know Lovejoy's address? I would be obliged.'

'Sorry, I've my father to see to. You might catch Lovejoy at The Ship taproom on East Hill.'

'Thank you, miss.' He paused. 'How may I recognise him?'

'Average everything,' Eunice said sweetly, 'except more down-at-heel.'

He was as staid as any city gent, wearing George boots – made of one piece of leather.

'Ta for the character reference, love,' I told Eunice. 'Who was he?'

'Tea auctions are confidential, Lovejoy.'

She told me on the way out, though. Mr Hennell, stock broker and antiques maniac, was known to wealthy private buyers in the Eastern Hundreds and had recently become Sandy's backer in developing a marina. Mr Hennell's purchase of Sandy's decanter was nothing more than a private scam. I erased him from my mind. Mistake.

Chapter Nine

brown: dead (fr. Brown bread, Cockney rh. slang)

Colo's milk float got me into town. Something Paltry said was worrying me. Today he would be on the river footpath, collecting money at the Castle Green cricket. The rain had stopped, *Dei gratia*.

Cricket takes three days, dawn to dusk. Crowds attract Paltry like marmalade draws wasps. Cars park on the greensward, throngs mill in, and Paltry trips about shaking his tin. He wears a label, *For My Opration Plese Giv Genrussly* (sic). Women want details. Blokes hurry on, desperate not to miss the game. Paltry swills the takings in the Marquis of Granby.

Arriving motors were churning the grass, throngs heading in. An idyllic setting. Swans glide, boats float, flowerbeds show off, children splash in the pond. Distantly our village's morris dancers downed their beers.

'Hey, Lovejoy!' Bosh yelled, our morris-master. 'We're one short. Straggo's late. Play for us?'

'Not me, Bosh,' I shouted across the footbridge. 'I'm still lame.'

They laughed. Their uillean bagpipes were warming up.

This is the English bagpipe. Morrismen use it because it's the only reed pipe that sounds beautiful however drunk the musicians. You do it under-arm, no blowing.

As I approached I could see Paltry among the cars, slithering on the wet grass, and decided to catch him.

Because I let infant cricketers cross the footbridge ahead of me, I didn't see Paltry die.

'Good luck, pal,' I was telling the last neophyte cricketer, when I realised something was horribly wrong. People were clustering where Paltry had been. I started to run.

A woman was screaming, two quick-thinkers tapping mobiles. Slipping in puddles, I ran to the mêlée.

By the time I shoved through, Paltry was dead. He was on the ground, his frock awry and his daft high-heeled shoes off. His wig was beside him, his collecting tin still in his hand. Two women and a little girl were staring white-faced at the carnage. Blood smeared the grass, men waving cars to stay away. A St John Ambulance man was calling to keep back, please.

Paltry had been crushed between two motors. One was a silvery thing with a grinning radiator grille wearing fragments of flesh like a bloodied mouth. A gent was wringing his hands and explaining, 'He jumped right out in front. I braked but...'

Can you jump in high heels on muddy grass?

He hid his face, overcome. I watched him. Thespians are never any different. They're born to it. St Nicholas is patron saint of bad actors. He has a lot to answer for.

'Use this.' Gentry had a travelling rug. He looked bored.

A kindly stranger covered Paltry's body. I noticed

stubble on Paltry's chin. How pathetic is that? The overcome gent was still acting distraught. Melodramatic. Killers often are.

Another man said, on cue, 'You didn't stand a chance.'

Any chance of prosecution? No. Of justice? No. Of being done for Paltry's murder? No. Of getting off scotage free, though? Sure, for murderers always depart laughing. Blood money fixes laws.

Firemen arrived and shepherded cars. I stood closer to the killer, who was giving his lies to some policeman who had finally bothered to come. The whole sorry panto was a sham. The oh-so-handy witness was calm, like any man of straw. In olden days, men willing to sell their election votes lolled by tavern walls with a straw sticking from their boots – hence the term 'straw man'. This witness didn't swap glances with the murderer. They're trained.

Odd fact: straw men are always female in the north, male in the south. My cousin in Lancashire runs a list of straw men. He calls it his Girl Panel: forty-two housewives, alibis to order. He takes thirty per cent. (Sorry. This sounds like a commercial.)

Liza, our town's reporter, rushed up. I pointed out the gent who killed Paltry. 'Got your photographer, Lize?'

'Shit,' she said. 'My fucking luck.' An Oxford sociologist, Liza thinks crudity is trendy.

'Borrow a camera and snap the perpetrators. I'll point.'

'Fucking brilliant,' she said, and did. She then looked. 'Perps, Lovejoy?'

Maybe Paltry knew something his killers wanted kept silent. 'Aye. One day, I'll send word. Promise you'll come a-running, OK?'

'Lovejoy?' she said uncertainly. 'Was it truly murder?'

I nicked a pencil and listed car numbers, makes, colours of vehicles until I got moved on. An ambulance took Paltry. I'd never seen Paltry in normal clothes. Was he really serious about Florida and a sex change? Blue lights flashed, no sirens. The police collected Paltry's tin. A constable asked, curious, 'What operation was this?'

'Dunno.' Well, I didn't.

'Did you see it happen?'

'No. I was too late. Like you.' And went on my way.

Hurrying down Long Wyre Street, I saw Big Frank.

'Who backed the tea auction, Frank?' I didn't mention Paltry.

Every tea auction needs an organiser, auctioneer, tyler – Eunice this time – and a wallet, as we call the hard man who funds any crime.

'Tasker. Nice bloke, Tasker.'

My heart reeled. 'Aye, nice bloke.'

Tasker is a quiet Irish geezer, smallish and thin. You couldn't guess his age if you tried. His face looks used up. Blue of eye, never raises his voice, and wears the same overcoat summer and winter. An Ulsterman of unswerving loyalty who wears an orange rose, Tasker has a slow sigh worse than a death knell. I told Frank so-long and shakily turned into Eld Lane and headed for the music I could hear. If Tasker realised I'd spotted the marred decanter... Would Eunice tell Tasker?

Ahead, I glimpsed Hennell, the stout gent who'd bought Sandy's rotten glassware. In the town square Sandy was already performing his lunatic dance, hoping somebody would talent-spot him and put him on TV.

'Isn't Sandy wonderful?' Laura's iron grip drew me under a coffee awning. I went with her, the weakest wimp in the Hundreds.

'No. He's a loon.'

She ordered coffees with an imperious gesture. Serfs leapt to obey. It's money. Laura seemed to be alone. For a tired moment I felt like telling her to leave me alone, but gave in and sat with her. Sandy was prancing round the fountain in a sequinned cape. His loony idea of fashion was red leather thigh boots, a copper breastplate and enough coloured sashes to sail the Cutty Sark. I saw little to admire.

'Oh, come *on*! He's divine! And he funded me when I needed it.'

'You know Sandy well?' So her Arcade meeting was a sham?

'He was marvellous. We became friends when my...' She was going to say husband, but cut out. 'Sandy will be invaluable in our project.'

Our project now? For the first time I saw her features clearly. Her cheeks showed that incipient Mach 3 drag, though it wasn't quite the wind-tunnel effect so noticeable after a sixth facelift. OK, so she was deadly serious about her mission. For mere vengeance, though?

'Sandy's on my team. He's vital.'

My spirits rose. 'Then why not marry Sandy instead?'

'He's no divvy, Lovejoy.' The waitress served two coffees. 'My husband would believe I'd marry a divvy – but Sandy?'

Mr Hennell joined us, huffing slightly and fanning himself with his hat. He carried the decanter box.

I said, 'Odder things happen, missus.'

Not often, but they do. I know Sally, a dealer from Argentina. She is crazy for Astro, an incompetent drunk. She's offered to buy him out of penury, his addictions and debts, and pay his wife off. Even Isaac Newton couldn't join those dots and make sense.

'Isn't Sandy magnificent?' Hennell gasped. 'Soon he'll release streamers and be a Greek goddess rising from fiery waters.'

Unbelievably, surrounding idlers actually applauded. I craved sanity.

'Amazing!' Laura said adoringly.

Sandy's embarrassing shows always make me feel I'm watching the sea trials of the *Titanic*. I'd not touched her coffee. 'See you later, missus.'

'Stay,' she commanded. 'Mr Hennell.'

Hennell parroted, 'Lovejoy. Your illegitimate son Mortimer verified an antique for Sandy.' He wiped his brow. 'Warm, isn't it?'

Mortimer did? Responsibility weighs you down. I hate it.

'I am the marriage lawyer you've no intention of visiting,' Hennell explained. I should have known. You never see a thin priest, lawyer or politician. They're all as fat as a butcher's dog. Meanwhile Sandy was splashing to Handel's *Messiah* music, the water gold-scarlet and Mel shovelling in colorant. More cleaning bills for ratepayers. People were yelling encouragement.

Laura added sweetly, 'Mortimer is therefore involved in the tea auction fraud. You may not care for Eunice, Lydia, Tinker Dill, Geraldo, Tasker, and the rest. Or even yourself. But you will save Mortimer.'

'It's called a set-up, Lovejoy,' Hennell wheezed. 'Sandy swapped his mint antique decanter for the faulty one.'

Laura rolled in the aisles. 'Isn't Sandy gorgeous?'

Gorgeous, was he, that idiot ponce who put Mortimer into danger? Now ice cold, I stared at Sandy's finale, *Yeomen of the Guard*, with him transmogged into a strutting guardsman before admiring sycophants. Two council workmen wearily moved in to clear the mess.

'Time for marriage talk, Lovejoy. Ready?'

Hennell yanked out a watch that made me weak with longing. I'd assumed my malaise came from his decanter. It was a pair-cased watch by Antram of London. He clicked it open and examined the champlevé surface. (Incidentally, *pair*-cased: inner and outer cases.) Mesmerised, I gaped at the priceless thing. Joseph Antram never signed his Christian name, just surname, even in the watches he made for King George the First about 1715. Champlevé only means the surface pits are grooved and filled with enamel.

'That isn't nicked, Mr Hennell?' I asked humbly.

Two similar Antrams were lately stolen, but hadn't yet reached the Art Loss Register. To date, the ALR lists 140,000 decent stolen items, which isn't much considering the vast annual turnover.

'Maybe,' he said laconically. Lawyers smile like they've never done it before. 'Do you want the Antram, Lovejoy? As a persuader? I can always get another.'

And he meant it. I looked from him to Laura.

'You the big bun, Mr Hennell?'

Bun is the northern dealers' word for the wallet.

Hennell gestured a modest oh-come-come with a throwaway smirk.

'I *contribute*, Lovejoy. I never *exploit*.'

'Excuse me, please.' Laura rose with that pretty movement women have. A man stands up like an expanding trellis, all creaks and angles, whereas females are fluid. I watched her go. Mr Hennell sighed.

'Isn't she a picture, Lovejoy? Women never recognise the man they're made for.'

Hello, I thought, was this unrequited longing? I know it, having so much of my own. I eyed Ginny, the waitress. I'd done her a favour when she was evicted from her grotty lodgings after a calamitous affair. I paid her to act as spam, meaning somebody to ask phoney questions about antiques. This is a quick way to identify rival dealers. They can't resist replying, to denigrate particular antiques, or to suss out other bidders. A spammer is always a she, incidentally. They can easily be spotted if they're bad actresses.

'No credit, Lovejoy.' She swung away.

'People think,' Mr Hennell began affably, 'that marriage has always stayed the same. Not so.'

'So?'

'Half of all marriages end in divorce. One mega-famous Hollywood actress even boasts of a marriage that lasted a mere fifteen *minutes*. Was it Zsa-Zsa Gabor? Now for the history…'

He would have been interesting if I'd listened. Instead, I watched Laura, and thought. We tend to forget that motive doesn't exist when nostalgia takes over. In May 2003, some Hapsburgs demanded back a schloss, plus

20,000-odd hectares of woodland. The grandson of the last Austro-Hungarian Thingy made a polite request: the nation's rules say it is compulsory to restore rightful ownership of possessions nicked in the 1930s. Ergo, said blithe legal phrases, the Hapsburgs were victims. Ordinary Austrians were outraged, said it all belonged to the people, so the Hapsburgs could get stuffed. The argument continues. My point: never mind motive. It's what you do that matters.

A bird I knew was a writer's wife from Leeds. She was an Aussie publisher, rich and pretty. The writer fell for another woman, – fights, divorce, mayhem. The OW was older and plain as a pikestaff, as folk say. His rich ex-wife quickly remarried back into her own elite circle – you still see her photo in glossies. The writer now drives a Leeds bus, and his OW cleans the village hall. They are happy. But is the beautiful rich lady publisher full of merriment? No. She never smiles in her pictures. So life really is as *you* see things. I think the Hapsburgs should stop griping. They, however, think they're victims. A researcher recently counted 'victims' defined by Human Rights pillocks, and totalled 109 per cent. Daft, or what?

'...so, you'll be divorced the next day, Lovejoy,' Mr Hennell concluded, finally catching my attention. He saw my confusion and looked his reproach. 'I just explained.'

'I'm not marrying anybody.'

Ginny immediately came over to earwig. 'More coffee?'

'Yes, please,' I said firmly. 'And biscuits. On credit.'

'Just this once,' she said, and moved away.

See? *As you see things.* Malthus touched on the subject and got nowhere.

Hennell's voice sank to a whisper. 'How many friends have you, Lovejoy? Twenty, thirty? List them. They could all go bankrupt.' He smiled as tumult broke out across the square, Sandy at Gilbert and Sullivan's 'Ruler of the Queen's Nav*ee*'. Sandy says shame is its own reward.

'You see, Lovejoy,' Hennell added kindly, 'Laura's scheme is a necessary sham that is vital to her. Just go along, and all will be well. I sprang Tasker's two sons.'

A gong stunned the world. Two pigeons fainted. People applauded. Mel revved the rheostat. Sandy re-appeared trilling, 'I am the monarch...' to guffaws.

Tasker? Breeding yet more psychopaths? Hennell beamed. 'So Tasker owes me. Your friends? Ruin, homelessness, desolation, Lovejoy. Or...'

'Or?' Here it came.

'Or you get a fortune. Help Laura for a few days, and your sprog Mortimer sails on. Your pretty apprentice Lydia stays alive.' The swine smiled. 'And Tasker...'

'Tasker what?' I asked, voice thick.

'Tasker gets told how you narrowly averted some disaster at the tea auction, et jovial cetera. Your little world carousels on.'

'What's the connection between you and Laura?'

'Lawyer and client, Lovejoy!' He leant forward confidentially. 'And you know how close those relationships can be!'

Prima waved from the bookshop opposite. I reached for the biscuits – gift horse and all that.

'I'll be at my cottage, OK?'

'Glad you're seeing sense, Lovejoy.' He snaffled the biscuits quicker than I could blink. Lawyers and clergymen always move fast for freebies. 'Thank you, young lady. On Lovejoy's credit, I think you said?'

As he rose to go, I asked outright, 'Mr Hennell. Did you top Paltry?'

His fat gut bounced with humour. 'Not personally. No good having a dog and barking yourself, eh?'

Always leave a sinking ship, I say. Grab the lifeboat before anyone else. I went hopefully towards Prima. Laura beckoned me from Sandy's merry mob. I pretended not to notice. I wondered who would pay for Paltry's headstone, and what to tell the stonemason to engrave. Him or her?

Chapter Ten

spam: false interest in antiques (trade slang)

Prima lives in a dream, hoping to find the world's most-prized antique. Greed makes us all lunatics. She uses her husband's gelt to fund private investigators to look into tales of fabled antiquities, so she has connections.

'I've a sniff, Prima.' I looked round like a spy.

'What, darling?' she breathed.

'Laura's husband – Ted, isn't he? – had sight of Good Queen Bess's portrait locket ring. You know the one? Opens to reveal miniatures of her mum, Anne Boleyn, and Bess herself. Close the locket and the two portraits kiss. Beautiful.' I almost filled up at the thought, being sensitive. Prima zoomed to the heart of the matter.

'God, what a *find*! I've heard of it!' She clutched my arm. I saw Laura frown, suspecting rival falsehoods. "Ted Moon, the collector who ran off when his wife won gillions? A missing girl from the sea estuaries? She's not dead, Lovejoy. We think Ted ran off with her. See Smethie. He taught Ted Moon jewels.'

'Eh? That's him.' I gazed at her with max sincerity. 'If

we find the locket, Prima, you and me'll go halves. It's gold, with rubies.'

Her face clouded at the thought of sharing. 'Of course, darling!' she cried. 'I'll get a man right on it! Love you!' And was gone. She would simply hire somebody to hunt my – no, *her* – rumour down.

Fed up with all that breathing, I went to find Mr Smethirst. I felt Laura's eyes burning me as I left the square.

Old Smethirst lives next to his sister-in-law whom he loves. His wife is pure malice, but who knows which came first, the hen or the egg? (Actually, scientists now say it was the egg because it was all mutated DNA, but much they know.) Has motive any power at all? Good Queen Bess once actually received a letter, currently in Greenwich, from Czar Ivan the Terrible. It was a proposal of marriage. Ivan blithely offered to poison his current Czarina so he could wed our Liz One. But who can swear the proposal wasn't dangled by Bess herself for complex diplomatic reasons? She is my womanest bird of all time. Cleopatra's my also-ran. Hen, egg, motives.

Mr Smethirst was in his workshop.

'Wotcher, Mr Smethirst.'

'Sorry, Lovejoy.'

He was at his shed workbench, covered in dust. He's always firing a kiln. I took over the bellows while he had a rest.

'Don't worry. No harm done.'

For a minute we spoke of Paltry. He heard me out and we expressed bafflement. 'What are you making?'

He survives on fakes. His factoids are usually culled from newspapers.

'A miniature scientific bathyscape.'

'A deep-sea diver's submarine?' His kiln was shoebox size.

'Ah. An American scientist invented a football-sized gadget that will sink to the Earth's centre. I call my fake Prototype XI. I'll sell it at Mildenhall.'

Mildenhall was once an American Air Force base, *mucho* secret. So far, so plausible. Except, how many scientists would his football hold?

'Isn't the Earth's core hot? Won't it melt?'

'I'm coating it in ceramic, like space shuttles.'

'Won't the buyer want to see in it?'

'No opening. I've stamped USAF on it. It's full of scrap iron.' He looked wistful and lit his pipe. 'Scientists reckon you only need dig it down fourteen miles, and it'll sink through the Earth's magma. Isn't that brilliant?'

Well, no. The scientist's original might do just that, but Mr Smethirst's scrap iron ball would just melt and send no letters home. Deceivers deceive.

'Ted Moon, Smethie. Why didn't the plod nick him?'

'That girl? Wasn't dead. Lovely. I'm glad she and him…' He cut himself off. 'I thought you'd know, Lovejoy. There's been sightings, like Elvis and Sir Francis Drake.' He blew a smoke ring, to my envy. I keep trying to do it with candle smoke. 'I wonder about his missus's win.'

That stopped me. He pointed with his pipe, keep going. I resumed pumping the bellows.

'You think she didn't win anything?'

'We'll never know. I knew Ted when he was a babby.

Good as gold, honest as you or me.'

'Pure, then?' I cracked.

'Don't joke, Lovejoy. Not all people are bad. I reckon she was playing away.'

'Laura had another bloke?'

'She was a right goer, if you'll pardon the expression.' Too many contradictions for me, and I said so.

'Young Edward was straight as a die. I lost touch, until Laura told me to collect antiques for her to show.'

I heard somebody coming down the path to the shed, so I shushed him and bent to my task, cunning smoothie that I am.

'D'you like my Regency silver tree, Lovejoy?' He gestured at the windowsill. 'Silver nitrate costs the Earth, though they always sell.'

'I've never seen an original Arbor Dianae.'

As I worked the bellows I inspected the glass globe. We think we have reached the epitome of civilisation. Wrong. The average Regency dame was talented. She played musical instruments, composed verses, quoted Milton's poetry, made any food or clothes you cared to name, preserved fruit and groceries for winter, identified plants, and made family medicines from opiates to laxatives.

And, I thought, she constructed her family's amusements. The globe was sealed, and contained a colourless liquid with, well, a miniature silver tree.

It was beautiful.

'Four drachms of silver nitrate in distilled water, four drachms of mercury, and that's it.' We dedicated forgers talk in old measures.

'And it just grows, eh?'

'I'll set it in resin so it can travel, then sell. Notice I've used old glass, for authenticity?'

'Good point.' I also like lead and tin trees, which are common, but silver glitters better. I love genuine fakes.

'I sincerely hope, Mr Smethirst,' Lydia said sternly from the shed doorway, 'no deception is intended. May I enter, please?'

'Wotcher, love. Mr Smethirst is giving it to charity.'

'That's right,' the old man said gloomily.

'Then I do hope its mercury is adequately sealed.' She smiled at my industry. 'How sweet of you, Lovejoy, to help with the kiln.'

Isn't it? I thought miserably, giving him the bent eye to keep quiet.

'I brought your travel funds, Lovejoy.'

'Where am I going?'

'Mrs Ellen Jaynor will donate to the Sick Baby ward, Lovejoy, in return for your services. Refusal is out of the question.'

'Oh. Right.' I thought wistfully of killing Ellen Jaynor. I could run her down in a dark alley, if my Austin Ruby got going and the chassis held out. I wish I hadn't thought those thoughts, in view of the deaths soon to happen. 'See you, Mr Smethirst.'

'Toodle-oo, son. Good luck.'

'Incidentally, Lovejoy,' Lydia said, as we left. 'Did you know the four expertises a Regency lady needed to grow peas? She sowed the purple variety of late pea, after soaking them overnight in warm milk. Then covered the drills in minced gorse, with mineral oil...'

'Very clever.' I didn't listen.

'You leave soon, Lovejoy.' She smiled brightly. 'May I come?'

'If you like,' I said, my heart suddenly singing, as romance books say. If Lydia was along, things might be not altogether ruinous. I'd have someone to take the blame if things went wrong. Life isn't always downhill, I thought.

Chapter Eleven

Castro: all right, correct
(Aus. slang, fr. Cuban, cubic, 'all square')

That evening I struck lucky. There are only two kinds of luck, antiques and women.

She came over. I was gloaking in the Marquis of Granby. 'Lovejoy?'

Not a bailiff or a debt collector. No irate husband in tow. Three plusses. I smiled. Her nose wrinkled, being used to better places, though the old Marquis is one of East Anglia's better dumps.

'How expensive are you for a night?'

The world stilled. Have you ever felt that strange sensation when slot machines go quiet and conversation stops? A noisy football team had arrived to carouse the hours away. I glanced round, red-faced.

'Er, for antiques?'

'Of course.'

Folk lost interest. She sat back, handbag on her knees. Her suit looked on its maiden voyage, hat and gloves in matching cobalt blue. Her eyes were so large they seemed to emit their own light instead of merely noticing the world's old used-up glim. Bonny, bonny.

She looked good enough to eat yet spoke like a tax demand. Her gaze was glacial. The hubbub returned. Tracy from Wigan laughed, all mischief.

'All right, Lovejoy, dear?' Tracy's never forgiven me. She once set up a dealers' ring for a coaching table at Herrington's. (Keep a lookout for these rare little centrally hinged folding tables, incidentally. They're mistaken for modern camping stools and furniture books forget to put them in. They're worth a mint.) What else could I do but nick Tracy's coaching table and sell it? I'd written her a really honest IOU, but women harbour grudges.

'Yes, ta, Tracy.' I put on a brave face.

'For how long?' she drawled. Everybody cracked up.

My lady rose with one-move elegance. I followed humbly to ironic cheers.

'Get my car.' The lady dropped keys into my palm.

'Er, I'm banned, missus.'

Angrily she snatched the keys and walked to a Jaguar that waited sneering at the kerb.

'I suppose I shall have to drive.' And as I drew breath for a snappy response, she snarled, 'And stop saying "er". Men don't dither.'

'Er, right.'

The Jag's journey took a millisec. We reached a night school, where myriads of tiny girls in ballet gear trooped and pirouetted. Noise filled a honeycomb of rooms thumping with piano, cellos, violins wailing. Infant musical genius was at work. Everybody we passed greeted my mentor with, 'Good evening, Miss Farnacott.' She swept into an office, flinging her hat aside. A secretary cleared off. I wasn't the only one scared of the Winter Queen.

'Sit.'

Like a dog. The door closed on the cacophony.

'You insulted my father, Lovejoy.' Those icy eyes fixed me. 'You sent him into a decline. Your explanation?'

So far the week had been the pits. Prison, speed-dating, Loony Laura's marriage proposal, arrests, my robbery at Eastwold, problems from the auction, Paltry's murder. The Free World had lost all allure. In fact, maybe prison had the edge. Now this Musical Avenger.

'Erm, I don't know your dad, missus.' My only Farnacott was George from Hong Kong, who passed on years since. 'If that'll be all…'

'*Sit.* You and that ignorant bint treated Father like a punkah wallah.'

Her mouth fascinated me. Fury made it a slit. Her eyes hooded. Wasn't there a snake that did that, or was it an eagle in that Ratisbon poem? Her features were smooth. Even white with rage she was beautiful. What, twenty-eight, say? I hadn't heard such out-dated slang for a generation.

'Who was she, Lovejoy? Don't try to protect her.'

Antiques dogma says never get between two warring women. Whoever Miss Farnacott meant, I didn't give much for her chances. Hang on, I thought suddenly. Old Smethirst had been mistreated. Bint was lingua franca. Arabic, was it, for a female?

'Sorry, missus, but I don't know who you mean.'

She rocked back. Everybody else sags when they loll, but not Miss Farnacott. Her body stayed shapely. I sat up to match the room's mood of subservience.

'My father's in hospital, Lovejoy. He had a heart attack after your visit to his workshop. Two things.' She leant forward. I leant back.

No hesitation now. I wanted to escape with one bound. She honestly scared me. I could imagine her gazing at the sun, and the sun giving up from lack of nerve.

'My father may seem like an old chickenwallah to your lunatic team, but he was once a gentleman of influence. Don't treat him like a kutch-nay. Understand?'

What the hell was she saying? I got the general idea. Her dad was a gent. I said, 'Yes, Miss Farnacott.' Kutch-nay was old soldier's slang for a nobody. Hindi?

'Two: My father stays out of your mad scheme.'

'Yes, Miss Farnacott.'

Those terrible eyes saw I was crushed and saw that it was good. 'No evil touches Father, or I shall have you hunted down by pig-stickers. You can go.'

Shaking, I made it to the door. I didn't ask for a lift back to town. Closing her office door behind me, I saw a crowd of little tap-dancers clattering down the stairs, the children laughing amid wrong arpeggios. The world was still normal. As I left, three miniature ballerinas passed wearing those frothy non-skirts that always remind me of Degas and biscuit-tin paper. One was saying, 'Let's ask Miss Farnacott if we can watch the principal dancers tomorrow.' They all cried, 'Yes! Lovely!' And they piled into Miss F's office. I drew breath to shout a dire warning – I mean, dragon's cave and maidens, right? We heroes know our duty. Then I glimpsed her looking up with the sweetest smile as the titches piled in. And the dragon said,

'Good heavens! My very best dancers! The answer is yes, darlings, whatever you want...'

The door closed. I reeled out through the press of jugglers and wandering brass trios. A dragon with a heart? The Winter Queen a secret angel? Not to me.

Plodding back to civilisation, I reflected on how the antiques trade is everybody's whipping-boy. It's wrong. Antiques are only as good or bad as people. Don't blame a penny for being in the wrong slot when you put it there.

People are people, the old saying goes. La Farnacott mentioned evil as if she knew it well.

Evil? You can only start with the beautiful Lady Alice.

This bad lass began as humble Alice Kyteler, the world's historical front-runner for true evil. Born in Kilkenny in the late 1300s, she had a succession of wealthy husbands. None lived long. In fact, they died with speed. Her last husband was Sir John le Poer, who one day noticed his hair and nails were tumbling out. His anxious children came. Neighbours realised they'd seen it all before. Lady Alice's rooms were searched. Poisons were found. The minute her cell door clanged in the pokey, Sir John recovered, and Holy Ireland confidently awaited a good, sensible outcome, like burning Lady Alice at the stake after a quick Ave Maria.

No way. The prosecutor was the Bishop of Ossory. Rich Lady Alice had lawyers, a tangled lot even in those far-off centuries. She appealed to the Lord Chancellor of Ireland. And, lucky, lucky, he was her kinsman, Roger Outlawe (real name; I'm not making this up). He got her off. She skipped the country.

The story's grand finale? *Her loyal maid Petronilla was*

burnt instead. The moral? Evil is a survivor, and innocence is not.

Not so antiques. They are so-o-o-o different. Remember that.

Maybe Miss Farnacott just hated men, I thought, trudging to town, hoping to cadge a free nosh. To gloak, incidentally, is to watch somebody else eat, in hopes. I classified Miss Farnacott: bonny, good with infants and dated slang, but murderous. Apart from that, she could be forgotten.

Couldn't be more wrong again.

Chapter Twelve

**divvy (n & v): one who detects antiques
without evidence**

Starvation has one good feature – it's cheaper. From town,
my cottage is five miles as the crow flies. 'Except,' like in
the Humphrey Bogart film, 'they ain't crows.'

Nobody in my cottage when I reached Lovejoy
Antiques, Inc. The *For Sale* sign was cancelled by a red *Sold*
stripe. I said a nervous hello to the empty garden, and no
silent son appeared from the mists. Safe, I slipped inside.
The gibbous moon's light was that slanting hopeless stuff,
so I did a lot of blundering for a candle. The candle was
put into my hand. Like a fool, I said, 'Ta,' then screeched
in fright. A match struck, showing Mortimer. I blistered
him while my heart resumed its normal service, what the
hell, etc.

'I came because of that lady, Lovejoy.'

He gave me fish and chips with mushy peas, a loaf, and
a flask of tea. I fell on them, my eyes on him in case he
wisped into the ether. His stealth comes from living in a
wattle-and-daub hut among reed warblers. For God's sake,
he owned the whole frigging manor.

The kilojoules kicked in. 'What lady?'

'The headmistress, Miss Farnacott. She's hired Terminal.'

Gulp. I'm scared of so many. '*Terminal*? Jesus. What for?'

'To track you. She is cousin to Judge Jeffries.'

Double gulp. Judge Jeffries is famed. Innocent or guilty, nobody gets off when he's on the bench. He once reported himself for a minor traffic violation and demanded the police take action. They lacked evidence, so he actually fined himself and docked his own driving licence. Miss Farnacott proved Charles Darwin was right. Genetics will out.

'Maybe it's time to emigrate.'

'Terminal's at the Queen's Head. I'll tell you when he leaves.'

East Anglian countrymen know the lore of leafy lanes. Mortimer goes one better. He knows things *without* knowing them, if you follow. Once, I had to meet him down Maldon way, loveliest of harbours. Mortimer was lying on the greensward, eyes closed, as I arrived and explained I was on trial again. Meanwhile, a yacht out on the North Sea started off in a new direction, sails flapping, and I wondered vaguely why boats did that. Mortimer – eyes still closed – said, 'The wind's veering, Lovejoy,' quite like we were in mid-chat. I said, 'How did you know what I was going to ask?' He said, 'The waves sound different. And your thoughts show.' Sure enough, the breeze changed. He once saved my life by this rum business. I think he's creepy.

'Do I deserve Terminal? Little me?'

'She thinks – excuse me – you are rubbish. It's her father.'

Shouldn't sons protect their dads, even if illegitimate? Terminal is a killer – he's said to have executed a paedo in Soho.

'Look, Mortimer. Things are out of hand. I worry about Eunice Whorwood, and suddenly Tasker is in the arena. I help Veronica at the Antiques Arcade, and some fat lawyer berk threatens me. I speak to old Smethie, and Terminal, who can break my back with an eyelash, haunts my hedge? I want out, Mortimer.' I spelt it for him, O-U-T.

'Miss Farnacott has forbidden you to visit Mr Smethirst. She hired Terminal to ensure your compliance.' Admin-speak. Mortimer would be great on some council.

'That's OK. I won't even try.'

'Ah,' he said, 'but—'

He maddens me. He folded the chip paper, wiping the table down with a serviette. I hoped for pudding. He just looked about for a waste bin. None. Mortimer was well brought up. *Requiescat in pace*, Arthur, you raised a tidy lad.

'Why the fuss?'

'Because Mr Smethirst has asked for you, Lovejoy. Side Ward 3A at the Beeches. He thinks he'll die soon, though the doctor says he will recover. He keeps trying to smuggle messages to you. Two guards stop him,' Mortimer added. 'Terminal's men.'

This meant yet more people wanting my help. I said so.

Mortimer leant forward. Here came something from the heart. 'Lovejoy. You really must get a waste bin.'

I blew up. 'Almost as important as a frigging waste

bin, is the problem of seeing Smethie without Terminal marmalising me.'

He smiled. 'Your solemn oath to Miss Farnacott did not last, Lovejoy.'

'You sarcastic sod. OK, when?'

'Terminal has started out for here. Come this way. No noise.' He snuffed the candle. When I dowse wicks they stink the place out. Not for Mortimer.

His hand grasped my forearm with surprising strength, and I was guided into the moonlight. Boards creaked over the door, presumably him replacing the slats. We went into the lane. I was tempted to sprint, but he stayed me. We moved through a marsh, then over somebody's lawn where Mortimer whispered to quieten some fool of a dog. We emerged into the light of our village's three street lamps. He hauled a bicycle from a ditch.

Me straddling the seat, he rode with silent intensity past our old church. He didn't even slow among the trees of Friday Wood, scaring me to death. We alighted at Fellham near the Fox & Stork.

'Go that way.' He pointed. 'Three miles, five furlongs is Mrs Fenwright's cottage. Knock. She will give you a truckle bed, and breakfast tomorrow.'

'Ta, er…' I once tried to call him son, but it came out wrong. Mrs Fenwright's cottage had to be on Mortimer's manor of Saffron Fields. 'How do I get in to see Smethie?'

'Morning, at four o'clock. You will be Male Charge Nurse Hargreaves.'

I said, stricken, 'That's bloody ridicu—'

Moonlight. I was talking to moonlight. One day, I seethed, this worm will turn. The first people I'd clobber would be bossy sons, illegitimate or not. I took the best part of an hour to wobble to Mrs Fenwright's.

There, I can report that Male Charge Nurse Hargreaves passed a restless night in an outhouse.

Dawn happens before it should. It had no right waking me at three o'clock on a cold frosty morning, urging me to a chill bath ('You won't melt, Lovejoy. Mortimer said you'd be full of silly complaints,' etc) and giving me an enormous breakfast. The attractive Mrs Fenwright stood me by the gate at ten to four. Even the moon looked knackered.

'Is Mortimer coming himself?' she asked, all eager.

'Dunno, missus.'

'You take care of him, d'you hear?' she said in the threatening way women have. Message: protect Mortimer at all costs. Lovejoy doesn't matter. 'Here he is!' she squeaked. A car appeared.

Mortimer alighted. No courtesy light, I noticed. We were secret. Mrs Fenwright beamed at Mortimer, then opened his jacket with a woman's proprietorial vigilance and tutted. 'You're getting thin. Don't people feed you?' She glared at me like I'd stolen the lad's grub. 'Won't you stay for breakfast, love?' Him, not me.

'Yes, please, Fenny. Have you any potato cakes?'

'Yes!' she shrieked, and rushed in. I hadn't been offered any. There's fascist discrimination about.

Mortimer ordered, 'Change into the male nurse's uniform in the motor, Lovejoy. This car will collect you after fifty minutes. The senior sister will simulate booking you on duty.'

Silently he shut the car door on me. How did he *do*

that? We drove towards town, me donning a horrible blue-striped uniform complete with a name tag. I felt a right prawn.

The Beeches is a smallish private hospital, new as a pin and shaped like a child's drawing. The driver said nothing, except when he stopped near a hedge footpath.

'Main door down there. Fifty minutes.'

'What if I get held up?'

'I'll break your legs. Mortimer wants you at the casino by eight.'

Casino? 'Of course he does.' I thought, Now what?

Rudely, he snatched the ball I'd made of my own clothes and drove off. I reported for duty to a senior sister in the staff office, and she signed the staff register. She didn't even look up, but asked if he was all right. Assuming she meant Mortimer, I said, 'Yes, fine.' She gestured me away. In the corridor I examined a wall chart. Side Ward 3A was two floors up. I didn't use the lift in case I met doctors barking commands in Latin.

Nobody was about except one nurse bent over her desk, screens flickering constant vigilance. Mr Smethirst was in a lone side ward. I slipped in and stood, feeling daft. He was like a pale, wizened fly in a web of polyester tubes. He had a medley of screens. I moved experimentally, saw myself appear on the nurse's monitor, and slyly shuffled out of the camera's view.

'Wotcher, Lovejoy,' Smethie startled me by saying.

'Er, wotcher, Mr Smethirst.' I tried for casual, but failed. Everybody spotted me before I knew where I was myself. 'Just visiting. You OK?' He looked terrible.

'Thank heaven you came, Lovejoy. I've not got long.'

'Got to keep out of the nurse's screen, sir,' I explained. Why had I called him sir? 'Want anything?'

'Get the recorder.' He gestured feebly. I found a matchbox-sized device. 'Press the red dot. Put it by my face.'

I obeyed, and sat on the floor among dangling bottles. I never trust gadgets. Batteries go wrong when I'm around, and I'm death to digitals.

'Lovejoy, I'm sorry about Laura.'

'No harm done, sir.'

'Stop that, son. Just listen. You mustn't join their daft plan, d'you hear? Don't be talked into it.' He struggled for breath. I watched anxiously, but he got going again. 'We've forgotten white tribes are doomed.'

'White tribes?' I thought I'd misheard.

'That's what history calls us. Why d'you think we came to England?'

'Er...' Did he want answers? I didn't even know the frigging question.

'Listen hard. The centuries have marooned us all. Like tide pools, full of strange creatures who should have left with the receding oceans. Instead, we live as anachronisms. Us tribes even taught our young to be full of hate. It's not right. You follow?'

''Course,' I said. 'Tough luck.'

'No, you don't, son. Keep recording. We forgotten tribes are everywhere in the Third World, though you'd be hard put to find us. Can you believe, we're even in America?'

'Good heavens,' I said politely, like you do when old people ramble.

'You're too thick to understand. No offence.'

'None taken, Smethie,' I said, well narked. I wasn't going to call him 'sir' after that crack. I'm not thick, just forgetful. I settled down. It was starting to sound like a chemistry lecture.

'Take the recording. Guard it with your life.'

'Promise, Smethie.'

He sighed. 'That's a load off my mind. You're hopeless, Lovejoy, but you'll keep faith. My tale will take twenty minutes. I was born…'

And off he strayed. It was a funny old drift, talk of Dutch folk (I think), Confederate battalions (I think), French-speaking Polish troops of centuries ago, whole countries betrayed by the League of Nations, diamond fields, South African politicos I'd never heard of, Namibia, and forgotten wars.

Coming to, I realised the clock had moved on and old Smethie was still whispering. I must have dozed.

'See, Lovejoy?' he was going on. 'Even the Great Silk Road left traces. We can't abandon duty.'

''Course not.' I tried to sound indignant. 'I always think that.'

'I'm done, son. Take the recorder. Transcribe it.'

'Right, sir.' Sir was back again.

'Good luck, Lovejoy. You're not bad, son. Just a pillock.'

'Thank you.' Thank you, for *that*?

'Their mad scheme, son. You can't take on the world for the sake of a few tide-pool tribes who don't even know they're extinct, can you?'

'How true, sir.'

'I knew you'd see sense, you daft bugger. Goodbye, son.'

Was that it? 'Ta-ra, sir.'

He did his long sigh, I took the recorder and I slid along the dim corridors to the outside world. I didn't sign Charge Nurse Hargreaves (i.e. me) off duty, which caused me not a flicker of conscience.

Four minutes from getting my legs broken, I boarded the car. I changed as Leg-Break drove me to a lay-by on the A12.

'That footpath to the railway,' Leg-Break said. 'The casino's there.'

He drove off without another word, miserable sod. I walked to Belfast Jim's tea-and-wad nosher, a transport container in which Jim feeds drivers hauling south from the Hook of Holland ferries. I had a stack of toast and marmalade. It felt like years since I'd had a bite in Mrs Fenwright's. I got a lift to town. Casino, indeed.

Odd things happen. I was crossing against traffic in a spectacular fashion – the town's roads are helter-skelter – when a bloke stopped me. Tall, he was impressively wizened like he was used to the torrid heat of East Anglia's baking sun (joke). I dragged him out of the maelstrom onto a traffic island.

'You nearly got done there. Traffic here's all one way.'

'Thank you.' He held a paper. 'Can you guide me, please?'

South African? He had that clipped, melodious intonation. Or Dutch? We get a lot on the coast. They drive on the right, whereas South Africans are lefties like sensible old us.

'Where?' The scribbled address was my lane, and *Ly*. For Lovejoy? Too much coincidence for me. 'Got a motor?' I dithered. 'A bus from the cinema goes every hour.'

'Thank you.' He had the clearest eyes you ever saw, long-range orbs of a hunter, and his skin looked pruned. Hot dry lands?

'Not much there,' I said helpfully. 'No inns. Just an old church and a post office. Will nowhere else do?'

'No, sir, and thank you.' No sirrr end thenk yoo. Polite definitely meant Southern African. Old Smethirst had mentioned there. What had he said, though? I'd not really listened.

Lurking by the Bull Tavern, I saw him catch the number 66 village bus. A stranger looking for me, with my address, asking me – nobody else, Doctor Watson – and speaking as if he knew Afrikaans? Had he come from where they had virtually no proper traffic at all?

I vowed not to go home for a bit, let the blighter draw a blank. Ogling Truly Newly's antiquarian window, I was found by Sandy and Mel. They told me I was to go with them. Mortimer said.

Chapter Thirteen

to bread: to spread bait (fr. angling slang)

'I always say,' Mel snapped as I boarded their monstrosity, 'once a harlot always a harlot.'

'Morning, lads.'

'Mel's *livid*, Lovejoy,' Sandy trilled, using a hand mirror, risking lacerating his eyeballs with mascara. 'Because I smiled at an Italian waiter.' He blinked a million flutters a second.

'Watch where you're going, duckegg,' I said.

Mel ground out, 'Do tarts *ever change*, Lovejoy?'

Their motor is a battleship. Inside, it is a multicoloured cathedral with a bar and TV, shimmering cerise, silver, blues. The roof wears grass (literally, that garden stuff). The bonnet is gold leaf, the body changing colour to match Sandy's mood. Today's hue was an electric emerald, with orange, pink and magenta streaks. The tyres are scarlet, and the windows leaded glass, stolen, Sandy says, from the Church of St Hanky-Panky. You're expected to roll in the aisles. He wants worship for this wit.

'Mind if I nap? I'm bushed!'

'No time, Lovejoy,' Sandy fluted brightly. 'We're due at the casino.'

Casino again? 'What casino, exactly?'

'Once a harlot,' Mel raged, so I switched off. Time the Great Healer must do its stuff.

'Butch people want you,' Sandy carolled.

'Harlot!' Mel boomed.

It beats me why they stay partners. They have an old house with barns for storing Art Deco and Art Nouveau furniture. They're great on treen. Sandy speaks a bizarrely – 'riah' for hair, 'eek' for face, 'jambs' for legs, and the like. His exotic mannerisms are an act, and very boring. He faints when somebody wears the wrong colours. Women love his company. Mel sulks, Sandy titters. They share extortion.

'We're backing your betrothed's plan, Lovejoy.'

'D'you mean Veronica?'

'No, moron. *You're* funding Veronica, remember?'

Another promise gone wrong. I'd forgotten.

'Money out, money in, Lovejoy,' he cooed. 'We're helping the shapeless Laura.'

'Hope it doesn't end in tears.'

Sandy pulled off Old London Road. 'Antiques can't lose. Hadn't you heard?'

'You'd be insane not to go along with Laura, Lovejoy,' Mel said.

We drew in beside a derelict railway siding. I couldn't wait to escape while Sandy made his entrance. An escalator comes from the car roof, Sandy swaying down it to martial music as Mel works recorded applause. 'Yeomen of the Guard' began. I heard Mel shout an angry, 'Lovejoy! Come right back!' but kept going.

Along rusting rails stood a hotel, newly restored from

the little country railway station it once was. New trees stood about, masking the roaring A12 East Anglia-to-London trunk road.

Assuming the hotel would house the casino, I crunched along the gravel and went in. Smiling girls welcomed me. I said I wanted the casino, please.

'Casino? I'm afraid there is no casino here, sir.'

Nobody knows what reception girls do, but there are always plenty to welcome you, then they waft about doing their nails. A display notice announced *Today: Convention of Ex. Disd Clns.* Well, I thought, hearing 'Beaux Gendarmes' playing to the unattentive trees, I'd try anyway, and Mortimer had said. I wanted to get this casino business over.

'Then the convention?' The only game in town.

'Consultant Suite 103, straight through, sir.'

An excited girl came rushing through. 'Sandy's doing his entrance!' she squealed, and the girls dashed away. One receptionist remained. She gave me a wry smile.

'Sandy owns a third of our hotel chain, sir.'

At the double doors I heard voices, two guttural, one a melodious Latino, and a woman's vaguely familiar voice. I knocked and entered. There were cards on a vast mahogany table, with people seated around it. Poker, was it? I never really know. Laura looked in control, her smart lime green suit showing off her colouring.

And an antique lay on the table.

'Lovejoy!' She gave the sweetest smile. 'At last!'

'Morning everyone.' Tough guy me, no concessions. And something really strange happened. Walk into a gathering where they've been talking about you, they don't look up. It felt weird. I suddenly knew I seriously mattered to this lot.

'I propose we introduce ourselves,' Laura said. 'Pierrilus?'

A stocky balding man gave a nod. 'Pierrilus Glinsky.' His expression warned me to watch my step.

The antique still lay there. I stared at it. It stared back, possibly thinking, What have we here?

'Hugo Hahn.' A tall man rose and looked me full in the face. Pruned, leathery skin. Almost skeletal, he shook my hand with a firm grip. Not the silly squeezing contest the young inflict on each other, but enough to say he could match anyone. He'd asked the way to my village. He too remembered.

The antique was still there.

Laura went saccharine. 'Donna?'

The other lady smiled a minimalist smile. 'Donna da Silfa.'

'M'lady,' I said, which earned Laura's sharp disapproval. The lady was slender as a wand and elegant enough for putting on your mantelpiece, last seen between two lawyers at Mr Kine's dungeons. Maybe from Gujerat, in India? Her dress was a gentle olive-coloured silk, with pearls that made my mouth water. 'I'm hopeless with names.'

'Francisco Polk,' said a slender seated man. Glitzy jewellery, rings, a mouthful of gold teeth, Savile Row clothes. No handshake.

The antique on the table was curious about me. I was curious back, having never seen a Baccarat 'sulphide' paperweight. These delectable rarities are the ugliest dusty red, except this contained a pewter-coloured hunting scene, a hound, hunter, tree and a stag. I prefer multi-cane 'carpet ground' weights because they are so happy. Hunts always make me feel like the prey, never the hounds.

A hugely fat black man darted me a sharp look and returned to his cards. He smoked a thick cigar.

'Hans Delius.' He spoke through smoke. 'Can we trust you?'

I tried to lighten the atmosphere. 'Most of the time.' Failure. Only the prune-skinned Hugo Hahn cracked a wry grin, his teeth pearly white.

The last man completed the set. 'Rico Rousseau.'

My mind reeled from the names, all of which I instantly forgot. Rico was bony, blue-grey eyes showing a startling clarity from a darkish face. His accent owed something to French, but what did I know? Donna da Silfa, though, stayed in the eye. You couldn't mislay her in a Wembley match.

Laura was beaming. 'Do sit down, Lovejoy, while I go over your antiques brilliance.'

I was getting used to obeying her. The players picked up their cards, and showed no interest in Laura's eulogy. She explained I could divvy genuine antiques, and even produced forgeries of my own. I looked at the antique. It was still staring back.

Mistrust was in the air, and I'd brought in ninety per cent of it. Laura listed a selection of my exploits. Cruelly, she went into detail over my prison spells. I thought her unfair, but didn't dare say so. Any one of them could have dusted me over. I would even have been glad to hear Sandy and Mel arrive.

'So you see, Donna and gentlemen, he's our scheme's perfect assistant.'

'What scheme?' I asked.

Laura went on, 'The scheme's tickety-boo and foolproof.'

'Er, excuse me. What scheme?'

'Will he go along with us?' Rico folded his cards and looked round the table. I felt narked at them for talking over me. They do that in hospitals while you're wrapped helpless as a tuppenny rabbit. Yet I seemed to be significant. Was it the same plan as Laura's – to recover her missing husband – or different?

'It depends,' I shot in.

'Of course he will,' Laura insisted.

Only Lady Donna spared me a look. She was so lovely. People have daft notions about older women. Magazine articles preach that youth is everything. I know different. A woman is a woman, and that's it. Donna da Silfa was older, fair enough, but she retained her elegance and poise. She was worth a dozen younger birds any day. Well, six.

'Lovejoy?' she said.

Into the protracted silence I said, 'Any antique dealer would jump at your offer. Me, I have a record. I don't have a team. I have one part-time apprentice I owe a year's wages to, and my only barker is a wino who sleeps in St Peter's churchyard.'

'Go on, Lovejoy,' said the lady. I began to love her.

'Two and two make four,' I said. 'But which four?' I kept going. 'Dealers won't touch your scheme if they know I'm in on it. And they'll all know before the day's out.'

'Who won the last hand?' Hugo asked.

The antique was still on the table.

'Me.' Rico showed his cards. Everybody nodded. He slipped the precious paperweight into his pocket. I gaped.

They had been playing cards for an antique worth a fortune?

Also on the table was a fake. Now I stared. Ivory, with a Chinese fighting cock in silver piqué work. The giveaway was its shape – the outline of a Queen Anne flintlock pistol lock plate with a scrolled M and an L. Wrong, so very wrong. Only one bloke turned out fakes like that, Fiffo in Birmingham. Clues were crammed in it.

'Whose deal?' fat Hans Delius growled, puffing smoke. 'For the Chinese antique this time.'

'It's not antique,' I said. 'It's fake.'

This earned several nods. Oddly no anger.

'Then my silver Georgian beaker,' the balding Glinsky decided, obviously bored. 'You all know it. My great-great-grandpa's.'

They all nodded agreement. 'Doesn't hold much San Mig beer,' Delius said. Chuckle chuckle. Laura and Donna watched me.

'Fifteenth hand,' flashy Francisco Polk grumbled in his American twang. 'I've lost every one.'

'Look, Laura,' I cleared my throat. 'If you're stuck, I'll join.'

'Are you sure, Lovejoy?'

'For a friend. Well, for greed.' It was hard, hard.

'Good.' The whole room relaxed. Why did I think they hadn't been playing cards at all? 'I shall take Lovejoy in hand.'

'Perhaps I should.' Hugo Hahn's casual was as phoney as my casual.

'No.' Lady Donna put in. Those eyes would look truly alluring over Honiton lace. 'I shall.' She smiled at Laura.

'You devote yourselves to mysterious legal things.'

As if on cue I heard Sandy coming screeching down the corridor, Mel booming commands and the receptionists laughing.

Laura was bright with annoyance. 'If you insist, dear.'

The deal was done. What deal, though? I hoped somebody on my side – Lydia, Mortimer – knew.

Chapter Fourteen

**dollop broker: one who stores illegal antiques
for another**

When I emerged, edging past Sandy's exulting entourage, the train was steaming, two footplate men stoking up. A familiar motor waited nearby: Ellen Jaynor, lately friend to Arthur Goldhorn. I stood watching the men on the tender. Ignorance was my own fault. What sort of bloke doesn't know he has a son growing up a few miles away in Saffron Fields? Cinders scrunched.

'Lovejoy, had news.' Ellen sounded apologetic.

'Ever since you came, all news has been bad.'

'Look. I'm free. I can give you a lift.'

Presumably another journey. I'd lost track. Had she been weeping? We walked to her motor.

'The Beeches. Mr Smethirst died twenty minutes ago.'

The doctor, Mortimer said, judged Smethie would get better. My old friend had been right, saying he didn't have long. Had Terminal's men been knitting in some corner caff?

'Right.' The windscreen fogged about then so I closed my eyes. Paltry and now Smethie. Did Mortimer know?

'If there is anything I can do, Lovejoy. Laura is on your side.'

'Ellen,' I said, 'shut the fuck up.'

Normally I don't speak like that. Things were getting on top of me.

'You *must* find Laura's husband. He'll be attracted to the antiques, but you're the bait.' She was pale. 'It's a matter of life and death.'

'Old Smethie and Paltry already know that. Where do I search?'

'Ted hunts antiques. You're the one to find him.'

'Will he be alone?'

Her lips set the colour of purple porphyry. 'He'd better not be.'

She drove me home and said my journey would begin eight o'clock sharp. I felt like saying, 'Trust me – I'm lying.' Old jokes are the best.

Breaking in, I pulled my divan down. I don't know how long I stared into space, but evening shadows were sliding along the walls when I came to. I drank water from the kettle, and sat outside. I'd given up all thoughts of hiding from Tasker, Terminal, anyone.

The thing is, people don't matter these days. Watch any film, and folk get shot all over the place. The audience simply chuckles and noshes popcorn. Somebody gets beheaded, the world says tut-tut. I'm told not to visit some old geezer, and can't be bothered so I go and... Except I hadn't heeded a blinking word Smethie said. I was reaching in my pocket when a stout bloke came puffing through my undergrowth.

'You're back, Lovejoy!' Hennell waddled over and sat

beside me with a gasp. 'East Anglia isn't supposed to be hilly.' He fanned himself with his hat. 'You've heard? Sad business.'

'His daughter, Miss Farnacott, hired Terminal's guards. Bastards.'

He seemed as down as I was. 'The hospital's fuses failed. Coincidence?' I didn't speak. 'People on blood transfusions, heaven knows what, yet the machines gave up.'

'Hospitals have fail-safes.'

'Those went, too.' He treated the world to his idiotic beam. Lucky old world. 'Sabotage.'

'How come you know all about it?'

He said, 'I'm Terminal.'

Long silence. I said, 'Eh?'

'Terminal's my company. Mine. We failed.'

'You're Terminal?' I almost ran for it, except he looked the least threatening bloke I'd ever seen.

'Our first ever failure, Lovejoy.'

'Did you really kill that bloke in Asia Minor?'

'No gossip. This means I must seriously take up the cudgels, what?'

'And batter who?'

'Mr Smethirst's enemies, Lovejoy.' His eyes roamed my brambles. 'Terminal doesn't accept failure. You,' he said directly, 'have an ally. Me.'

'Some ally. You let them kill Smethie.'

'As did you, Lovejoy. Remember that.' Maybe he had feelings after all? He gave a shrill whistle without needing fingers. I admired him for that. 'Oh, Lovejoy. Do you remember any details about the people whose cars killed Paltry?'

'I have their numbers written down.'

'Let me have them, old sport. Starting point, what, what?'

'I'll find it. I never throw anything away.'

'Leave a message marked Terminal with any hotel shroff, old boy.'

Yet more out-moded slang. What *was* I getting into? A shroff is old colonial for anybody on the till. 'Right, Mr Hennell.' I watched him go. If he was Terminal & Co, I was safe, right? Except old Smethie hadn't been.

Veronica came from the back garden. She always looks timid.

'Your brambles tore my tights, Lovejoy.' She stood. 'I waited. He might have jumped to the wrong conclusions.'

Which were? I didn't say it. 'I'm too down for visitors, love.'

'My husband is really cross, Lovejoy.'

My robin came onto the bough of a small apple tree. It has this knack of bouncing up and down while its head stays exactly on the same coordinates. Does that trick help hunting? I'd ask Mortimer. He'd know. Nature teaches us things.

'He thinks I should be making a fortune,' she said despondently. 'He got me a council cleaning job.'

So? The robin dropped like a stone and yanked a worm from the grass, leaning back. Normally I'd have rushed inside for cheese, Lovejoy to the rescue. Except I had no rescues left in me.

'My husband likes everything in order, Lovejoy. Knives in the cutlery drawer, labels on bottles. He dockets every penny. I suffocate.'

'Mmmh.' Could doctors tell if somebody was suffocated *before* the hospital electrics failed?

The robin flew into the hedge, its prey dangling.

'I envy you, Lovejoy.' She sounded wistful. 'Men can do exactly what they want, and don't give a fig for anybody else. I wish I could be like that, just not care about other people.'

Other people see truths.

'I suppose it's a man thing. It's us women who are put upon.'

'Yeah, right.' Tell Paltry and Smethie that.

She stooped and peered. 'Are you all right, Lovejoy? Have I upset you?' She looked about. 'Should I stay and cook something? Perhaps we'll cheer up. Have you got anything in?'

'Mmmh.' I hadn't. I'm lying, trust me. 'Come to bed, Veronica.'

Next morning something was pushed under the door. I heard a lady's voice murmur. A motor dopplered to silence. Birds were already tweeting, the light grey. I turned on my side. Veronica looked at me along the pillow.

'Should I see, Lovejoy?' She blushed and said, 'I mean the post.'

All news being bad news, I wanted her to leave it where it was, but women answer phones, fill pots, make beds. What would the plod do if they caught Smethie's killer? Fine him ten pence, then give him a free ride home? Since Laura came, I'd got allies, but things had become calamitous. Veronica would have to fight Lydia to a standstill, and no woman had ever yet defeated

Lydia. 'Course, women land me in more trouble. It's just life. There couldn't possibly be a connection, could there? Veronica returned to the divan clutching a dainty embossed envelope.

'It's from a lady, Lovejoy. Foreign. Rich. Does she collect antiques?'

'Not really, just sits elegantly by while friends gamble for rare antiques.'

'I'll make your breakfast. You have no eggs, Lovejoy.'

'Mmmh.'

She did that screech with which women signal that it's cold, and grabbed her clothes. 'You've no bathroom.'

I already knew that, so I said, 'I know. There's a bucket near the well.'

She moaned. 'If we make a packet – you divvying, me charming the punters – there's a reliable builder down Stanway.'

Reliable builder? The old joke: It took over five hundred years to erect the Great Wall of China – but we've all had trouble with builders, har-har. Veronica had only joined me ten hours ago, and already she was babbling insanity. I opened the envelope. Inside, an ornate card.

'Oh, hell,' I told Veronica. 'The tax man cometh.'

Her eyes filled. 'Lovejoy, you poor thing.'

Lies rushed in to help. 'This is what comes of kindness, Veronica. My poorly great-aunt's in an old folks' home in South Gotham. I've had to sell my Staffordshire slipware dish. You remember it?' I grew so sad about my noble sacrifice my lip actually trembled. 'Twenty inches wide, brown with ochre-coloured squiggles.' I almost filled up. 'My sacrifice was worth it.'

'Oh, Lovejoy, you're so sweet.'

Well, I am. I made the story up. One of those old slipware pieces (about 1780, give or take) would keep anybody in luxury. If it wasn't a pack of lies I would really have been kind. As it was, I've no great-aunt.

'I'll bring something, then we can do the contract.'

'Er, contract?'

'Our partnership, silly!' She trilled a laugh. 'Have you forgotten?'

As she faffed about, I read Donna's card:

Dear Lovejoy,

Good morning. Please join me for our tête-à-tête at ten o'clock to start our journey. This invitation does not include your strumpet. D da S.

Her description of Veronica seemed a bit strong, but I had enough wars without fighting Veronica's as well. I called out to ask what the time was, as I had to go to the tax-gatherers. Twenty minutes later, I made heartfelt vows of unfailing loyalty and unswerving devotion, and felt quite moved. Jacko in his coal lorry delivered me into the hands of strangers.

Chapter Fifteen

gloak: to wait in hopes of charity (Eng. dialect)

Donna da Silfa's motor was better appointed than most hotels. The driver was a dark hulk whose eyes hid behind thick lenses. We set off on the Great Trek that would solve Laura's problems.

'Fleggburgh, Norfolk, wack,' I told the driver's neck.

Windows slid up, isolating me and Donna da Silfa. She observed the townscape as we trogged northwards, past dwellings, churches, students drifting to the Art College.

'To think your Queen Boadicea crucified 70,000 of you here.'

'She was a bad girl. Terrible temper.'

She smiled. 'You and women, Lovejoy! Not an unswerving patriot?'

'Them old historians,' I said.

She quoted glibly, 'Very flat, Norfolk.'

Her Noël Coward quip worried me. She meant to lighten the proceedings while I worried about Paltry's murder and Smethie's unexplained death.

She explained, 'Noël Coward. I thought you'd know it.'

'Captain Bracegirdle.' I thought that would shut her up,

but she only laughed and clapped like a little girl.

'I told them you *are* worth hiring!' She settled back. 'Could we not just stay at some lovely riverside hotel? The scenery is awfully drab.'

Countryside is horrible. Squirrels kill birds. Foxes slaughter hens. Owls eat shrews. Hedgehogs chew slugs. Charming lambs frolic on the way to the butcher. I don't get the hang of rural enthusiasts. Have they never heard of concrete, for God's sake?

So Donna da Silfa chose me, and not Laura. Did she secretly know why Paltry was murdered?

'You're so serious, Lovejoy. Are you abducting me to some sordid tryst?' She laughed, a pretty picture. Sunshine showed off her fantastic colouring.

'A fairground. Some bloke I have to see before Laura's quest.'

'Ugh! Candyfloss, children being sick on the Big Dipper? Ugh!'

Donna da Silfa was difficult to tolerate. 'My gran told me about women.'

We passed a canal-lock gate where once I'd nearly got shot, blubbering surrender. Mortimer saved my life, guessing cowardice was my normal.

'And what did your gran say?'

'Women live by the clock.'

She dwelt on it, allowing Gran a moment. 'Did she explain men too?'

'Yes. Men have heads full of jolly robins.'

Another delightful laugh accompanied by pretty gestures of applause. I wondered how much of Donna da Silfa was herself, and how much was performance.

'Lovely! And how true!'

The two men who killed Paltry, though. Accents always intrigue me. It may be only an inflection overheard on a bus. Then, quite unbidden, I think, Yeah, that lady was probably Canadian, because she spoke the word 'about' as if reining a pony in. My mind's jolly robins cheeped pointlessly on. Except sometimes one robin sits still and thinks, What's wrong? and then, Why did nobody tell me? I was to hunt down this Ted Moon, trap him with antiques I had to take on trust, while wedded to the hate-filled Laura. And what had it to do with forgotten white tribes?

'My maid is following with whatever clothes I might need.'

A motor had caught us up, a dark-haired lass driving.

'Your grandmama was right, Lovejoy! Living by the clock! No time to rush and buy new outfits.' She sighed. 'It must be so easy being a man.'

The trouble was, Gran never did say which clock, and every woman's clock is wound different. Yet it was us men who fixed the world on Greenwich Mean Time.

'Tell me about being a divvy, Lovejoy. Is that the word?'

Now, she'd just admitted she'd hired me because I was the only divvy they'd heard of.

'You already know. Doing it makes me feel ill. That's all.'

'I am starting to understand you, Lovejoy. You deliberately miss the point of what a woman says. Is it skill or innocence?'

On the defensive again. 'I'm a bad thinker.'

'You're the divvy, though, our private detective.'

'No, Donna.' I hadn't been paid yet, but did not remind

her. 'A detective must be *suspicious*. A divvy must be *right*.'

'Was I wrong to hire you, then?'

'An infallible detective is a fake. A bad antiques dealer is a fake. Opposites, see?' God, she had lovely eyes. 'See you later.' I made to kip.

'Please don't leave me alone.' She took my hand. For the rest of the journey I stayed awake. During the hour-long drive I kept singing to myself songs from when I was little, like, 'Clap hands, Daddy come, bring his baby a cake and a bun…'

People do daft things.

On time, we glided smoothly into Fleggburgh. It's the smallest of villages, but spread about. We arrived at the fairground. I was thrilled.

'Hey ho, come to the fair,' I rejoiced.

'Lovejoy! This is a penance!'

Women see climate as somebody's fault. Lydia is the worst, assuming I make the elements unseasonal when she's dolled up.

'Stay in your motor, then.' I went, smiling, into the silent fair.

The site covered an acre. It might have seemed eerie to some, but only because people associate a fairground with marquees full of people and all the fun of. Lights should be on, I thought with nostalgia. The carousel was there, its hobby horses frozen on their gilded poles, red nostrils flared, ready to gallop as polyphones piped reedy melodies.

Donna slithered after. 'Lovejoy, you left me alone!'

'Wotcher,' a bloke said. 'You Lovejoy? They passed word you'd come.'

'Wotcher. Pete?'

Every fairground owner is called Pete. Who knows why?

He was momentarily taken aback by Donna. She looked ready for a typhoon, Paddington Bear in wellington boots and a yellow sou'wester.

'Got a sec, Pete? Gossip, please.'

'Sure, booy.' He was middle-aged, heavy with the responsibility of being East Anglia's fairground master. 'Three streets, see? Ovens in the marquees.'

We entered through canvas flaps. Benches were placed round the cold boiler and iron ovens. I smiled.

'We had as many as two hundred in here on a rainy day, Lovejoy. Know what sold best?'

'Black peas.'

'Right! Nice to meet a customer!'

My mouth watered. 'Nothing like tarry black-pea soup for a cold winter.'

'We tried hot dogs, burgers, them Indian triangles. My fairground women lost heart.'

We emerged into slanting rain, to whimpers from Donna, and walked the rows of stalls: Roll-a-Penny, Hoop-La, the Magic Man who told fortunes for a penny. There was even a cylinder piano by Hicks of Bristol from 1860, with its original veneering. Pete gave me an old penny. I chose the Victorian, 'Why Do We Have To Part, Jim?' The machine whirred.

Pete could not hide his delight.

'I keep it in good nick, hoping buyers will back us.'

'No luck?'

He shrugged. 'They want computer games, ethnic dancing, God knows what. Can you imagine?'

'No.' I truly couldn't.

The Big Wheel was still there. He went sad when I asked if it could still go. 'Health and safety laws did for it. They said people might not enjoy it in snow.'

'Then they wouldn't come. Didn't you say that?'

Pete perched on the steps of the Caterpillar. This showpiece is simply a snaky circular train. A crinkled green canvas covers the seats, so you're completely enclosed as it rolls to wind-bag music. You could snatch a kiss – more if you were fast – before the hood flopped back exposing you to the speculating eyes of waiting crowds. It was real culture.

'Times have changed, Lovejoy.' Pete went into the old fairground barker's lament. 'Youngsters can't enjoy themselves. Oh, they whoop it up, get sloshed and sick up all through the night. I know,' he added with feeling, 'with two of my own. But they don't *enjoy* themselves.'

Donna da Silfa exploded, 'What rubbish!' Pete looked up, his eyes wrinkling in his smoke. 'Rubbish, Mr Pete. Like your fair.'

'How so, lady?'

'Look at it!' She stood there dripping in her yellow slicker, comical, if she wasn't jeering at Pete's heartbreak. 'It is cheap and nasty. Pennies, to throw balls in a bowl? Going round in circles to hurdy-gurdy music?'

'It is beautiful, lady.'

'Self-pity, Mr Pete! Sell this tat and get a job.'

She gestured at the Win a Goldfish! stall. Racks of glass bowls, but no goldfish gaping out, thank God. There was even a What The Butler Saw, and automata that played Victorian national anthems to Flags-of-all-Nations. Glorious. Pete longed for vanished times.

The only difference between us was he longed for one particular thing and I hungered for all antiques. This is the reason collecting is a disease. Never start, because you can't recover. Someone who begins collecting matchboxes or Egyptian pendants is gripped by fever. It turns into a hatred of rivals. Collectors will kill for that last Britain's Home Farm toy ('Set of Nine, a Patriotic Wartime Toy' of 1940) horse and roller, no joke. If a collector won't go to extreme lengths to add to his store of tremblant brooches in emerald and diamonds, then he isn't a collector. He's merely greedy. Recently, a French philatelist murdered a competitor for a Hawaiian stamp, to make up the set.

Donna da Silfa was concluding her tirade. 'You're a grown man! Pull yourself together!'

She clearly thought the Palace of Delights, and the Rare Exhibition of the Truly Exotic, so much garbage. I thought it moving enough to touch a politician's heart. For sheer discharity I'd never known anyone like Donna. I had thought her elegant and sophisticated. Now, I saw cankerous malice in a destroyer. She had designs on my world, and everyone else's world as well. I honestly felt scared. Never mind what Mortimer and Lydia urged. I wanted out.

'See you at the car,' I told her. 'I'm done.'

She moved away, tutting and grumbling. I let her leave then asked Pete after Ted Moon. The reason I'd found Pete was simple: he was our Three Counties fairground master and would know more gossip than all the rag-and-bone men put together.

Pete pondered a minute. 'Aye. I knowed him. Nice geezer. He'd lately separated. He used a Brum street faker for handies.'

'Where did he go?'

'He mentioned Derby. Knowed a bonny Irish whore madam.'

'Ta, Pete. Much obliged.' I had my link.

'Can you help me, Lovejoy?' Pete was staring at the grass, ashamed. 'I'm done for. My missus left.'

These are fatal moments. I usually lie through my teeth and say OK pal. Among those century-old machines and dripping canvases, I felt their collective antique eyes on me.

'Mebbe,' I said. My mind screeched, What am I saying? I said, 'How long we got?' And what's this *we?*

'Month.' He looked about. 'I've only one caravan left, a nag, and two lads who mump here. They do odd jobs in case a buyer comes a-calling.'

'How come the lads don't get nabbed?'

'They escaped from an Irish industrial school. What can you do?'

The scandal was still boiling across The Water, where orphans were punished by devout religious orders just for being children.

He knocked his pipe out, its dottle fizzing on the drizzled grass. 'The bank closed me down. I lose the fair and Grampa's mill.' A ramshackle farmhouse stood nearby, crumbling. It had a decaying old waterwheel, its paddles and spars askew. Timbers projected like tired teeth in the wattle-and-daub. 'I took out loans. All done.'

Two youths were waiting nearby with the terrible reproach of the young. One lad held a dejected horse. We were all wet through. I thought of Laura's promised gelt.

'Maybe, Pete.' Christ, had I just promised?

'Ta, Lovejoy.'

He touched his hat and walked away. The two lads fell in beside him. The horse gave me a sad look back, the parasitic bastard. Animals make me feel really narked. What else did a horse do except chew grass? It should get a decent frigging job. Everybody wanted me to save them, the idle sods. That nag lived in ladyland. The serfess took Donna to the car under an umbrella.

'With you in a minute,' I told her, and ploshed back as far as the Grand Emporium of Delights. I went in, and there it stood.

This very fair used to come to our village. I loved the Faventia Street Piano, made in Spain a century since. It looked for all the world like a colourful handcart with projecting green-yellow handles. Twin barrelled, it could plonk out twelve tunes. Adapted to electric, its flex was easy to plug in. I got 'The Blue Danube'. Spinning your lady partner in a reverse turn on wet grass is a pig. I waltzed slowly and alone to the pong-pong melody. I'd last danced with a lass who left to marry a pub landlord.

Hard to concentrate, with that exquisite Spanish red-grained wood beckoning. This was how religion should be, really uplifting. The lady came into my arms, me humming the melody and... Lady?

Donna danced well, turning with grace. The Faventia must have felt so happy.

The old tune clonked to a close. I spun her, feeling a duckegg. She curtseyed. I told the street piano so-long. In the car, me dripping wet, Donna told the driver to go to some hotel. I asked if I could have something to eat there.

It was all ready for us. Our old Queen Empress was

the only person in history to sit down without looking to check there was a chair (note: there always was) but Donna da Silfa came close.

At the Norwich hotel a change of clothes was laid out ready, a maid checking she'd guessed the sizes right. I had a bath. The housekeeper took out my clothes at arm's length, which narked me. I'd just come from fascist dungeons, for God's sake. I was still seething when I went down to nosh.

Donna da Silfa had already chosen. I was starving. The soup was cold, and my grumbles made the waiter gape, but he didn't have to eat it. He tried telling me the soup really should be freezing. Donna quickly apologised and made him bring some hot instead. Bloody cheek. If I'd been paying I'd have gone somewhere else.

'I'm truly sorry, Lovejoy. I should have checked.'

The grub was quite good, which made me think their Frog chef had picked up the knack of cooking. Donna tested much of it, and sent one dish back. I went red when she complained. Oddly, the waiters seemed to love her. When she approved, two waiters slapped palms like they'd won a medal. Waiters are truly strange. I could understand me being bowled over by the exquisite Donna da Silfa, because I'm a scrounger on the make, but a waiter is only somebody who fetches plates. I waded through the fancy dishes, each of which she inspected with her critical eye. I went round twice, in case I got hungry again later. Honestly, Woody could have learnt a thing or two, picked up some recipes for his Sloven Oven.

Donna told me to rest, as she had to speak with somebody. We had six hours before 'the others' were due. I thought, Hello, more strangers? No antiques shops in Fleggburgh, so I went upstairs and stretched out on the bed after removing my shoes because superstitious grandmas never really go away. I woke to find Donna murmuring reassurance and helping me off with my shirt.

I'm not proud of everything that happens, because beggars can't, can they? I just wish I had more chance to control things. She wasn't in that much of a hurry after all. Derby, though?

Chapter Sixteen

grockle: tourist (West Country dialect)

She was short of breath because I lay on her. 'Young women are too obvious. Mistake, no?'

'How come?' I rolled aside.

'You want to doze, Lovejoy.' She licked me, words taking turns with her tongue. 'I love a man's sweat. Now I tell you all.'

Par for the course. Women inventing jobs.

'First I shall explain why I hate the young. Then you shall understand about us forgotten white tribes. Learn while you doze.'

I groaned. 'Don't tell me. You know an Inca jungle city full of tribal gold? I'm sick of con tricks.'

'I and my friends *are* the lost city, darling. *We* are your treasure.'

After some time I came from the post-love pit to find her smiling a welcome.

She began speaking in that attractive accent. I thought, Here it comes. Bound to be Pythonesque. Donna da Silfa had been truly inventive making smiles.

Her features showed a Bollywood elfishness, which

makes a woman seem only toy bones beneath a beautiful skin. 'I tell you this because you love women – old, young, all the same.'

'Women are never the same.'

'I stand corrected.' She gestured at the sight, us barely covered by the sheet, mocking.

'Women are the portal to bliss, love. Don't let on.'

'You men have no idea of reality. I had to force those men – at the casino by the train?'

No smile now, so this was her most serious truth. I worry about this kind of thing, because women persuade me to become their disciple.

'The mistake girls make,' she said gravely, 'is to think reckless hilarity is their only purpose. Stupid.'

What can a bloke say? I wondered if priests in confession ever interrupt penitents and say, 'Hang on a sec. Go back to where you met this bloke…'

'Personality, Lovejoy, is not like water, the clearer the better.' She shook her head, agreeing with herself. 'No. Transparency is the quality of a herd. A woman should always hold back opaque fragments of herself unseen by men.'

'OK,' I muttered. Forgotten white tribes, though? Smethie said this. It niggled.

'A woman must stay beyond analysis.'

'Good old mystique again? The eternal woman?'

'Does it make you uncomfortable?'

'The young learn sooner or later, then older women had better watch out.'

'Yes, but far too late. By then, they've become thirty-nine-year-old frumps wondering what's gone wrong. Like

Laura. They hanker – hanker is the right word? – for when they were all-conquering lovely belles, wondering where that happy riot has gone, when nobody comes calling.'

'That's unkind.'

'It is true, Lovejoy. Tipsy tarts are vile, disgusting tramps. I could have turned out like them. Circumstances decreed otherwise.'

'Maybe they mirror you, some other time, some other place?'

'I like to put it another way.' Bitterness came now. 'They carouse from fifteen to forty, and become older women cackling inanely at TV shows and swill tequila. Your word is "chavs", no?'

'Not all.'

'Not *quite* all,' she amended. 'Laura is definitely one. They wonder where the carnival has gone. Most men,' with a sharp glance along the pillow, 'don't have sufficient character to forgive, Lovejoy. You do.'

'Wrong.' I spoke because I was fed up. 'What right have I to judge? Gawd, I can't even judge myself.'

'You imply I'm wrong?' She smiled and stretched. Loveliest sight on earth. I climbed back to reality. 'Like your dud fairground, Lovejoy?'

'I loved them,' I said sadly, and swung off the bed, feet to the cold floor. Donna reached for me, easily evaded.

'Come back. We've hours yet.'

I dressed and marched out. Ten paces and I was mad at myself. Her and her meandering philosophy. Young women grow older. So what? I sat sulking in the hotel lounge because her driver was guarding the exit.

Twenty minutes later, Donna da Silfa came and sat beside me. In that measured voice, she calmly told me about the forgotten white tribes.

Thinking about it now, there's no way to avoid gender differences. A woman overwhelms a man. Imagine elections, where all votes are in, yet the two candidates for president wear ghastly smiles not knowing who's won. That's my feeling when a woman superwhelms. I don't understand the process. I only know it happens.

Forgotten tribes, though? I felt like one myself.

'You've seen those tide pools, Lovejoy. Imagine one miles inland, no longer connected to the sea. Teeming with strange creatures – crustaceans, fish, sponges – unlike any other living things. And why? Because the sea has ebbed and gone.

'You know what's truly sad? Those weird shellfish and exotic fronds, trapped in their tiny tide pool, firmly believe they are the whole world. In fact they are extinct. They just don't know it.'

Her smile was grievous. 'What if one creature suddenly realised the terrible truth? I am one.' She resumed after a pause. 'The Dutch burghers of Ceylon are one group. People say Sri Lanka now. We Portuguese are too.'

'You're Portuguese? Whereabouts?'

'I have never even seen Portugal, Lovejoy. I live in Sri Lanka.'

'Eh? Oh, right.'

'All the tribes in our scheme are descendants of forgotten settlers. Distinct and proud. We have…' she hesitated, went for it '…class, Lovejoy. No English liberalism, please, that Germans call *Manchesterturm.*'

'Didn't the Dutch and Portuguese roam the globe in the olden days?'

'Of course. Now, their descendants hang on, in derelict old people's homes. And each tribe is distinct. Like we, and the Landesi.'

'Where is Landesi?'

'Olandesi was the Sri Lankan word for Holland. Landesi came to mean Dutch. Would you believe, darling,' she said earnestly, 'the old folk argue who is the most Dutch among them?'

'Seems a waste of time.'

'Don't dismiss us tribes, Lovejoy. We represent untold profit.' Her lips parted. 'Just as you represent our survival. I see my frankness makes you uncomfortable.'

I glanced at the impassive driver.

'Did you notice a card player who seemed American?'

I ran her casino people through my memory. 'That gambler bloke?'

'Straight out of some American Confederacy film? *Gone with the Wind?*'

'That's him.'

She laughed, clapping her hands. 'He is native Brazilian! His tribe is literally from the USA Confederacy, after their Civil War. He has never been to the United States, as we tribes in Sri Lanka have never seen Lisbon or Amsterdam.'

'Go on.' I began to feel as if I were staring into a tide pool of extinct creatures left stranded by receding seas.

'I can tell you about all of them, if you wish.'

'Later, maybe.' With any luck, never.

She was enjoying herself. 'And did you notice anyone who looked faintly Polish, from Warsaw perhaps?' She was mischievous. 'I see the penny drops, Lovejoy. Yes, a Pole born in Haiti. His ancestors were a Polish regiment sent by France's all-conquering Napoleon. Haiti,' she explained prettily, 'was once French Saint Domingue.'

'Are you all – no offence – remnants?'

'Of course. Our saddest is Namibia's lost white tribe. Hugo Hahn? They migrated from the Cape of Good Hope in 1868 to Namibia. The League of Nations guaranteed them a republic.'

'Namibia? Hot desert with all those diamonds?'

'They produce their legal documents at the drop of a hat. Think of us as Faces in our tide pool, darling. Guadeloupe's Blancs, Jamaica's German tribe, the Basters of Namibia, the Landesi and Burghers of Sri Lanka, the Welsh of Uruguay, all dreaming of our so-called homelands. We all grew up hoping our homelands would one day take us back. In vain.'

'Can't you just catch a plane to, well, wherever home was?'

'We wish, Lovejoy.' Her eyes filled. 'Would they welcome us?'

'There are more?'

'Sixteen groups, from all over the world. We here are delegates, elected to speak for humanity's forgotten fragments. All we have is our identity, and our ancient possessions. One is Jewish, from the Yiddish-speaking enclave of Birobidzhan, that the Soviet Union established in 1928 on the Trans-Siberian railway. It had its own oblast, a province four hundred miles north of China's city of Harbin. So many.' She turned her lovely eyes on me. 'All bizarre species.'

'Like younger women?'

She nodded. 'Except the world has changed beyond recognition. We lost tribes know we are finished. You are our instrument to bring us into the modern world, Lovejoy.'

'Shouldering sixteen lost civilisations? Sorry, no.' Moments ago, she was exquisite. Suddenly, she was a dangerous old bat. 'Not me, love.'

'Too late, Lovejoy.' She signalled. The driver went for the car. 'Your task is to rescue us from our rock pools so we can swim free in the world.'

'Donna, I'm a scruff without a bean.'

'We tribes have realised what we possess.' She instantly became young again, the way women can. 'Antiques, Lovejoy. Antiques like you wouldn't believe.'

Three limousines were drawing up the hotel drive. The gang was all here. Donna rose to go out to meet them. Casually I drifted to the loo.

A minute later I was out the back way, escaping from lunacy.

Chapter Seventeen

fiffer: a dealer who works on percentage profit

Before day broke I was in Birmingham, courtesy of a hitchhike. A street worker who faked handies could only be Fiffo. And Ted Moon's shop was in Brum.

I arrived like a drowned rat in heavy rain and made my way to the Bull Ring, Brum's shopping mall where I went, shivering, for a breakfast of everything of everything.

From noon until dark, I washed dishes in a nosh bar, my forte. That night I slept in the campers-and-packer stores next door. My employer made me feel highly valued.

He said wistfully, 'I only hire drifters. Teenagers won't work. Stay.'

'Ta, Ahil,' I told the silver-tongued tyrant. 'I have a duty to a friend.'

'Duty!' he wept. 'What do the young know of duty?'

And so on. I headed for the city centre – fountains, taverns, entertainments. Fiffo's another of life's weirdos.

He was in the Friday market, where street actors strove to get noticed by passing movie moguls. Droves of actors, and not a single mogul. Fiffo's forgery skill is stupendous. He does piqué. (Say pee-kay, or buyers think you're uneducated.) From honesty, that ultra-rare bird, Fiffo shows his talents in the open. He is kept by Camille, who sells Fiffo's fakes and pays him in kind. She keeps the money.

One of Fiffo's pieces had been on the Faces' card table. If I wasn't so thick, I'd have maybe reached Fiffo earlier and saved Smethie, but I am so I didn't and I hadn't so I couldn't. Fiffo had included, in the Chinese fighting cock piqué design, a florid curlicue. To me it was like a flag day. It was the outline of a Queen Anne flintlock pistol plate, with a single M and L, for Mortimer and Lovejoy. Immersed in the exotic flourishes, they would go unnoticed except by another forger.

Fiffo was saying to bored spectators, 'Piqué is beautiful. Ladies love it. My design is about 1690, but China did it earlier.'

He works on a tray. Minuscule silver dots, a spirit lamp, and tortoiseshell, ivory, or even deer horn. Fiffo scorns plastics, Ivorine and the like, though heaven knows I've used enough synthetics.

'Is that real ivory?' a man demanded, an aggressive do-gooder bent on wrecking the world.

'Yes.' Fiffo smiled. 'And it's older than your great-great-great-grandad. Why?' He paused, a dot of silver in his tweezers. 'Will you bring the elephant back to life if I stop working?'

'An elephant had to die for that!'

'Like the cow that provided your shoe leather? And the animals they tested your hair dye on? And the dogs they tested your aftershave on? And the pigeons they tortured to check your aspirin?' Fiffo eyed the man. 'Or your wife's cosmetics?'

The man strode off in anger. Other watchers faded. 'I'd hoped you'd be shaving some piqué posé, Fiff.'

'Wotcher, Lovejoy. About bloody time.' He waited as a toddler came over, oooohing, wanting a piece of the action. Its mother hauled it off. 'Nar, son. I've no money to buy silver.'

'Didn't Camille get a fair screw from them foreigners? You did a lovely piece, Fiff.' Camille was obsessed with money. The age-old problem in loving relationships is who keeps whom.

Fiffo is the only jewellery faker-maker who does perfect ancient piqué. He's a rough-looking bloke who's worn the same jacket as long as I've known him. He used spectacles now. No dandy, Fiffo.

It was his turn to sigh. 'She's taken up with a city councillor.'

Camille uses politics like stepping-stones, meaning she makes progress and colleagues stay immersed in the cold effluvium. She's beautiful so it's OK. The wind veered. Returning rain touched my nape. People began crowding into shopping centres.

'Still together, though?'

'For a while.' He set the spirit lamp under the miniature metal pot, plopped the ivory in and closed the lid. In a few minutes the ivory would grow soft. I'd often wondered if he used a design or worked from flair. I'd be copying him as soon as I got a minute. 'Only Fridays. Don't know how much longer I can thwole it.'

Thwole is to endure. To explain, Camille and Fiffo

were lovers. She recognised his unique talent and started marketing it, for herself. She was a councillor, and met other political scroungers. Her relationship with Fiffo waned. Fiffo gave her an ultimatum: all or none. After all, he slogged while she whooped it up with other corrupt politicos. She offered him a deal. Cohabit once a week, and Fiffo worked in the salt mines. From there, one full night shrank to half a day. When last I'd heard, it was a fleeting hour, Fiffo being slotted in, as it were, between better offers.

'See, Lovejoy,' said this sad genius, 'she's always out clubbing. She even bollocks me for not having stuff ready. She exports to the Continong. She forgets to come, then she's on the news with some bloke.'

There's a horrid expression for a bloke who is completely in thrall to a woman's body. I won't write it here. It's *multo* crude, and Gentle Reader of Tunbridge Wells will write more angry letters. I felt a terrible sympathy. Drizzly rain glistened on his face. The little spirit burner fizzed its raindrops.

'You once told me that any woman can have any man, Lovejoy. I laughed. I know now it's true.'

I hadn't realised back then that Camille was his bird. It was at a Weller and Dufty auction, where I'd been hoping for a Queen Anne flintlock. I'd just learnt that Mortimer was my son, and Fiffo said, 'Bless the lad.' Hence the M and L in his design, to warn me.

'Safe here?' When Fiffo nodded, I started, 'Them foreign geezers.'

'That's why I clued you with the piqué posé, see? Camille's taken up with the tall South African. She's in deep there, Lovejoy.'

'How many are there?'

'Half-dozen and tarts. They've got too many antiques to shake a stick at. Their lawyer's called Laura, Ted Moon's missus.'

'What about Ted, Fiff? Topped a lass and got off scotage free?'

'Ted? Don't believe it. Hang on.'

Fiffo felt the metal pot, and with tweezers lifted out the ivory sliver. He pressed each silver dot into the soft ivory. In minutes, a silver chrysanthemum grew, his thick ungainly mitts creating a work of genius. I almost filled up. A true artist, aping the work of ancient craftsmen simply to keep his lady love. Didn't seem fair.

'I like the piqué point,' he said as he worked. 'I keep going as long as the ivory stays soft. Some forgers use dilute acid, so bloody sloppy. It always shows.' He grew indignant. 'What if it was a piece for a pretty woman's necklet?'

'Well, yeah.'

'Everything for cheapness. It's not right.'

A uniformed plod came up. 'What you two doing? Planning a robbery, are we?' He harf-harfed like in children's TV.

'I'm demonstrating, Constable.' Fiffo showed his plastic permit, Camille council issue.

'OK, lads.' The ploddite wandered off chuckling at his merry quip. The ivory had gone hard, gripping each silver dot. It would take a lovely polish.

'I've got to do four by tomorrow, piqué posé strips. Fancy some grub?' He gave a sad grin. 'Or a job?'

* * *

We had fish and chips in newspaper – the only way. Not a patch on Woody's.

Fiffo's house was a small terraced place with a shed in the yard. A dozen photographs of Camille adorned the walls, one lit by a blue votive light. A shrine.

He spoke with pride. 'She's a beauty, eh?'

And he was right. Photography isn't art. Point a camera and click, end of message. With Camille you were already there. Not like painting a portrait. Suddenly guilty, I looked about while Fiffo brewed up.

'Your portrait's in the other room.'

'Oh, really?' I went casual.

This is my trouble. I went through. She truly was exquisite. I felt my heart lurch. Not a patch on Gainsborough's portrait of his missus, the greatest portrait since the world began. I'd posed Camille as if she were startled, and caught the beginning of a smile, in a cerulean blue shawl.

'Good, eh?'

'Oh, aye, Fiff.' We sat. He gazed at the portrait.

'I've had it, Lovejoy. This order is her last. Then she'll scarper.'

'How come? You're a gold mine.'

'She's coming into a fortune from these strangers.' He was choked.

We all have a serious problem called love. It's deadly. My question is, can you paint a woman's portrait without falling for her? Some artists claim they stay remote, and answer yes.

I'm in the no group. You *can't* paint a woman's portrait without falling head over heels. You just can't. No, *nein, la, non*, and nay verily. It is impossible not to fall. I ahemed.

'Look, Fiff, mate. Those piqué posé clues on the ivory to tip me off. Why didn't you just send word by some night haulier, as usual?'

'I couldn't risk Camille finding out.' He never took his eyes from her portrait. 'She's mad for a tall cowboy bloke.'

Hugo Hahn. My face must have betrayed me. Fiffo grimaced.

'She'll leave soon as she gets the gelt.'

'Gelt from what, your forgeries?' He looked shifty. I got narked. He'd sent for me, by his Chinese *You Shi* design, and I'd trogged up here. 'Tell me, Fiffo. What d'you want me here for?'

'I'm scared they'll top me.'

That made me stare. 'Kill, Fiff?'

Now, Fiff is not given to exaggeration. I know I go over the top, things I say, things I do. It's my way. But Fiffo's your true plodder. The finest forger you'd meet in a long march, but still your mundane slogger who had perfected his talent. Camille was just bad – or good – luck, depending on how you looked at it. Like, is it better never to have loved and lost than, etc, etc?

'Aye. Kill.'

A super headache began, my vision flickering zigzags. I couldn't stand another of my mates getting snuffed.

'She's sold this house. It was my dad's.'

'How can she? Doesn't it take weeks?' In Germany, I've heard, you can buy a house in a single day, so efficient are they, and I daresay the Yanks do it over coffee, but our creaking old kingdom takes literally months.

'I only found out by accident.' He stared into the

distance. 'At an exhibition of American Art Nouveau jewellery. The Yanks love Egyptian and Byzantine colours. I was sketching away, and saw Camille with this bloke.'

It was a sad tale of skulking and hotel registers.

'I even caught her at it, Lovejoy. She rents two council flats to herself, worse than Harringay councillors in London. She lives with him.'

'It isn't a capital crime, Fiffo.'

'You know why they call me Fiffo, Lovejoy?'

'You conned the old fifty-fifty?'

He invented a con trick when younger, though now it is everywhere. It works like this: He'd hang around car parks and find a car with the house keys inside. He'd don an official's armband and help the housewife carry her shopping. She'd not be able to find her house keys. 'I'm sure I left them on the dashboard,' etc. Guess what? To her enormous relief, Fiffo would 'find' them! She'd be so grateful, unaware that he'd taken an impression. With her key, Fiffo would then ransack her home, but only if his escape odds were fifty-fifty. If her husband was a copper or a similar crook, he'd simply move on.

'Know what my odds are, for my survival?'

'I never gamble, Fiffo.'

'Hundred to one against. All my life I've gone with half odds. Except for Camille. I just didn't think it would end like this.'

'You certain?'

'I've heard, Lovejoy. I can't escape. I want you to take my stuff so the craft doesn't die.'

We talked a bit. No, he didn't know how he'd be killed. No, Fiff had no intention of making a run for it.

'Old Smethirst didn't make it, did he? And he was one of them, poor old sod. And Paltry. Who'd go to all that trouble, for a nerk like Paltry?'

Sickened, I left when it got dark. He gave me Ted Moon's address. I walked miles through rainy old Brum.

So many things are chance. Kings, tyrants, and even epidemics, are simply a shake of the dice. Like Sarah Martin.

This lass was only seventeen when she fell in love with our dashing young Prince William Henry. A rector's daughter, from Loughton, Essex, the pretty maiden was ruled out when the prince wanted to marry. He became William the Fourth, of course, and died without leaving us an heir. His niece became Victoria, our Queen Empress we know all about. But Lady Luck hadn't finished with Sarah. Lovelorn, she turned to scribbling, and in 1805 dashed off a ditty. *The Comic Adventures of Old Mother Hubbard* was an instantaneous success and is still with us. Collectors give fortunes for the original issue. See what I mean? Chance. Just when a plan is certain, Dame Fortune chucks a spanner in the works. As I ploshed through the streets of Brum, I remembered Tinker telling me, 'Bad luck always has a bit of good. You've just to find it.'

The address was in a parade of shops. *Edward Moon, Antique Dealer to the Stars & Royalty, estd AD 1672*. I smiled. Ted's sense of humour, putting royalty second to Hollywood. The date was an even bigger joke. By my guess, he'd been a dealer for only six months before...

before what, exactly? Answer: before 'a girl went missing, believed dead'. Chance again? Had Ted zoomed off *before* Laura won the lottery? Or, stranger still, after?

The locks were firm, chains across the doors. An off-licence was open, and a laundrette held hopefuls praying for clothes to come out unscathed. I went into the off-licence and asked the woman about Mr Moon.

'Ted's gone. Women arguing over one man is disgusting.'

'Oh dear.' I did my tragic pose. 'He promised me a job.'

She eyed me. Her brow cleared. I must look a pillar of respectability. 'He went off with the other woman.'

'What did she look like?'

It was a fill-in question to give me time to think. I was surprised when she said, 'Nicer than his missus, that's for sure.' She served two customers, young blokes in a hurry, tins of ale.

'No idea of his address, then?'

Her eyes narrowed. 'You the council again?'

Again? 'No. I'm from East Anglia.'

'Sorry. Odd about Ted, though. My cousin Clara's girl saw him last week down the mall.'

'The Bull Ring?'

'Talking to some street pedlar. She said hello, but he hurried off. I think he's done a moonlight, not paid his rates.' She sniffed. 'The cost is a scandal. His missus was a lawyer, common as muck.'

'Somebody told me she was nice.' A sprat to catch a mackerel.

'Nice? She won the lottery. Took a grand house somewhere and brought in a load of foreign cronies.'

'Thanks, Bonnie.' Her name was on her badge. I hesitated, but duty called. 'Pity Ted's shut down. I'd have liked it here.'

She smiled, not giving an inch. I went to break into the empty shop of Edward Moon, Dealer to the Stars.

Chapter Eighteen

to top: execute, kill (Lond. slang)

The shop seemed decayed in the faded light. I felt dispirited. Some places I burgled looked pretty depressing, then turned out brilliant. And even in the grottiest there's always something worth finding. Chance again. I got in using a fallen slate. I'd learnt this trick as an infant. Make sure your slate fragment is thin, it'll slip open any old-fashioned lock except the Joseph Bramah.

Going into a strange place is weird. I wandered from room to room. A faint street light shone in. I tried the electric, but fascists had commandeered the supply. I had no torch, of course, being a duckegg. I was about to go upstairs when somebody put a key in the lock. I flattened against the wall.

'Evening, Lovejoy.' A click, and all was light.

'Er, evening, missus.'

'Is there *nowhere* to sit?' She carried an electric lamp, one of those things you stick to the wall. 'No,' she called to footsteps plodding after. 'Wait outside. Is the place empty, except for this idiot?'

'It's clean, lady,' said the voice of one whose business

was serious toughness. Mr Hennell's men, of Terminal fame?

The front door closed. I hadn't realised how young Miss Farnacott actually was.

'Sorry,' I said, and explained when she stared, 'No chairs. I hadn't expected visitors.'

'Shut up. Don't talk as if *I* were the fool.' She perched on a stair. 'Now, what do you charge?' She passed me a second lantern and pressed hers to the wall. It clung on obediently. I'd have done the same.

'Charge?' My hopes rose. 'For divvying antiques?'

'For finding who killed my father.'

'Old Smethie?' I apologised. 'Mr Smethirst?'

'Think faster, Lovejoy. I'm a busy woman.'

That hurt. Had she followed me to ask the impossible? Maybe I should simply agree to do whatever she asked, then lam off the instant she'd gone. I cheered up.

'I hired assistants to track you, Lovejoy. I shall instruct them to capture you if you abscond.'

You abscond from prisons and remand. I was legally free. I kept wondering why Fiffo had chatted to Ted Moon and then not told me.

'I reckon it was Mr Moon did your father in, Miss Farnacott. He's supposed to have killed a lass.'

'You are as stupid as you look. Ted Moon was too kind to do anything like that.'

She knew that? How? 'Right.' I tried to absorb her faith.

'Lovejoy, you shall locate the murderer, and I shall instruct you where and when to eliminate him.'

'Er, eliminate?'

'Kill,' she said impatiently. 'How much is it?'

My headache jogged a warm-up lap. 'I don't do things like that, missus.'

'No? Then I am seriously misinformed. I know all about you. The woman you eradicated? The killer on the Isle of Man? The two who perished in Switzerland?'

'I can explain, missus.' I get narked when people bring up past accidents. It's not proper logic. And it's unfair.

'Only idiots *explain*, Lovejoy. The fact that you *escape* the law is highly relevant. Your scale of charges, please?'

'I'll do it for nothing.' Lies seemed the way to get rid of this psycho. They say to humour them.

'I insist on paying. The labourer is worthy of his hire.'

Scripture provides excuses for anything, if you look.

'I'll need expenses. After that, it depends.'

She nodded. 'I understand. This is enough for a month at decent rates. Please keep receipts. Will you need to go overseas? Haiti? Guadalupe? Namibia? Sri Lanka?'

'Er...' Those places had nothing to do with me.

'I expect you will, if Father's killer absconds.'

She passed me an envelope. It felt like a wadge of bunce.

'For undue expenditure use that card. Contact me any time, night or day.' She gazed at me. I stood there like a lemon. A woman's features are exquisite in subdued light. The old portrait painters often used one candle, or a carriage lantern, rarely natural daylight. It shows how ignorant we are of faces nowadays.

She went aggressive at my stare. 'What?'

I'd start her portrait with olive green underpainting, no oil, only turpentine. Maybe two layers, then a one-tenth oil in turpentine. The serious problem would be her dress colour on her shoulders. Maybe a lace bertha? I'd have to think.

'I learnt you were Father's friend. But do not eliminate his killer without calling me first. You follow?'

'Yes.' I pretended to go along with this malarkey. Maybe she trusted me in some mad way.

She beeped a mobile. Immediately the shop door crashed open. Her plodders entered. 'I have finished here.' She commanded, 'Return me to the airport.'

'Yes, lady. What about the mumper?'

A mumper is a tramp who sleeps rough. They meant me. I drew breath to argue but she left without a glance. The door slammed.

At least I had money now, and two lamps. I went for a big fry-up to annoy Doc Lancaster's lunatic health plans, and decided to sleep in the shop.

One odd thing, though. The feeble light from Miss Farnacott's little wall lamps kept catching on a dot on the floor. Like I said, the place was so clean you could have done an operation anywhere. I knelt. The spot definitely shone. I moved the light and it vanished. I moved it back and it showed again. I struck a match, touching the flame to the minuscule spot. After a second or two, the dot changed. I thought, Aha. Somebody had been doing lapidary gem-cutting in Ted Moon's shop. Ted himself maybe? One more piece of the jigsaw. I put it into my memory, and slept.

In case of burglars I barred the doors. You can't be too careful.

Chapter Nineteen

to shuff: to illegally move antiques between auction lots

On the way to the lunacies, I reminded myself of a ghastly tale. It too involved an antiques hunt I'd been hired for.

Three years back, I'd met the wife of an international playboy. His hobby was exploits, caves, racing. He was in the glossies and on TV. Twenty-eight, Christina lived among their *dolce vita* pals. Like the Romanov Czarina of All The Russias, she took it into her pretty head to treat her man to a wonderful present. While her hubby was breaking speed records in South America, she hired me to find the world's superbest antique. He would then adore her more. The following conversation, I swear, ensued:

Me: 'That's daft. He's crazy about you.'

She: 'Get going, Lovejoy.'

Me: (sensing icebergs ahead) 'What antique am I hunting?'

She: 'An antique to stun the world.'

Are there dafter ways to make a living? Not a lot. Off I went. Her agent paid on the nail – travel, meals even. I lived on the cholesterol of the land. And, God knows, I hunted.

Three days after starting, I found Christine a rare Imperial Chinese carpet, Ch'ing Dynasty, interwoven with precious metals. I could have got it 'for a song'. Antique dealers never actually use this expression; if they do, they're dud. The vendor recognised me as a divvy, so agreed to let it go for only a king's ransom. I rang in, thrilled.

Me: 'Christina, it's rarer than a dancing duck. Unbelievable.'

She: 'It's not expensive enough.'

Too cheap? I had to lie down. Recovering, on I went. A weird pattern began:

Me (Manchester): 'Missus! I've found you a mint – *mint!* – Pennsylvania walnut longcase clock, painted metal dial, 1800…'

She: 'Only the price of a new Rolls Bentley? No, Lovejoy.'

Me (in York): 'A Flemish sixteenth-century tapestry costing the same as a yacht?'

She: 'Onward, varlet. Too cheap.'

Me (more icebergs): 'Chippendale furniture?'

She: 'No. Too cheap.'

A rare mass of Regency silver? Too cheap.

Ancient Greek bronzes, Russian paintings, English glass? No, no, and thrice no.

Finally, worn out, I visited: 'Christina, I'm jacking you in. Your barminess is turning me to crime. I'm tempted to buy *anything* overpriced. Other dealers defraud. Not me.'

And I returned to shaving in cold water at my garden well.

The following week, this bombshell: 'I've found it, Lovejoy!' She showed me a vase. I gaped.

A millennium since, Egypt produced lustre jars. Only

simple, true, but tenth-century Fatimid lustre work moves your heart. Pale umber trying to be russet.

'It's fake. No vibes.'

'It can't be, Lovejoy. I paid a fortune.' She purred, mentioning the price of a Kensington house. I almost fainted.

'Christina. See the scrolly pattern? It doesn't connect with the creamy decoration of the belly. Ancient Egyptian potters didn't make that mistake.'

'Nonsense!' She explained, 'I've met a *brilliant* young man who owns a Middle East shipping line. The Customs and Excise know him.'

Back reeled my battered brain. 'Christina. Would Customs, grimmest of tax-gatherers, let a bloke make untaxed profits, because they *know him*?'

I bussed her goodbye, and lost contact. Much later, I saw her in a drossy auction in Mildenhall. She looked like a bag lady. Whifflers had arrested her for pulling the shuff, shifting small items between lots. It's the most pathetic trick in antiques. You see it in every country auction.

Christina was now divorced. Her wealthy importer – so pally with Customs, note – was now jailed. She said, eyes shining, 'He's innocent.'

From Egypt? No, he'd never been further east than Harwich. Shipping line owner? No, a shelf stacker. But his friend in Lowestoft made his ancient lustre pottery. 'My plan, Lovejoy? Why, find a priceless antique and get him freed.'

And her husband?

'Would you believe it, darling? He harbours a grudge, because I sold his firm and racing cars. I *told* him Salil's

Egyptian jars were valuable. He simply wouldn't listen…'
See the fallacy? Christina, jealous of her hubby's jet-
set, decided to outstrip them all. She couldn't trust me
(a scruffy dealer, right?), so she trusted some fraud who
couldn't tell a Corot from a carrot or a ruby from a booby.
Gold is in the eye of the beholder. Remembering, I had a
disturbing sense of doom about Donna.

Yonks later I told the taxi driver, 'Here, please,' alighting
near a headland above the North Sea. I went down into a
place full of people I liked.

At the mouth of the River Deben there is a marina,
near the North Sea. A holiday township is set among
breakwaters. In summer it serves holidaymakers with nosh,
boats, pubs and bingo halls. The area dwindles in the dark
of the year. It's then that I visit, because into the empty
chalets and flaky-paint taverns drifts a tide of refugee
entrepreneurs.

This strange lot needs space and quiet. They hardly
speak, are broke, lack food and money. Say hello, they
just stare. They're an odd bunch. Some hope to discover
rare crustaceans, or hunt long-sunken galleons. Others
write poetry, compose Beethoven's Twelfth Symphony,
or even his First. Others are quite mad, striving to crack
DNA mutations without interference from science. One
communicates with sea witches who abounded in 1641.
Another lives for the day when his home-made machine
will photograph the warplanes that flew out to dreadful
combat in the Second World War, and so prove some
psychic carousel. They pinch the electricity and never tidy
up, but so? They live out their dreams. If dreaming was the

worst we got up to, the world wouldn't be in such a mess. I say leave them alone. Dreaming saves us all.

Tansy is first to arrive. As the swallows leave on Michaelmas Eve, Tansy comes to East Anglia's winter shores. I often wonder if she clops in on some mule, rifle across her pommel. Or maybe – this is more likely – peeps timidly round the faded pub corner worrying if she's early.

Anyhow, Tansy is a missionary, Milton's saving goddess Sabrina Fair.

Tansy works in a London supermarket, does extra shifts on Bank Holidays. She lives on scraps to save money. She labours in a garden, bedding plants. She also proofreads for some publisher, and provides him with what she calls 'special solace'. Tansy doesn't charge him, as that would make her a prostitute, she explained. No, she simply expected her publisher boss to recompense her. If a 'solace' session took three hours, she hoped for three hours' money.

And when the winter winds blow chill over the sealands, Tansy resigns and heads for the deserted township of Mehala Bay, bringing money and her unique brand of saintliness. Meaning she breaks in, plugs into the electricity, and gets ready for the dreamers to hove in.

They arrive without a bean, bringing maybe a few clothes acquired from other peoples' washing-lines. Tansy instantly starts cooking. A grocery down the coast learns of Tansy's return by the peculiar osmosis of East Anglia, and carts in vegetables, eggs, meat. Soon her caff-cum-grocery booms. Except there is one unique factor. Tansy's creates an instantaneous rush on an uninhabited coast, and gives her meals away.

Tansy *gives away* all she has earned with her year-long supermarketing, proofreading, solace sessions, gardening centre, all her sleepless summer travail. I prayed she would have arrived, because she was my one hope for unbiased news of the foreigners tightening their noose round my neck. They'd even forced Mortimer and Lydia to obey them. What chance had I?

Mehala Bay showed signs of life. People clustered about a caff that glowed with purloined electric power, a scent of cooking drifting with the breeze. I headed for it, saying hello, and shaking my head when asked if I was seeking some lost herb, missing planet, or apparition. 'Sorry, no,' I said, 'but good luck with your, er, Maya codes.' England is eccentric, they say. Who was I to argue?

Tansy was serving stew. Without a word I stood to and began washing up. She can never get enough help. If I sound like a crawler, I make no pretence. I am. Tansy has a husband who long since spotted that he'd married a saint, to his profound disappointment. Edburgh runs a booking agency for overseas groups. A workaholic. Talk to Edburgh, you lose the will to live as he explains the ins and outs of tourist bookings. The only problem is that Tansy sees her task – to feed the world's eccentrics – as heaven-appointed; Edburgh regards her drifters as dead-legs. I'm not knocking Tansy. She does more good than all the priests, politicians, doctors and social workers on earth. Not difficult? OK, fair point, but Tansy'll get to heaven and the rest of us aren't exactly odds-on.

She had her stew recipe tacked on the wall, from Mrs Beeton's *All About Cookery* (revd edn): *Soup for Benevolent Purposes. Ingredients: an ox-cheek, any trimmings of beef, which may be bought v cheap (say 4 lbs), a few bones,* et gruesome cetera.

I rolled up my sleeves, chopping and peeling whatever seemed sufficiently bulbous to need a whittle. The rush came, eventually subsiding about seven o'clock. I was knackered. Tansy came over smiling, brushing her hair from her forehead with her wrist the way women do, pleased.

'Phew, Lovejoy!' she said. 'Was I glad to see you! I'm done for. Have you ever seen so many thinkers?'

To Tansy, her thinkers will all turn out to be Newton, Saint Alban, George Boole reincarnate, and maybe a Shakespeare or two given encouragement.

'Got a bit of grub left over, love?'

'What am I thinking of!'

She rushed about. We shared a meal. I asked after Edburgh. She gave me glowing reports. I said I was pleased. We drank. I asked if I could stay. We left the door open so geniuses could help themselves. Tansy and I made smiles the previous year, so I made the same assumption this time. Before retiring, we made a dozen breakfast starters for early risers. Tansy wrote out a notice telling visitors how to switch on the oven. I'd no idea how complicated a kitchen can be. No, truly. Cooking could wear you out.

The weather improved during the night. We were roused by dawn drifters starting a communal breakfast. I was tired, so dozed to the sound of waves and phrases exchanged by far-out mystics. I needed essential facts from Edburgh. Tansy could be wheedled.

* * *

By three o'clock, we'd fed the lambs and fed the sheep and stopped for our own nosh. The last thinker was a bird who always sat facing the wall. Daniella had been coming ever since Tansy began her mission. She always wore a shapeless marquee and dark glasses, had her meal, then froze, nose inches from the shredding plaster. I said hello. She only mumbled.

I began ferreting. 'Why does Edburgh never come, Tans?'

Her eyes narrowed, instantly suspicious. 'What're you after?'

'Nothing.' When all else fails, go for honesty. Tansy would get it out of me in a trice anyway. I try to be a wheedler and become the wheedlee. 'I'm in a mess, love.'

'I heard. Those foreigners, Lovejoy.' She took my hand. 'Finish your nut cutlet. It's good for you.'

'Right. It's, er, really splendid, Tans.'

It wasn't. I forgot to mention that Tansy was the world's direst cook. Enthusiasm and a heart of gold, but grim. She once sighed, 'I can't boil an avocado, Lovejoy.' Various scholiasts usually took over once the season got under way, producing enough kilojoules to keep body and soul together. Our midday nosh had been cooked courtesy of a lass working on a thesis proving Jane Eyre was actually ancient Assyrian. A patriarch who studied Arthurian legend and who one day would locate Excalibur, to cosmic rapture, was the comi chef. The meal was crap, the kitchen a shambles. I would clean it up.

'What a mess.' Tansy's lovely features smoothed in sudden understanding. 'Lovejoy, you're not the antiques dealer they've co-opted?'

'Well…'

'Those antiques? Lost tribes and all that?' She reached for my hand. 'Lovejoy. We've been, ah, well, er…'

'Friends?' I offered helpfully.

She went red. 'It's scandalous. You either live in a country or you don't.'

'True, true.' What the hell was she on about? 'Except, two old friends of mine got topped. It's irritating, Tans.'

'Mr Smethirst? He was originally their boss, Lovejoy.' She looked at the kitchen debris. 'My flock eat at six. Time we started.'

'Boss?'

'Them forgotten tribes. He was a leader.'

'He can't have been,' I argued. 'He got knocked off.'

'Why do you think they killed him? He saw how lunatic they were.'

'How do you know, Tans?'

'Edburgh himself books in the important groups.' She smiled a bleak smile. 'Don't tell Edburgh, Lovejoy, or he'll know I blabbed.'

'It's a deal.'

'He had a time finding Somnell House. They were so picky.'

'Did Smethie and Edburgh argue?'

'Mr Smethirst turned against the whole thing, and opted out. Others from the Old Raj took over. Edburgh had six – six! – meetings. 'Course, he doubled the price.'

'Well, why not?' I sounded all indignant as if I really understood. I got curious. 'What did Smethie do, Tans?' East Anglia sometimes functions like a village.

'He so loved tradition, antiques, Lovejoy. Nostalgia,

see?' She gave a winsome smile. 'Like here, Lovejoy. My children.'

Yes, I told myself miserably, Tansy loved them as individuals and children. That's saints for you, I suppose.

'Did you ever meet him?'

'Mr Smethirst came to our house to sign the lease for Somnell House. Edburgh wanted proof their syndicate had the money. They paid on the nail.' She looked away. 'I didn't like them. I thought them weird.' From Tansy it was formidable testimony.

We got up and I cleared away while Tansy went for a lie-down. I did my best sorting vegetables but can't bear touching raw dead things. Oddly, Daniella, without a word, began preparing the stew. Had she overheard? Face obscured by enormous spectacles, enveloped in her marquee, she was Miss Frump. I went to help Tansy to rest. I'm charitable that way.

When I came to, Tansy had gone to the wharf where a fishing boat was docking its catch. I put cutlery out for the evening rush. Suddenly Daniella was beside me, nobody else there. She just stood, amorphous and goggle-eyed, looking at the floor. The silence lengthened.

'Oh, er, ta, Daniella. All done, eh?'

Nothing.

'Er, how's the…?' What the heck was her dream/theory/plan?

'James Joyce.' Her voice was a whisper. 'He didn't exist, you know.' Her eyes filled, to my alarm. 'They want to ruin Irish town design. I just heard they won't publish my book.'

'Oh, aye.' I remembered. She'd once told me this lunacy in mind-bending detail. I thought her barking. Her *magnum opus* was a mere 4,500 pages. 'I'm sorry, love. It was really...interesting, Daniella.'

'You believed, Lovejoy. So I'm going to help you.'

'Oh, ta, love.' If her reward was a copy of her giant tome, I'd wait for the film. 'Er, are you Irish?' Not another of the lost clans?

'No. They conceal the proof in a secret Dublin office.'

'And you spotted it!' I thought, What the hell am I saying?

'Lovejoy, Somnell House is full of armed people.' She looked at me through bottle lenses. I recalled her droning on about James Joyce.

For a second it didn't sink in, then I yelped. '*Armed? Guns?*'

'They practise with them. Lancashire, the Fylde. They own a Blackpool hotel.' She looked downcast. 'Don't get in their way, Lovejoy. They might oppose my theory.'

'Thank you, Daniella. Don't give up hope for...for your thing.'

'Thank you, Lovejoy.' She bussed me. 'You're a dear.'

'Ta.' Lasses like Daniella make you go red. She said shyly, 'Please give my regards to Dr Castell.' And when I looked surprised, 'He was my Cambridge University supervisor. He didn't believe me, either.'

'Silly old him.'

That was it. I stayed another day. More barmy drifters ambled in. One or two had antiques. Only one mattered, a carved ivory figure of Shakespeare, Victorian but none the worse for that. It would keep Tansy's entire colony in fuel for the winter. I phoned the sale through Stoker Prod in Sudbury, who sells such thefts. I refused a fake Edward Hopper painting (labelled *Paris, 1899*) of a figure in a theatre. Wrong date. Good forgeries are fine, but dud fakes are truly naff. Ever since London Tate Modern held their badly run Hopper exhibition, fakes abound. It narks me. If you're going to fake, for God's sake fake right.

Without saying goodbye to anybody, Tansy and Daniella included, I stole away. Goodbyes are a nuisance. They can stop you running if you aren't careful.

Chapter Twenty

bunce: bundle of money (Romany slang)

Isn't money strange?

Sitting looking at the bunce Miss Farnacott gave me in Ted Moon's derelict shop changed my mood. Money is just paper rectangles (actually cotton) yet we'll kill for the wretched stuff. Look at the 50 million zlotniks nicked by that gang in Kent – they risked everything in that snowy February of 2006. Dreams.

We also gamble. Like Laura, lottery winner and addicted gambler. Our National Lottery is confidential. NHS records, love affairs, bank accounts, are all freely available. A woman who sleeps with the rich and famous hurtles to sell her story to the TV for gelt. People promising confidentiality *are lying*. Nothing is secret. Our vaunted 'secret elections' are a laugh. A bloke near my village sells personal voting records within hours of a General Election. I'm not making this up. (It isn't me.)

The clever city of Lydia in Asia Minor invented money. Rome took hold of the notion. *Pecus*, meaning cattle, gave us 'pecuniary', coins being stamped with goats and whatnot. Everything has circulated as cash – shells, paper, massive stone discs, tobacco, teeth, bags of salt, gold and silver. The goddess Juno Moneta is talked up as the pretty moon goddess who guards children and females, but Juno had a really horrid side. She married Zeus, the big banana on Olympus, without telling her parents. OK by me, but ancient chroniclers wrote her down. She had a ferocious strop on her, and hated the children Zeus fathered. Zeus was a ladies' man and put it about. Juno became a goddess of thunder.

Women have enormous faith in it – Goddess Juno Moneta's influence? I don't know. Just listen, though, to studio audiences, seventy-nine per cent females, note. Not all money is spent with decency. Forty-one lavatory blocks in the European Parliament Building, Brussels, show cocaine usage. UNESCO has built a costly Japanese garden in Paris – for themselves, of course, not the likes of us taxpayers. All politicians snort in the money troughs.

Miss Farnacott shelled out this wadge without a quibble. For revenge? Poor choice, though a bereaved daughter might want heads to roll. I once knew a lady who harboured hatred. We were dining in the George, when Michael, the manager, stopped at our table. He said, 'How is Hannah?' And explained, 'The crash?' The following ensued:

Marianna (my food provider, pro tem): 'Crash? Hannah?'

Michael (hostelry owner): 'Haven't you heard? She has terrible facial injuries. Scarred for life. My chef, Jem, saw it happen.'

Marianna (sweeter): 'Will she live?'

Michael: 'Yes, thank goodness. Sorry.' (He meant bringing bad news.)

Marianna: '*Please* don't apologise, darling. How fabulous!'

Michael (not getting it): 'We were all so relieved.'

Marianna (brightly): 'Yes! Champagne, darling!'

Michael (still not getting it): 'Yes, m'lady. That's exactly the attitude! Celebrate Hannah's survival!'

As he wafted on, I said, 'You bitch, Marianna. You're *glad*.'

Marianna (fluttering yard-long eyelashes): 'You're so innocent, darling, you're positively refreshing!'

And she drank the whole bottle. I couldn't touch a drop. Their dispute arose when Hannah, Marianna's bosom friend, said she didn't think Marianna's dress should have had sleeves *quite* that shape. The war began. Is vendetta rational? I don't think so. Marianna was furious I didn't join in her glee. Marianna eventually bribed estate agents, so Hannah lost heavily selling her bungalow. The bribes cost Marianna a mint. She thought it worth every penny.

Money, I thought, deciding to find Quemoy at the Dog & Duck, is supposed to have its own emotions. Wrong. My law is: *Money feels nothing.* That's another rule I wish I'd remembered, when life got harder and my troubles worse.

It was the following day.

The Dog & Duck had no sign of Quemoy. I got a pasty and a swig in the taproom, earning nods of recognition. I didn't ask for him. Rumour in East Anglia acts like pheromones to the Great White.

Fifteen minutes later, he slid onto the next stool, then noticed me with a theatrical start.

'Goodness gracious,' he declared, rep theatre on a bad day. 'If it isn't Lovejoy!'

'Wotcher.' Yet more dated talk.

'You have a sufficiency of imbibation?'

Did he mean a drink? The uncomfortable thought came that maybe he too was one of these disgruntled tribes.

'Busy?'

'Indeed I am, Lovejoy. Keeping the old mitts in, what?'

'Oh, right.' I asked if he would suss out another location.

'You're sure there will be no comeback?' He smiled.

Maybe I was agreeing too often with too many people. When they come from the Nationalist Kuomintang islands, and have criminal connections… Still, his English was hell of a sight better than mine. Why quibble?

'Have you the address?'

The babble in the Dog & Duck is always at max decibels. We couldn't be overheard.

'Somnell House. Is it in the Fylde?'

His face did not change. 'Got it,' he said. 'How soon? And how much?'

Quemoy is a creature of habit, and normally only asks the fee. His '*How soon?*' surprised me – he'd never asked before. We talked, he agreed. He said expansively, 'Hey, Lovejoy, what are friends for?'

We were such good friends. Or even spiffing chums. He promised me the Somnell House data in two days' time, collect from the Dog & Duck. Usually he took three hours – another warning bell. I kept up a light banter and got him laughing like a drain. I left at seven o'clock for the town bus. I needed to find Daniella from Mehala Bay, to interrogate her anew about Dr Castell, then about Somnell House, Lancashire.

The bus was on time, so not all omens were quarky. Now I'd finally got started I felt content. Bollocking Mortimer could wait.

Somebody sat beside me, silent until the bus turned at Leavenheath.

'You found Quemoy, Lovejoy?'

'Nosey little sod. Why ask if you already know?'

'Language, please, in public.'

'Here,' I said, narked, 'why do you pay no bus fare?'

Mortimer looked surprised. 'The bus company operates through my manor, Lovejoy. The driver is embarrassed when I offer to pay.'

'Then why do they charge me, you chiselling sod?'

'Because you are irrelevant, Lovejoy.'

He remained mute. Once in town, I headed for the Minories, an ancient house full of paintings where genteel vegetarian suppers are served by parish ladies. He came along, and eyed the wadge I flourished.

'Please tell me what transpired, Lovejoy.'

'Harken unto my words,' I said, then wished I hadn't been sarcastic because he went red and one of the ladies tut-tutted at my rudeness. 'Sorry.' More apologies. I told him everything, including Miss Farnacott's donation. I offered to let him count it. Politely he declined.

'What with that Ellen Jaynor stalking me, you, Lydia, Laura, Sandy, Tasker, that incompetent Hennell, an impending marriage, and Miss Farnacott talking tickety-boo Edwardian threats, I'll be finished before I start on those forgotten white tribes.'

'Ah,' Mortimer said. He didn't even glance up, yet one of the serving ladies sprinted across. 'Do you have cane sugar, please?' he asked.

'Silly me!' the lady gushed. 'I'll forget my head next.' And sprinted for some.

'Thank you.' He gave her a shy smile. She simpered and went to brag of her triumph to her mates.

I asked wearily, 'What does "Ah" mean this time?'

'Dad was one, Lovejoy. Of the forgotten white tribes.'

That shut me up. Now, Arthur Goldhorn wasn't forgotten or lost at all. I knew where he'd lived, where he was buried. And where Arthur's missus lived in riotous profligacy among gilded youths. In short, I knew everything about Arthur.

'Dad was born here, in Saffron Fields. Grannie was a Baster. They formed the republic in what is now Namibia. Recognised by the League of Nations. Grannie left all kinds of mementoes. I have them.'

'Antiques?'

'Not for you, Lovejoy. Dad guarded them. Even when you…'

'Look,' I said, narked. 'Don't bring that up. Some murderers die by accident. It isn't always me.'

'If you say so,' he said politely. 'Which is the reason you must serve Mrs Ellen Jaynor loyally. She is a Burgher of Ceylon.'

My brain felt it was floating free in a neap tide. 'Whose side are we on? Knowing might help me to survive.'

'We must find Ted Moon. Which is why you must go to the Formula One in Sunderland before going to Lincoln Cathedral.'

'Sunderland? Lincoln?' Not Derby?

'Ask any motor persons for Mr Gentry.'

'What do I want from Gentry?' I felt ill.

'A proper explanation, Lovejoy. Please ask that precise query.'

'Right.' This, note, was me taking orders from my sprog, whose feathers were still damp. 'Then what?'

'Lincoln. It's their flower show.'

'Do I nick some daisies?'

'Please leave tonight. I shall inform Miss Lydia. You do not have time to go back to Mehala Bay.'

'Very well.' (This, note, was me taking…etc.)

'Travel alone, please. You have sufficient finance, I see.'

'Very well.' I went to pay. When I turned, he'd left. I asked the counter lady which way he'd gone.

'Sarcasm,' she told me frostily, 'is the lowest form of wit.'

One day I must find out who said that first and what the hell it means. I went home via the bus and looked up how to get to Sunderland. Somnell House could wait. But this time I took a precaution. Time I put me first.

I phoned the Welcome Sailor on East Hill, and told Tinker to go to Mehala Bay.

'In secret and fast.'

'Where are you going, Lovejoy?' asked the loyal old soak.

'Me? Motor racing in Sunderland.'

'Christ Almighty.' His cough sounded like a distant avalanche. I held the phone away from my ear against contagion.

'Then we're flower arranging in Lincoln Cathedral. Bring Tansy.'

'Lovejoy,' he whimpered, 'I've no gelt. Where'll I get the train fare? I've not had a beer for—'

Try to help people, you get exploited. I put the phone down and went for some grub. I had a long journey.

Chapter Twenty-One

zlotnik: unit of any country's legal currency

The Formula One in Sunderland was about as secret as UN corruption. I was dazzled on the platform by posters.

'Is that today, mate?' I asked a geezer in an anorak. He was admiring a huge motor racing advert.

'No,' he said wistfully. 'Practising. At Blaydon Fields. I've to go to work.' And as I went to the ticket barrier, he added, 'Sunderland deserves its own motor circuit.'

I agreed. 'The council should do something.'

The Fields turned out to be mayhem, throngs ogling pieces of metal, and cars that looked like they were melting. All this, to drive cars in a circle? I get depressed by mankind's idiocy. There's a group in Mexico who, at a cost of millions, will race 1,500 miles above Planet Earth. These X-racers will zoom round and round in the Bright Blue Yonder, boring us all witless. Why?

Back on Earth, I pretended interest among these deranged saddos.

'Trouble?' I asked one lot.

'You wouldn't chuckle,' a bloke said morosely. He wore an orange overall hung about with spanners, his four assistants all equally unmerry. 'The practice cancelled.'

Motors stood on asphalt surfaces in the paddock. There simply was no circuit, but I went along in the cause of solidarity. Sundry pantechnicons loomed, cables strewn everywhere.

'It's the weather. The suppliers are late.'

'Terrible.' I kept up a litany of sympathy.

They talked gloomily of engines, when not one engine looked fit to go.

'Anybody seen Gentry?'

They were impressed. 'Do you know Gentry? Manager's tent.'

Gentry was among effete snobbery in a marquee, being served with canapés and cocktails. He broke off and came towards me.

'Ah, he's here!' I felt riff-raff among the nobs.

'What am I here for, Gent?' I kept my voice down.

'To advise, Lovejoy.' He was really pleased to see me. 'About the profit you'll win us ex-pats.'

Suddenly I felt weary. Everybody expected me to haul money in over the transoms when I'd no net. Ellen Jaynor, Laura, Donna da Silfa and her lost Faces, Dr Castell and Penny, Uncle Tom Cobley and all. Pete wanted his travelling fairground saved, and now I was responsible for dud engines littering Sunderland. It was too much.

'Is that all, Gentry? I resign. Ta-ra.'

He grasped my arm. 'Shouldn't do that, Lovejoy, old chap. Not good for your health. Think of Paltry.'

What was that? 'Eh?'

'Paltry put his foot in it. D'you recognise anybody here? He overheard a chat, and put the wad on us.'

'Put the wad on' means to blackmail. 'You?' I

couldn't believe it. 'You did Paltry?'

He sighed. 'Joint decision.'

Everybody was talking world championships. One man stood out. I'd last seen him giving testimony to a baffled plod near Paltry's body. A bloke next to him had the frigging nerve to give me a wink. Dressed to the nines, London tweeds, a gold watch that could have settled the National Debt. He was the straw man. I'd told Liza, the local reporter, to find out where he was from. She'd drawn a blank. Now here he was, among the racing elite.

'It was me put Penny Castell on to you for that mask thing her husband wanted from Eastwold College.' Gentry chuckled. 'Good value, is Penny. You'll have already found that out, eh, Lovejoy?'

What was worth killing a sad transvestite and old Smethie for? Couldn't these loony expatriates simply sell their fucking antiques and head for the hills?

'I still want out.'

'Don't even think of it, Lovejoy. Tomorrow you cross the Pennines to complete the job. We all go together.' He rubbed his fingers, meaning money.

'No deal.' I tried to speak like an aggressive Yank out of a Dashiell Hammett novel. It came out a bleat.

'I'd hate to have you erased, Lovejoy.'

'Is that a threat?'

He smiled in surprise. 'Why, yes.'

The witness raised his glass as I left the marquee and Gentry rejoined him. They had a good laugh. I heard them across the paddock.

* * *

Only an ill wind blows *nobody* some good. People say that. I got a lift back to the railway station – red-brick arches, so similar to that in my home town, probably the same Victorian builders – and caught the train to Derby. I could reach Somnell House later, without more murderers telling me what I had to do.

Like Penny, I always decide sex on my own. It's not true, but I felt good thinking it. I prayed Fionuella would still be in Derby.

Many towns vanish without telling me. It happened to Derby. Familiar shops were now kebab fast-fooders, a library a rush-nosher, an outfitter's a tat shop. The one good thing about Derby was Fionuella, a let's-pretend 'Irish' madam whose Genuine Antiques Emporium fronted her working house.

She never closes. The special house was her main income. Her girls specialised in sex machines. Its income was massive. Fionuella pays taxes based on phoney accounts.

I knocked and was admitted on the buzzer. She was at her desk among a load of dud antiques. Dud, except for one drab little cup that shone like a beacon.

She didn't even look up from her ledger. For a second I wondered if it was a pose, as if she had been expecting me. But how could she?

'Fifty an hour, sor,' she intoned. 'Sure to God indeed.' Lustrous black hair and London Blue eyes, and as Oirish as Lucrezia Borgia.

'That much?' I said.

She penned numbers. Double-entry system, exactly as the city of Florence invented in the Middle Ages. A creature of habit, Fionuella.

'All night is two hundred, sor, beggorah.'

'Can I choose the girl? I'll have you, Fee.'

She'd got contact lenses. Her face lit and she engulfed me in her cleavage.

'Lovejoy!' Her accent was gone. She's as Cockney as the Bells of Bow. 'You really want a girl? I've new Balkan grumble. I've got a city councillor coming at eight.' She smiled elfishly. 'Going to apologise, Lovejoy?'

Two years before, I'd divvied a collection of Davenport glass. John Davenport's porcelain was long out of favour, but he did one thing that beams through all history. August 1806, with the nation barely recovered from the death of naval hero Nelson, this potter patented a new way of engraving glass. It's simply a picture scraped in a coating of ground-glass paste stained with Aleppo-gall ink, and the glass fired at low heat after wiping the paste away. A kid can do it. Or any careful forger.

Fionuella had seduced a high clergyman (think a Church of England bishop, and you're there) out of his Davenport glassware collection. I'd travelled to Derby, divvied it for her as authentic, and she sold it for a gillion, buying a boutique which she changed into a brothel. She promised me a few groats, and never paid. Narked, I'd stayed away, until now. I looked about for Davenport pieces.

'I'm waiting, you bastard.'

Had she got the right end of the stick? *She* had defrauded *me*. When I'm desperate, my true character shows through.

'Sorry, Fee.'

She re-engulfed me in that crevasse. A fake mystic topaz

brooch added insult to injury by pricking my cheek. It didn't half hurt.

'Then I forgive you, Lovejoy.' *She* forgave *me*?

'Ta, love.' I came up for oxygen. She uses enough cosmetics to camouflage a frigate.

'Look, Lovejoy.' Demure now, changeable as the seasons. 'I'll let you in to number 18. I have the top flat.'

'You live in the er…?'

She smiled modestly. 'The girls don't have the skill, ignorant cunts. No fucking sense. I have to drill them on the bloody sex robots. One girl almost lost it on the Montreal Machine. Christ Almighty, all she had to do was stand in it. She went mad. No control. Even Sandy laughed at their antics.'

Sex robotics are the rage. You can hire every known automated – indeed automatic – device. And they aren't all in houses of ill repute. Retail shops sell them.

'Right, love. Finish your accounts. Can I look round?'

'You and antiques, Lovejoy!'

She bent over the ledger. She doesn't use computer accounting. I wandered as she grappled with the two sets of books. One was for VAT, the other falling a logarithm short of the Inland Revenue's expectations.

The antique that drew me stood on a 1930s pottery sheep. The cup looked for all the world like a small pewter dish. I licked my finger and tasted the inside. My mouth turned bitter. Unmistakable.

'Got anything good, love?' I said, flannelling.

'Shush, Lovejoy. Nearly finished.'

The slate-grey cup slotted neatly into its case. Unseen, I slipped my belt through the handle, so my jacket covered the little thing. Hands in pockets, I wandered, then told Fee I'd drift round to number 18 – you never use the word 'brothel' in the trade.

'OK if I have a drink there first, Fee?'

'Sure, Lovejoy. Tell them you're my dick for tonight and not to charge you. I price drinks worse than terrible.'

'Thanks, Fee.'

'Love you indeed sor,' she said mechanically.

Carefully seguing from her shop so as not to reveal my cased cup, I left. It was worth half her premises, and maybe more with provenance.

In a small hotel I told reception girl my car was stolen. Cash settled her anxiety. Alone in my room, I examined the cup. Fee should have had it valued.

Back in the harsh sailing days crews lived atrocious lives. Sea battles, foul weather, invading practically everywhere on earth, and they endured maggoty ship's rations. Captains did somewhat better. Rum was the source of cheap calories. Naturally, constipation was the enemy.

The antimony cup was born.

Captains bought cups made of antimony. Antimony pills were purgative. Drink a swig of wine from an antimony cup, and constipation ended. This cup was antimony, the fitted leather case genuine 1750. A ship's captain's purgative cup enabled a skipper to last out long voyages. The cup could be used again and again.

An antique like this would buy a house in the right hands. Or, I thought with a wry smile, the wrong. I reckoned Fionuella owed me, and I held a fortune in the antimony cup. Maybe I could pass it off as Nelson's own?

Fionuella had kept my share of her patent Davenport collection of glassware, so I was simply evening things up. I had no qualms. Comforted by this morality, I went round to number 18.

Chapter Twenty-Two

to put the wad on: to blackmail

Next morning, I offered Fionuella a fortune – I hoped to make a lot from secretly selling her (read *my*) eighteenth-century antimony cup – to drive me to Lincoln. She accepted with alacrity. She had regular clients there. And I sincerely honestly *don't* hint at a Lincoln clergyman, or the iniquitous bilge written about cathedral staff in the *Church Times*.

She drove. I looked at her, suddenly realising I didn't know her at all. Like I said, I'd known Fionuella two years in passing. She hadn't been wary then, yet here she was vigilant as a badger. Was I the only duckegg thick enough to trust her?

Another thing: I'd no idea she knew Sandy and Mel. See how your mind leads you down cul-de-sacs?

We stopped after an hour, she wanting to call at a farmers' market. Chatting about prices, vegetables, she was surprisingly expert.

'We'll have a bite here, Lovejoy,' she said. 'I'll get some provisions, in case.'

'In case of what?'

'Oh, nothing. Got to eat.'

Was I just lucky to be abducted by a gorgeous madam? It could have been known killers. Had she been too willing to accept this Lincoln trip? We stocked up with emergency rations, in case of 'nothing'. We ordered tea, sea bass, vegetables and a slab of Impossible Cake. I noshed while she went to phone her working house, something forgotten.

'World War One cake,' she said, smiling. 'My gran taught me. No dairy produce, no butter or margarine, no lard, no flour.'

A cake with nothing in it? I gazed at it admiringly. Heavy as lead. 'Can I have some more?'

She laughed, relaxed now. 'You're a gannet, Lovejoy.'

If I hadn't known her so well, I'd have said she gazed at me with cynicism, but I'm wiser than that. Double-shrewd, that's me. I wish I hadn't thought that now.

'Do you still see Femmy? The Audubon prints. You left me for her, remember?'

'Oh, aye.'

Women remember things. Honestly, it was not my fault. It had been Fionuella's. She'd thrown everything she could lay hands on. I left at a run. She'd cut my chin with a Woolworth vase.

Femmy was inordinately rich, meaning she spent whatever, whenever and wherever she liked, had four businesses, and a husband who owned banks near Lisbon. Or Cadiz? Somewhere there. I'd been invited to join in a cruise on the River Douro, but hopped off near Salamanca when her sister wanted to join in our night-time activities. I never did get the Audubons. Lucky I'm not bitter. I could remember Femmy's antiques, and that she'd had a boob job the size of Scafell Pike. Yes, I'd liked Femmy.

Fee waved her hand before my eyes. 'Come back, Lovejoy.'

'Sorry. I was thinking of Scafell.'

She smiled with fondness. 'You're sentimental, Lovejoy. I like that. Time to go.'

We arrived in sunny Lincoln after two hours and booked in as Mr and Mrs Voce. She flashed her plastic card.

'Fee,' I began as she unpacked. I noticed she had two suitcases and a heavy shopping bag. No antiques, though. 'Why here?'

'You had a job on here. Didn't you say that?'

Couldn't remember what I said. Passion rubs things out.

Her stare seemed absent and cold as a frog. My thought recurred about how little we know people.

'I've really loved your company, Fee, together again.'

Suddenly she embraced me, and wept buckets. Real sobbing. My shirt got wet. What are you supposed to do when a woman weeps for nothing? I'd assumed her mad careering meant we were OK. Instead, she cried like her heart would break. Memory's to blame, I often think. I couldn't remember Fee ever weeping. Fee in a temper, of course. Fee chucking things, sure. But Fee sad and sorrowing? Never in a million years.

Except in Lincoln?

Over supper I listened to the diners. This flower thing seemed a big occasion. Flower arrangements were everywhere, flower videos showing in lounges. The place was crowded by ladies worrying their husbands would crush their displays unloading the van, all that.

'Big do, eh?' I asked the waitress.

'Oh, yes!' She was thrilled. 'My aunt's come in all the way from Spalding.'

The head waiter came over. 'Are you in a flower club, sir?'

'Ah, no. Just here for the, er, daffodils.'

'Good,' he said doubtfully. Fee did that matronising smile with which women show they're making allowances for men's stupidity.

'We've to be up early, Lovejoy,' she said after we'd spent time in the bar. I was sick of the damned flowers. 'Best to say nothing to anyone. Understood?'

'What if people ask me?'

'Tell them about daffodils,' she said with sarcasm.

She didn't use to be sarcastic, either. Which raised the question: why did I feel part of her plan, not vice versa? Was it my animal appeal? I put on a show of being happy, then slipped off to a payphone. I managed to reach Tinker, thank God.

'Mehala Bay?' he croaked. 'Gawd, Lovejoy. Them cold estuaries kill me. My rheumatics—'

'Tinker. Get pedalling.'

Fee and I were very close that night. I was jubilant, though she wept more buckets as dawn came. She rose clear of eye and firm of lip, and we left at nine.

Daffodil time.

Flowers aren't much of a mystery, though women go mad for them. Our village has a team. They compete against neighbouring flower guilds and win (or lose) cups. But where is the art? Whole books are written about how to stick them in a pot. Truly. It's all my eye and Betty Martin. Flower plus pot plus water, leave the coloured end sticking out, OK? Life is busy breathing so get on with it.

But if you're a flowerer, Lincoln's your jaunt. Don't miss it. I knew I'd be bored sick until I could clear off. Ted Moon and the Faces would be here somewhere. Find the link, then collect my money.

'Every six years?' I marvelled. 'Bet they forget when it's due.'

'Silly. It's famous.'

I doubted that. A six-year flower show must be different from the Nottingham Goose Fair and All Hallows E'en, because they're engrained in the national consciousness. Some become immersed, like our old Martinmas, which blends with Armistice Day. You can tell when a 'day' or an 'eve' has made it because folk say a date's nickname, like New Year's Day instead of January First. I said all this. Fee ignored every word.

'Isn't it beautiful, Lovejoy?'

The cathedral truly is stunning. If you're new to cathedrals, go and see Lincoln. Its Chapter House is enough to amaze. That tracery in stone, those dazzling surfaces. I was ready for its vibes, for hadn't we seen those high outlines across the Fens, at the crossing of Fosse Way and Ermine Street, those prehistoric tracks? My wariness vanished at Lincoln Cathedral.

Feeling distinctly queer in the ancient place, I went wobbly near a small exhibition stand. Clammy, I found a pew as Fionuella moved swiftly into the floral throng. You couldn't see the cathedral's interior for flower stalls.

A middle-aged lady was seated nearby. 'The scent setting you back?' she said.

'Er, it isn't that, love. It's that stand, I think.'

'Lincoln is better than York Minster.' (Tip: Lincolnshire folk always run York Minster down.)

I'd had enough urban warfare. Lincoln Cathedral's lighting is crap. York's is better.

'You a visitor?' When I nodded, she said bitterly, 'They turned my stand down.'

'Your stand? Flowers?'

'I wanted to do King Stephen and Maud.'

'The Period of Anarchy? Don't flowers stand for peace?'

Our land has had its ups and downs. One of the downest was after 1135, when King Stephen was crowned. Grandson of the Conqueror, if I've got it right, he was opposed by Maud. This empress invaded us and marauded against Stephen. It's a period so grim our collective mind wants to forget.

'So why reject my display?' she demanded. I wanted an aspirin, not a scrap. 'Look at Scunthorpe!'

I racked my brains for Scunthorpe's part in our civil wars. Were they pro-Stephen? I have a map in my cottage.

'Their flower club has stands everywhere!' She made her voice a simpering whine, mocking. 'Byzantine cones depicting spring, can you believe? Lincoln's club is the same. Ingrates!'

I thought, Wars over flowers?

'So bo-o-oring. And Grimsby's flower stand is rubbish. Henry the Eighth. How dull is that?'

Well, no. Henry did wonders for London's sewers, and

was the last monarch I'd call dull. Several queens and his sons would agree. I noticed a lady looking down from a gallery. In shadow, she seemed fixed on me, but the light was poor. I wondered if somebody was standing with her, but I get shadows wrong.

Mercifully, my unexpected companion lowered her voice.

'I never take sides,' she confided. 'But King Stephen was too weak for his own good. Letting Maud go? What was that all about? She was a right bitch.'

Now, this was a thousand years ago. I went, 'Mmmh.' My peace shattered, I was looking about for escape when the lady said something vital. 'You feel the same about Stand 149.'

The reason I'd tottered was a battering from antique vibes emanating from Stand 149, between the Guilds' Chapel and St Anne's. I eyed her, wondering if she too was a divvy.

'Foreigners aren't eligible. I'm glad you hate it too.' She was fuming. 'They butted in with *seven days to go*. And got given Stand 149. I'd been shortlisted. It's horrible, little bits of glassy stuff with scraggy flowers. Call themselves the Overseas Flower Fans of Lincoln.'

The vehement lady pressed her hand on my leg, perhaps only for emphasis. I realised how attractive flower arranging could be.

'Can you do that?' I asked. 'Butt in?'

'Of course not!' The Guilds' Chapel was on the way to St Hugh's Choir. That was the direction Fee had taken, scurrying through the crowd. Looking for one particular stand, like say 149?

'Flowers deserve symbolism, don't you think?'

'Well, yes,' I agreed. 'Blossoms, after all.'

'There! If *you* can see it, why can't they? The foreigners made a donation. Lincoln Cathedral is corrupt. They'll do anything for a clipped shilling.'

'I've heard that.' I glanced up at the gallery. The staring woman – did I know her? – had moved. There was that deep shadow again. Perhaps another flower enthusiast, or a cathedral guide? 'What was your display, love?'

'It was exquisite. *Amaranthus purpureus* is so difficult. The symbolism was perfect.' Her eyes filled. 'Love-Lies-Bleeding, and the Indian Prince's Feather variant. My husband, Rich, does me a beautiful folio. My third rejection.'

I worked it out. 'Three sixes? Eighteen years?'

She found a hankie, sniffing. 'A Derbyshire lady got the foreigners in. She's the deacon's bit of skirt.'

'Foreigners.' Stand 149. Anything to do with Fionuella?

'A flighty mare from Ceylon vamped the deacon. And bribery. They called Stand 149 *The Future is in God's Safe Hands.*'

'Sadism.'

The woman in the gallery was still looking down. My task was now more identifiable. It stood in Stand 149. My chatty friend's hand kneaded my knee in her anguish, but duty called.

'Would you mind if I look at its, er, symbolism with you?'

'I'd love to!'

Two sincere flower arrangers together, we headed for Stand 149. A verger stepped up.

'No, sir, Mally. Please follow the arrows, south aisle.'

'It's all one way,' Mally explained.

We hurried past the displays as quickly as the throngs allowed. I suddenly felt desperate. We were heading away from 149, that verger and his bloody arrows. Then somebody screamed, the voice oddly familiar. I looked up and the woman in the gallery fell. It was like slow motion.

People screamed. I don't think back over horrors. They are too difficult. I fled alone into a small chantry and sat, shivering. It was Blaise's chapel, patron saint of woolcombers. The walls were covered with murals by Duncan Grant, only finished in 1958, so not antiques. Oil on fibreboard. They could easily be nicked by evil night-stealing footpads, though the thought honestly didn't cross my mind. I was shaking and remember retching. Visitors try to identify the famed Bloomsbury Set who were his models, like was it Virginia Wolfe's face or not?

The sight of that falling girl's look of despair wouldn't leave however hard I tried. I sat trembling from fright. I imagined she caught a glimpse of me as she tumbled, knowing in that final moment that I hadn't saved her. Me, no use to anyone. I retched into a hankie.

Eventually, looking through the grille, I recognised the visceral tomb of Queen Eleanor of Castile. Properly Leonor de Castilla, she was our King Edward the First's missus and rode with him to war. Queen Eleanor was loyal. Fables tell how she saved his life in a dagger fight at Acre. A tough bird. His grief, when she died up the road at Cross O'Cliff Hill, is the reason we have so many crosses as place-names. Everywhere her bier's procession paused for the night, a cross was erected – hence Charing Cross.

Thoughts of death among these lovely flowers made me feel I had malaria back again.

Further down the cathedral was where the imaginary 'Little Saint Hugh of Lincoln' had a shrine. He was dreamt up by hysterical people who took it into their heads to blame Lincoln's Jews for ritually crucifying some poor Christian lad in 1255. Bollocks, of course. The goons rampaged, wantonly destroying Jews' homes in the usual daft epidemic. Thinking didn't stop my shaking. I tried to work out what I was doing, sweat dripping down my chin. A kindly cleric looked in.

'Shaken, are we, sir?' he asked. 'Terrible accident. The young lady fell from the cross gallery at the north-east transept. We have a tea shop here. If you go…'

Tea solves most things, my gran said. Once, I shot back that tea didn't, and she clouted me for giving cheek, with, 'Don't answer back.' She'd only meant tea gave you a moment to face up. Over the next hour, my trembling diminished. Weak as a kitten, I pulled myself together. To face up.

Chapter Twenty-Three

tom: jewellery (tomfoolery, fr. Cockney rh. slang)

Mally was easy to find among the folk milling near the west doors. I needed her now.

Mrs Mally Winthrip was Lincoln born and bred. I said she was being marvellous, and how lucky I was to be with her when it happened.

'That poor woman. Why do you think she did it? She had a camera. Maybe she…'

'Leant out to take photos? Yes. Accidental.'

She eyed me. 'You don't suppose…?'

'Deliberately? No, impossible. She…'

She wasn't like that. I held it back. Tansy had so much to live for. The winter refuge at Mehala Bay for misfits. Because Tansy was a saint, who did not shirk. Others shirked, did, do, will. Like me.

'Because women don't. In a cathedral?'

If Tansy could have afforded a camera, she would have sold it and made nourishing beef stock to make vol-au-vents.

Also, I could have told Mally that I'd sent Tinker to fetch Tansy to Lincoln, nearer a cache of priceless antiques owned by foreigners who left deaths as their spoor.

'You and I share similar convictions, Mally.'

She coloured a little. 'The accident has lost me any chance now, to show my Period of Anarchy display.'

I steeled myself. 'Pity I never got a decent look at Stand 149.'

'Oh,' said this wondrous woman, 'We can get in. I'm on our Structures Committee.'

'Are we allowed?'

'I have the bleep code.'

As if conscience niggled, I hesitated, then pressed her hand. 'I wouldn't want to get you into trouble, Mally. But the cathedral must go on.'

Corny, but it persuaded Mally. 'After all, our city has withstood far worse.' Her lips thinned. 'Like that bitch Empress Maud.'

'I often think that, Mally.'

We were admitted with astonishing ease. A verger allowed us to walk right up to Stand 149. I felt the familiar ache in every muscle that serious antiques give. Police were flocked round yellow tape across the north aisle where poor Tansy had…I grabbed hold of Mally's arm to steady myself and gazed at the display.

'Isn't it ghastly, Lovejoy? The minds of people who made this up… Brains like ragbags.'

Blood-stained brains, the minds of killers. 'They've killed the very best of living things,' I said brokenly.

Mally stared, eyes wide. 'Lovejoy! You're actually…' She found me a tissue and we were let out into the bright day by the same verger. 'I'm so sorry, Lovejoy. I was thoughtless. You are even more upset by the display than I am. How sensitive!'

I showed a stiff-upper-lip bravery. I quite like praise. 'I'm like that.'

'Though men *are* the most sensitive poets, aren't they?'

We sat on a bench where the shops began. 'I hate to see wrong done, Mally. Living things are friends.' I didn't mean flowers.

'You poor dear!' she crooned. 'Relax, Lovejoy. Take your time.'

My forehead in her neck. 'I'll have to wait another six years. Heartbreaking.'

'No, Mally. I'll make it quicker. I promise.'

'How? The show only lasts a few days.' She sounded doubtful, and I hadn't a clue what to do.

'Heaven is on our side, Mally.'

Donna da Silfa's group did Stand 149 for me to spot and approve. How many other watchers were also there, and who they were, I had no way of knowing. International buyers maybe? Auctioneers?

'Er,' I managed to get out.

From a floral point of view the display was dud, zilch, *null*. Mally kept up a whine about this pattern, that Hogarth curve, colour balances. For me Stand 149 was the dawn of a new world. Only one in four flowers was real. The rest were artificial, man-made.

'You're as upset as I am. It's a scandal.'

My voice was strangled. 'I haven't the words, love.'

My resolve grew back. Whoever had flung Tansy off would pay dearly. I would be peaceable about it. Some things can't be shelved simply because it's nice when troubles go away. That morning in Lincoln I came to my senses. No more flowers. Whatever happened now, I'd have to stay focussed.

I had a goodbye meal with Mally. Then we parted, and I bought some paper and coloured pencils. No trace of Fionuella. Odd, that. I shelved thoughts of her, for Stand 149's display was everything Donna da Silfa had promised.

Sketching in the hotel room with a thick B4 pencil, I outlined the antiques, lettering them as I went. It was the most breathtaking show of antiques I'd ever seen. The flowers were simply the Faces' admission ticket. I made notes on the scale of it all.

This was my job, I realised: to prove the antiques were genuine and worth what they hoped. I'd never seen anything like them. Nobody else ever had, either.

The memory caused a toxic delirium.

Divvying is always grim – malaise, sickness, even rigors. TV antiques-show presenters pretend they have the gift, but they are simply forging career moves to encourage another series. To Mally the stand must have looked strange.

A pair of neat corner cupboards, but straight out of Ince and Mayhew's 1752 book, originals beyond rarity. Those masters designed them to blot up the angles in a lady's parlour. These ecoinears would each buy a house. I'd only ever seen one such pristine pair, and they had been heavily restored. Those on Stand 149 were exactly as they'd left the hands of those geniuses. Ladies overseas had nurtured them through generations. Sketching them took an hour.

With them stood a so-called roundabout, the famous 'burgomaster chair'. If you see one now, it's sure to be a machine-tooled replica. The stand's was 1695, give or take,

Dutch East Indies pattern. Their cane-bottomed seats seem strange (sitting, you get sticky in the tropics). Unbelievably heavy. Move one, it's hernia time. Lavish scrolly carving. You could hide a herd in the acanthus foliage on the six – *six* – knees. The four Indian Raj variants were beautifully light, all ivory, so you could blow them away with a breath. Exquisite.

No more furniture, just those. I felt as if I had come across a Rembrandt or a Gainsborough in a garage sale.

A footfall creaked the floorboards in the corridor outside my room.

As if those weren't enough, the artificial flowers hammered the final nail in. I'd never seen such a mass of rare gems. I needed serious advice on those, for the gemstones *were* the blossoms. I could only list them.

We assume diamonds reached Man when little Erasmus Jacobs found his 21.7 carat 'shiny stone' in 1866, and mighty South Africa's great diamond boom started, leading right up to the recent 603-carat 'Lesotho Promise' found by the eagle-eyed Miss Agnes in the Letseng, the world's highest diamond mine. Yet Indian diamonds were known to the Ancients. In a priceless Japanese Satsuma bowl were flowers with diamonds in the Ceylon-cut. This old cut was wasteful. The modern brilliant-cut is one of the most economical. And one calyx showed a giant rare blue, exactly like the Hope Diamond.

Rarer still was the alexandrite got from the fatal Ekaterinburg District. See one before you buy any other jewel. It spoils you for all the rest.

A faint draught touched my nape. *Somebody was now in the room.* I kept on drawing. I was on a roll. Alexandrite has tricks of startling beauty. By day, it's mostly greenish. In candlelight it turns a startling blood red. Its colours seem uncontrollable. I knew a rich lady once, a beautiful Hollywood actress who lived in Endsleigh Gardens (and if you think The Contessa, you've got her). She thought her ring was an odd emerald, until I showed it to her by lantern light. You must sell your whole estate to buy a two-carat stone.

Tanzanite, unbelievably in a genuine Regency pendant, was supposed to have been 'discovered' in Tanzania in 1967, but one large blue on display was in a Regency scroll setting. The USA political embargo business in the 1980s bled prices to death.

I heard a faint tap of a heel.

'Who was the silly cunt', I said quietly without turning, 'who cleaned the tanzanite with ultrasound?'

Silence.

'If it was you, love,' I went on, 'I'll spank your bottom. Only ignorant sods use ultrasound.'

'Hand-cleaning costs the earth even in Zimbabwe, Lovejoy.'

'Didn't you have the sense to look it up? Tanzanite is simply blue zoisite. It goes muddy and is permanently ruined in ultrasound cleaners.'

'Isn't it time you saw sense, Lovejoy?' Lydia said, exasperated.

'Wotcher, Lyd. Time you got here.' Turning, I put my face into her belly. She leapt away with a cry.

'Lovejoy! In a public building!' Lydia would always be Lydia.

'Tansy got killed.'

'That's the reason I hurried here, Lovejoy.' She would bollock me any second. I braced myself. 'To make sure you do nothing outrageous. Tinker told me of the poor girl's accident.'

'The sod didn't show. I told him to bring Tansy here.'

'Language, please. Leave it to the police, Lovejoy. Tansy fell photographing the flowers. The police say so.'

Yeah, right. Strapped for a groat to feed her multitudes, Tansy buys the most expensive camera then falls to her death so her people can starve? I looked at Lydia's blue eyes with all the innocence I could muster.

'You're right, Lyd. I'm just upset.'

'There you are, then!' She looked at my drawings. 'Nice.'

'Yes. I thought', I invented quickly, 'I'd illustrate a new edition of my antiques book.'

'Good idea. Time you settled to some real work.'

'You know, Lyd,' I said, 'you're absolutely right.'

'Lydia, please.'

I rolled my drawings into a cardboard tube I got from the hotel reception. At a rough estimate, three hundred and eighty priceless gemstones, all in their original settings from the past four centuries, were displayed on Stand 149, a sprinkling of ancient Roman and Greek among them.

'Can we go by the cathedral, say a prayer for Tansy?'

'Of course!' She filled up. 'What a lovely thought!'

It's hard not to think of loot, or have I said that? I put two and two together so often, that four offers few surprises. Have I said that too?

Chapter Twenty-Four

woman: any non-dealer, male or female, among antiques
(trade slang)

We went down to Lydia's car, loot on my mind. Money was the main thing for those Faces trapped in their historical Time lacuna. We're *all* trapped by money, let's remember.

It isn't of much interest, except to numismatists who fight over the design of pellets round a Saxon silver penny. Yet the fur flies. Add money to anything, and it ends in uproar. We are in there too, no matter how holy we pretend to be.

Think of any museum. Just the place to blob out, if your train is late or it's teeming down. Then answer this question: is any great museum or gallery untouched by scandal? Or *hasn't* been suspected/accused/aware of thefts while amassing treasures? *Are any of them honest?*

Not on your life.

All museums and national galleries stand shamefaced in the dock when you talk robbery, art theft, and the menace of loot. Money is their theme. Despite the problems of Christie's and Sotheby's, and of the harrowing trials of the mighty J Paul Getty Museum in Los Angeles and the denunciations of the St Petersburg Hermitage's noble (and morally correct) policies, the antiques trade surges on. (And I'm really glad Getty of LA is returning forty artworks to Italy. No, honest – we all are, right?) Relics have become priceless. Tomb robbers flourish. Museums compete, and the weapon is gelt, plus treachery. It's the ugliest business on earth. It is greed, this lethal world of antiques.

Esteemed curators demand sunroofed Porsche SUVs (think California, and I really am pointing the finger here), look as saintly as Sir Galahad, but that old niggle begins – *are they honest?* And prosecutors slither out of the woodwork, lawyers oil into night offices, accountants dangle on telephone wires, and suddenly the gallery is closed with police on the doors.

Planet Earth is a celestial body preoccupied with examining its own innards. Why is this? Because antiques rule. They rule by money. You gave your lovely lady a jewel. But would she be as pleased if it was paste?

And the answer is…?

Driving with Lydia, I dwelt on the image of Donna da Silfa's tribes, all people with mind-bending antiques passed down families. OK, I'd got that bit. Yet to me, they were still Faces in the Pool, ethnic descendants in far-flung countries and yearning for some old motherland. It seems strange, hankering after old homelands you've never even seen. It's almost as if Americans suddenly started longing to return to England, Italy or wherever. There are boring jokes about this – 'Ireland (Germany, or Sicily, Savoy, etc) is a country whose people live everywhere else singing about it,' and so on. Sentiment is perpetuated by those yawnsome anthems hysterical crowds bawl at the Olympic Games and rugby internationals. For me, nationalism is the ultimate drowse. It's great to harbour admiration for, say, ancient Egypt's culture, the Han Dynasty, Stonehenge, or Shakespeare, but only *because it's interesting*, not because it's rabble-rousing. There's a difference.

Thinking ends where money begins. And love ends where money begins. And loyalty ends where... Money stuns. I include me, I'm ashamed to say.

I'm no good when people ask an antique's value. I always reply, 'You have to laugh at those *Antiques Roadshows*, when some lady says of her George the Second 1759 silver London hallmarked cake basket, "It's a family heirloom. I don't care about money..." She's screaming inside *"How much?"'* (The answer, to save you worrying, is US$ 27,500, but by the time this ink dries...) Filthy lucre isn't as filthy as all that.

Money is now the only question. Hence our total barbarism. Loyalty? Forget it. Marriage? Divorce is its natural consequence. Truth? Outdated myths that died with Grampa. Decency? Vanished when Grandma sighed her last.

So could I really blame Donna da Silfa's lost Faces, for selling up? Not really. They were determined to swim out of their landlocked tide pools into the sea of life. We'd all decide the same, cash in and scoot to the sin bins of Europe or the mighty US of A. I felt worn out by ridiculous thinking.

When we swung near Lincoln Cathedral (a giddy 7 mph, Lydia concentrating hard at the wheel) I suddenly lost all reason. I saw Mortimer. Here in Lincoln? My trustworthy, dependable offspring, Mortimer?

He was on the greensward by the giant west door. People were loading Stand 149 into a pantechnicon. Hugo Hahn, the tall Namibian, was supervising the loaders.

Lydia drove on by in whirlwind progress, her delicious tongue protruding from the corner of her mouth. I'd never felt so alone. Mortimer represented honesty and decency. In short, Mortimer was everything I wasn't. Until now? Surely to God the lad wasn't as deceitful as me after all?

I was in a state of shock. And Lydia, epitome of grace, was here, in on everything without my knowing anything. Why was he so friendly with Donna da Silfa's merry band, who'd murdered my lovely Tansy?

'Hang on, Lyd,' I said suddenly. 'The hotel key. Stop here. I'll phone.'

'No, Lovejoy. I gave it in as we left.'

'I'd better check. Park there.'

I alighted at the traffic lights. She tut-tutted and drove pacily on to a line of shops. I dodged into a close. She'd not be able to follow, not without parking and hunting the streets. She would then zoom home in a rage. Same old same old, folk say. I got breathless rushing down Lincoln's steep slope. An ancient coffee house bridged a river with swans.

Stoke's Coffee Shop was right in the middle of the city, and stood over the River Witham. The crowds of shoppers made me feel safe. Lovely copper cowls over a fire burning in the grate, with a cheery lass to serve.

She said brightly, 'We call this the Glory Hole.' She meant the swark flow beneath the Norman arch. 'The

Murder Hole, old folk still call it. Changed it for tourists, see?'

'Good idea,' I praised faintly. Why was Tansy killed? You don't kill saints for nothing. Except motive is always nonsense, nothing to do with what folk actually do.

'Been to the Flower Festival?' she kept on.

'Lovely,' I told her.

Looking over the thoroughfare, I thought of gems, the most precious objects known to man. I needed help from a gems expert.

Trying to focus my ragbag mind, I closed my eyes, trying to remember my birthstone. Didn't it relieve headaches?

'Sapphire, Lovejoy,' somebody said. 'Relieves pain.'

Had I been mumbling again?

'Traditionally,' his voice went on, 'Zodiac for Libra – you are Libra, Lovejoy? Last day of September? – is the peridot. Its planetary influence comes via the sapphire.'

'You little sod. Why were you chatting to those killers?'

'Lovejoy, responsibilities do not disappear when you get bored.'

'I'm going home, Mortimer.'

'No. You must rob their mansion house.'

'Last robbery I got nabbed, almost killed, then abducted.'

'That's no way to speak of friends.'

I opened my eyes. The caff was almost empty, the counter girl watching us warily. I hoped she hadn't heard our conversation. I saw her eyes flick from Mortimer to me, as if spotting some resemblance.

'Friends?' I said bitterly. 'My gran used to say, "Lord,

save me from mine helpers."' I thought a bit, went red and added, 'Er, I mean your great-grandmother.'

'You can tell me about her. I should like to know.'

'Any mansion house in particular?' As if I didn't know. 'If it goes wrong it's your fault. Just remember that.'

'Your team should be ready.'

He helped me to my feet. I caught sight of myself in a wall mirror. Haggard, looking off the road. I really was rubbish. Beside me, Mortimer looked fresh, astute, learned. I felt a weak glow of pride, quickly suppressed. I was right to be sorry for myself. He didn't care a tinker's toss.

'Has it to be me?'

'Of course.' His tone hinted that I was being ridiculous. 'You're the one who gets everything right.'

'Who told you that?'

'Dad's old friends.' He held the door open for me.

'Thank you, sir,' the girl called. 'Please come again.'

She meant Mortimer, not me. I think these young girls are too cocky for their own good. Too forward, Gran would have said, or, if especially tuttish, too froward (sic).

First off, I'd throttle Tinker, if ever the drunken sot showed up. He'd got Mortimer into this unknowable shambles.

'I'll need to suss the place first.'

'Not, I hope, to ask Quemoy for details, Lovejoy. I rather suspect Quemoy might not be entirely trustworthy.'

'Right,' I said, broken. The squirt was giving me orders now. That's how far I'd sunk.

Chapter Twenty-Five

to uncle: to steal (fr. nick, Cockney rh. slang, Uncle Dick)

'What about Lydia?' I asked in the taxi. It was late afternoon. 'And Fionuella?'

'Miss Lydia is less hardy than some,' Mortimer said gravely. 'I have not had the pleasure of an introduction to the latter lady.'

Thank God for that, I thought fervently.

'As for the private detectives, Lovejoy, they must mend their ways.'

It was said with sleet in his voice. I felt the chill.

'Here, sir? City mortuary?' The taxi driver wasn't asking me.

'Correct. Please wait.'

His eyes fixed on Mortimer in the mirror, and he silenced. I was narked. How come everybody obeyed a sprog, but never me? It's not right.

We alighted, some cars pulling away. I eyed the place uneasily.

'What are we here for, Mortimer?'

'The coroner, please,' he told a uniformed guard.

The man conducted us into the building where a bald

man rose in a fluster to greet us. The place was sparse, creamy walls with plaques. He shook Mortimer's hand. Hopefully, I hung mine out. He ignored me.

'Glad you made it, sir. Yes, the deceased can be viewed. The young lady has already arrived. Your driver may accompany you.'

'Thank you for making the arrangements, Doctor.'

'Yes, thanks,' said the driver bitterly, aka me.

'I shall wait in case you have any questions.'

A thin, cachectic man who looked as if he was gasping for a cigarette led the way. The mortuary was cold, breath steaming, the whole scene made worse by those horror-film lights. We went through two sets of double doors. An exquisite girl was standing there. She gave Mortimer a hug, to my annoyance – she at least twenty, and him hardly hatched.

'Hello, sweetie,' she said in a husky voice.

'Is it she?' Mortimer asked respectfully.

'No, thank God.' Had I seen her before?

Mortimer said, 'You must be so relieved, Etholle.'

The exquisite girl said, 'Yes, in case I had to pay for her frigging funeral.'

'Etholle, we do not forget the sad demise of the poor deceased.'

'If you say so, sweetie.' She sounded bored out of her mind. 'This is miles from any-fucking-where. I'll wait.'

'Hello,' I said. 'I'm Lovejoy.'

She turned her beautiful gaze on me. 'Oh. Right.'

That was me done with. I followed Mortimer in. There lay poor Tansy, a sheet covering her. She looked…well, gone. Not one flower for a saint who had fed the eccentrics of East Anglia, and seen them safely through dark snowy nights.

Somebody had killed her. What was worth a whole saint? I stood looking.

'Tansy?' Mortimer said.

Sometimes it is hard to speak. I looked at her hair.

Once, some of us slum urchins went to see the body of a dead friend. We did that back then. The parents let us in. We little children stood looking at the poor lad in his coffin. He'd choked on a fishbone. I can see Brian now, waxen in frothy white garb, looking as though he was having to work hard at being asleep. Poor Tansy was relaxed, her hair glorious. I hadn't noticed it during her life, even though we had…

Somebody had done this violent thing, and I hadn't stopped it. What would happen to her eccentrics, waiting for their dinners by the winter sea? The light of the world had gone out.

'We can go now,' Mortimer was saying over and over. He had the sense not to touch me.

'So long, Tans. See you soon.' I said it to the whole place more than Tansy. We left. The attendant closed the door.

Etholle was waiting. Men locked up after us.

'What's up with that berk?' she asked Mortimer. 'Is he crying?'

'He's got a cold,' Mortimer said. 'Allergic to flowers.'

'It's not my sister in there, is it?'

'No.' Mortimer paused. 'Lovejoy's friend.'

'What now?' She sounded bored sick.

'Go and bring your sister, please, Etholle.'

'Oh, fucking hell,' said this charmer. 'Do I have to? I hate the crazy frigging bitch. Can't I just phone the useless mare?'

They seemed to have written Tansy off, and meant somebody else.

'I would rather you went, Etholle.'

'I haven't any money,' she said in a sulk.

'Yes you have. Bring her north,' Mortimer told her, a Churchillian imperative.

The ignorant cow flounced away – actually *flounced* out of a *mortuary*. We left, thanking the coroner. I signed a paper offered by his doleful acolyte, feeling a traitor to Tansy.

The taxi driver said nothing, just drove on without instructions.

'You stay at a hotel, Lovejoy,' Mortimer said. 'Then head north tomorrow.'

'Go and get who?' I couldn't help asking. 'Lydia?'

'No.' He said no more until we drew up at a hotel. I could see the cathedral in the night sky. 'Go to Blackpool. The New President Hotel.'

'Who has she gone for?' I asked again. 'Somebody I know?'

'The World Champion Sex Pole Dancer.'

My mind didn't even bother trying. He bade me a polite goodnight and the taxi gunned away. That, I told myself angrily from the hotel steps, was my underage by-blow giving orders like Marlborough before a battle. Everybody simply did as he said, the little sod. Me, they ignored.

Sex pole dancer? I didn't even know the crummy beginners in the local pubs, let alone a – *the* – world champ. How the hell did he even know any? I'd box the little sod's ears. He should remember he wasn't too old to… *What was I saying?* It was time to give up parenthood, and I'd never really started. I'd be telling him to wash behind his ears next.

In the hotel I tried phoning Tinker. No go. I tried Lydia, no luck.

A room had been paid for and somebody had delivered clean clothes for me. No pole dancers, though. Sadness is compound. Grief always brings its friends. Stop being sad about one thing, you have plenty more sorrow to be getting on with. I tried to sleep. Tansy slept. I didn't.

Six o'clock I roused. The girl on the hotel reception gave me an envelope with a train ticket to Blackpool. First Class? I'd never travelled posh in my life. I caught the London train, and pretended to the inspector I'd mistaken the train. It didn't work. He made me get off a hundred miles down the line. Narked, I boarded the next southbound, and reached London. Blackpool could wait.

Tansy was dead, so I had duties of my own.

At the Gem Institute I asked for Arona. Etholle treated me like dirt, Mortimer saw me as a duckegg, and Donna da Silfa and her Faces in the Pool wanted me as a money spinner, fine. Let them all get on with their madnesses.

Arona came into the foyer. Her expression fell. 'You bastard, Lovejoy. They said Inspector Kine.'

The security guard advanced to threaten.

'Er, Kine couldn't come, Arona. I've an urgent message.'

'It's all right, Nev.' And as the guard relaxed, 'I've no money so piss off, Lovejoy.'

And she turned on her heel.

Arona has never trusted me. If she were drowning and I sailed to her rescue, she'd gasp, 'What's the catch, Lovejoy?' It all stems from when I sold her sister. It was to a drunk in East Cheap who owed me. I'd been desperate, and her sister thought it up. Saphie was always up for a lark. She'd met me afterwards in the Lamb (Dryden's old pub, still there) down Long Acre and demanded half the gelt.

'It's those gems.' I tried to make tears, failing, and I can't make my lip tremble. 'Tell them I'm sorry.'

She paused, but by then I was leaving.

'What?' I heard her call after me. 'Lovejoy?'

Head down, I walked into the street, brave Sidney Carton to the guillotine.

She caught me up. 'What gems? Tell who?'

'Don't pretend, Arona,' I got out, all bitter. 'I know it was you. Nobody else knows precious gems like you do, so don't mess me about.'

Her eyes narrowed. Luckily it was drizzling, and a woman hates rain on a rising wind.

'Lovejoy. If this is another of your—'

'Yeah, that's right, Arona.' This time I really did get bitterness in. I sounded great. 'That's it. I'm never truthful, am I?'

Illusions don't work. I knew I was disposable. They killed saints. They'd not think twice about me.

She glanced about the street. It was off Little Britain, where Wesley knelt praying for a miracle when his sister was trapped in a burning house. (A brave workman clambered in and rescued her as Wesley praised God, religion doing its usual fraud.)

'Come back, Lovejoy. I'll hear what you have to say.'

Looking as if I was suspicious, I gave in. 'OK. Ten minutes. I have a train to catch.'

Arona got her coat. We went to sit in St Botolph Without – its proper name. I proved my sincerity by putting some gelt in the box. I love the old place. Baby John Keats was baptised in its font, which I always touch, hoping his gentleness will rub off on me.

Gentleness hasn't reached me yet, but there you go.

Chapter Twenty-Six

**rounder: a fake antique sold repeatedly at auction
(trade slang)**

We sat in the old London church. A few city people were in. They looked holy while plotting the assassination of rival banks. Arona whispered in the voice of love – not for me, but for gems.

How strange people were. Attractive and brainy, gems to her meant money.

'Supposing, Arona,' I began in a whisper she leant to hear, 'a friend told me he'd seen a group of gems in settings proving they were centuries old.'

'How many? What stones? Which country? Where?'

'Hang on. I'm only supposing, right? Say, four hundred.'

'What, big? Little? Which?'

'One was a massive diamond. Bluish, from where I... where *he* was standing.'

'Your friend, right?' She nodded. 'Draw me how big it was.'

On her palm I drew a rounded outline shaped like one of those balloons barmy people fly in.

She shook her head. 'Your *friend* is having you on, Lovejoy. No such thing. Except the bluish Koh-I-Noor. And that weighs 105 carats.'

'Plus a cushion-shaped brilliant-cut diamond half as big again.'

'What grade? P3?' She sneered. Gemmologists hate stones crammed with inclusions.

'River. Over Wesselton Top.'

'Good God, Lovejoy. Your pal was drunk. Look. The way pure gems are cut is critical. No modern gemmologist would cut a highest grader into a cushion-shaped brilliant.'

'Why not?' I asked, all innocent.

'There are fashions in cutting. We opt for the brilliant-cut now. Like, the elongated step-cut is a truly ancient way of cutting emeralds. It fell out of fashion. Now?' She smiled, well into her subject. 'Now we call it the *modern* cut! Hilarious!'

'Hilarious,' I agreed gravely, because there had been at least three step-cut rectangular emeralds on Stand 149. 'What's the biggest diamond you've ever seen, Arona?'

'Disney's *Snow White and the Seven Dwarfs*, Lovejoy.' She chuckled at her witticism. 'Oh, I went to see the Orlov in the Kremlin about ten years since. Dome-shaped, named after…'

Named after Count Orlov, yet another lover among Catherine the Great's thousands. Arona told me the tale, 189.6 carats of dome-shaped diamond as big as a quail egg.

'Really?' I said, going all impressed. 'I thought that was the Regent.'

'Don't, Lovejoy.' She shivered. Never mention the

spookiest diamond on earth to a gem expert. 'Lucky we're in a sacred place, Lovejoy. It used to be called the Pitt Diamond. It's still in the Louvre. An Indian worker in 1701...'

...cut his own leg open, to smuggle the diamond out of the mine where he worked. A British sea captain murdered him and sold it for a fortune to Tom Pitt, who governed Madras. The sea captain took his own life from remorse. The stone went to the French Regent, Prince Philippe...

'They say it's evil.' She glanced at her watch. 'Look, I've to get back. I've examiners coming today.'

'One last question. Alexandrite, Russian setting, eighteenth century. Were they cut in cushion shapes back then?' cunning, cunning Lovejoy asked innocently.

'You've got that wrong, Lovejoy.' Her eyes grew dreamy, as did mine at the thought of the seven-carat alexandrite gleaming among that massive shoal of jewels.

'Why, Arona?' Still innocent.

'A peasant called Maxim Koshevnikov first found some emeralds under an uprooted tree in the Urals. They dug, and found alexandrite too. Nordenskjold named it for Prince Alexander, who became Tsar Alexander the Second. It's beautiful. Every woman longs for one. Pure emerald by day, by candlelight a lovely ruby. Think how a woman imagines herself, entering some banquet wearing one! As night candles shine, the stone turns into passionate scarlet...'

She ahemed and looked guiltily at the high altar.

'It's pleochroic,' she went quickly on. 'Chromic oxide, replacing other chemicals of the chrysoberyl group...' and so on.

My mind switched off. This superb gem is rarer even than diamond, and shows the odd phenomenon of twinning, two crystals joining as they formed millions of years ago in the Tokovaya River region of the Urals. The one I'd seen was *still in its twin form*, something I'd never even seen.

Not only that. It was set into the surface of an iron vase. After his wars, Peter the Great switched the Tula munition works to making domestic things like candlesticks. Catherine the Great, resting briefly from her lovers, kept the factories going, but that all ended with her death in 1796. The ironworks had developed a clever but unmistakable rosette pattern. The blinding alexandrite on Stand 149 was set so. Priceless doesn't even come close.

Now, if it was only discovered in 1830, how come it was in genuine metalwork made in the previous century? That single fact would change the study of precious stones for ever. And the Ekaterinburg mines were almost exhausted in the 1920s, so the world depends now on lower-quality finds in Sri Lanka and Brazil. I felt ill from greed.

Arona was still rabbiting on about different ways of cutting gems: '...so if your friend saw an Old English double-cut, which we call the Old Star, he must have billionaire pals! So wasteful...'

'Arona,' I interrupted. 'Do people still use Wood's alloy?'

'Old-fashioned gem-cutters do. Why?'

'Ta, Arona.' I rose. 'My friend was making it up. Can you believe some people?'

Uncertain, she said, 'Lovejoy?'

And I walked out. The dot on the floor of Ted Moon's

shop had become as fluid as mercury. Wood's alloy melts even in hot water. At least I'd had the nous to spot one clue on my own.

To Blackpool, I thought, and the World Champion Sex Pole Dancer.

On the train at Euston, I listed the females who were likely World Champion Sex Pole Dancers. It was difficult, for all women are beautiful to start with.

Lydia was out, though spectacularly gorgeous. Fionuella was a good possibility, though she specialised in, er, a more direct approach to eroticism. I counted ten, maybe eleven, who would perhaps rise to the occasion, but some were busy, one was in clink, and the rest had problems of their own.

Veronica? She couldn't hack it. Tansy, poor Tansy, was not available. Yet it had to be somebody I'd met, for Mortimer knew her. Who? I kept thinking of women I had known at the various places along the route. Like, Watford meant a pretty dentist whose hobby was illegal hare coursing and who bought early silhouettes. These paper cut-outs are highly valued if pre-1815, the year Miss Barbara Townshend published her little book on the art of making 'shades' and 'profiles'.

Macclesfield to me was Rafaela, who collected Victorian photographs and who built sculptures of fictional murder scenes. I really liked Rafaela. To my indignation she married a schoolteacher from Whalley. Crewe was Isobel, a night-school lecturer on the Spanish Civil War who sold houses to visiting ambassadors, hated taxmen but loved sexual fetishes.

There was one point worth more than Arona's views. Blood diamonds – you've to say 'Conflict diamonds' now, so the UN can carry on betraying truth with its phoney Kimberley Process scheme – are illicit diamonds sold to finance murderous wars. The KP has forty-five nations, plus the EU, certifying diamonds as 'clean'. Ancient gems would predate the blood diamond wars, right? The price would soar beyond counting.

Blearily, I woke at Manchester and changed for the stopping train to Blackpool, the Coney Island/Las Vegas/ Atlantic City of our industrial north.

Chapter Twenty-Seven

to mogga: to mix randomly

Blackpool. I felt pushed from pillar to post as I went along the seafront looking at the changes since I was a little lad. Back then, the great thing was Pablo's ice-cream. No mills, no moors, just the Big Wheel, Pleasure Beach, the Tower so like the Eiffel, piers sticking out to sea, crowds hustling on the promenade. It's up for a World Heritage Site nomination.

It looked grander yet grubbier. The streamlined electric trams always fascinated me, looking straight out of Flash Gordon's wars versus Emperor Ming. Fishing fleets used to sail from Fleetwood, but no longer. There wasn't the same passion to revel, just a passive drift to boozers and shows.

The shows seemed curtailed. Like, some comedian's GIANT SEASON was billed as running 'Ten Whole Days'. Once, favourite stars filled theatres for twenty continuous weeks, no break except for Sundays. Now, I saw with resentment, each entertainer was labelled *Television's Own Superstar!!!* Without TV, stardom did not exist. I sat on a waterfront bench near the New President Hotel, wondering why I had come. I'd been had by everyone.

Three deaths, all avoidable if I'd been bright enough. All my fault. All 'accidental'.

And I was baffled by this World Champion Sex Pole Dancer. Yet Mortimer, arrogant little know-all, gave the impression that I too must know the lass he'd told the luscious Etholle to fetch. And he'd been cool enough to send for Etholle to check that poor dead Tansy wasn't her sister – presumably the famous lass? Leaving aside whatever reasons Mortimer needed an exotic sex performer for, somewhere along the line I'd been duped. The speed-daters? That attractive Joanna? Chloe, or somebody from the Arcade? My guesswork was never up to much.

Another niggle. Etholle seemed *scared* the dead girl might be her sister. How come she needed Mortimer and me to identify the dead girl? Mortimer had been in touch with the coroner beforehand. Not yet adult, he'd needed me to sign for Tansy – or did that still apply, now infants were adults without growing up?

One other thing. Why was Tansy in a dangerous choir loft? And where was Fee?

Everybody pretends they are something they're not. Like Fee, say? A French geezer on the news won 6,000 euros in a casino, and felt invincible. He gambled on – and lost half a million. He is suing the casino 'for not stopping me gambling'. True story. He saw himself as Lucky Luke, when he was Dudley Duckegg. Pretending. We all do it.

And take the Dutch. Holland is ram-jam packed with soulful eco-friendlies. Didn't they turn out Vincent van Gogh *et al*? News item: a hundred Dutch enthusiasts laid out 23,000 dominoes, to claim some record for making a bonny falling pattern before cameras. Planning took a month. A sparrow flew by and collapsed the pattern. *They shot the sparrow.* See? Compassion is good for reputations – until it's inconvenient, then vengeance rules.

A bill poster was busy pasting up a notice: *ONE NIGHT ONLY!!! OUR VERY OWN WORLD CHAMPION SEX POLE DANCER!!!* The venue was a famed tavern between the Tower and North Pier.

Crossing over, I asked the bloke, 'Who is she?'

His eyes glazed. 'Miss Erosa Sexotica? Only the best sex-dancer bird ever.'

'I think I'll go.'

'You've had it, wack.' He resumed his brush-and-paste work. 'Sold out in ten minutes. There's ticket scalpers about, already charge ten times the face value. Watch out for forgeries.'

'For a pole dancer?' I made sure of our wavelength.

'You've never seen her,' he said. 'I have. Shift your feet.'

My feet shifted, I found the New President had booked me in. The manager reverently passed me an envelope. Inside was a ticket for the Miss Erosa Sexotica, World Champion Sex Pole Dancer. Unbelievably, the ticket was embossed in genuine gold leaf. I thought, God Almighty, the ticket alone was worth it. I went and bought some new clothes, hang the expense. But, I thought uneasily, who exactly was paying? Debts give me hell. What if the benefactor turned out to be Mortimer himself? I assumed it would be those Faces. Any one of their precious gemstones could buy Blackpool.

Up in my room I slept a while, unfortunately dreaming of a group of pale faces floating in a deep pool where slowly they were dragged down... I woke drenched in sweat. Not fear, just knowing that if anything happened to Mortimer I would kill the perps and giggle while they drowned. And after what they did to Tansy and Old Smethie, even worse. Paltry was a traitor, but who was I to judge?

At four o'clock, I rose, had a bath, and got more or less togged up for the show. By five I was on the starting line. Then a message slid under my door.

Nobody there when I looked out. The message read:

Dear Lovejoy,

You and I have never actually met. I am the 'murdering swine' – you know, the supposedly missing dead girl from East Anglia? I understand you work for my ex-wife. I appreciate your efforts to locate my whereabouts. Could we meet? I shall try to run into you at tonight's show, when Miss Erosa Sexotica comes out of her enforced retirement.

Yours sincerely,

Ted Moon

It was signed and dated. This was serious evidence. He was a careless murderer to write a confession. Unless…

That 'enforced retirement' troubled me. How could the most worshipped sex performer in the world be forced to retire? Didn't such dancers merely hang up their spangled G-strings and buy a Greek island? And what power was great enough to swing her back into action? I was impressed. Whatever had been set in train by the three murders it must be heap big medicine.

The hotel gave me a proper meal. Once, all grub in Blackpool used to be fish, chips and mushy peas with a

Knickerbocker Glory. It was sophisticated now. Posh grub is something of a minefield. You never quite know what's going on in rare dishes. Still, it made me match-fit. Two hours to go before the show.

It isn't often I tog up like a tuppenny rabbit. I felt dressed to kill – no, I meant dressed to the nines. Sorry, Gran, I mentally apologised, I often make mistakes like that. Maybe.

Though 'maybe' only means 'maybe not'. I think I said that first. I'd check when I got a minute. Maybe the OED still had people who read?

The crowds were denser, dusk intensifying the excitement and hordes streaming past North Pier. Passing trams were packed. Blokes grabbed my arm asking, 'Here, mate. Got a ticket for Erosa?' I lied no. The money they were offering was beyond imagination. I kept up my untruthful refrain along the promenade. Pubs were crammed, spilling out onto the pavements. Progress was impossible so I walked among the traffic, darting out of harm's way of adventurous motors. Worse than a Cup Final. On the way I saw the world's most fantastic thing. I saw a sun-dog.

It stopped me as if I'd hit a wall. A sun-dog is a rare double sun. Seen at sunset, it brings good luck. Out to sea the sun was setting – *except there were three*. Three suns, I mean. In clear weather, you normally get two suns, one real, the other its reflection. This third sun just hangs between the two, same size and brilliance as the others. Supposedly the result of suspended ice crystals, the sun-dog is an extra reflection. Little things cheer you up. A good omen! I'd never seen one before.

The huge building where Miss Erosa Sexotica was to dance was full of excitement, bodies jammed in doorways. The theatre stood behind its tavern, which bragged ten bars. Lights glittered on the façade in that irritating moving fashion. I asked a bunch of blokes where the stage entrance was. They laughed.

'Hoping to see her, wack? They've got it screened off.'

'Any chance of a ticket?' I asked.

They fell about, popping tins of beer and repeating my question like it was the funniest crack in ages. The show must hold, I believed, answers. Any day now Laura's minions might force me into her shotgun marriage, and what then? The Faces-in-the-Pool plot would never be solved. Worse, Tansy's murderers would get away unscathed.

Seeing as I didn't know what Ted Moon looked like, I was on a loser. Hour and a half to go before the eight o'clock start. Hawkers were selling beer and lemonade, making a fortune. I bought a drink for an arm and a leg. A gravelly voice hit me.

'Lovejoy? Get me a swill, son.' Tinker, shabbier than ever, his filth clearing a space as if by magic.

'Tinker? How the hell did you get here?'

'Your Mortimer sent word.' I bought him three tins of ale, paying enough for a UN bribe.

'Who'd you bring?'

Tinker grinned, revealing corrugated brown stubs of teeth in his wrinkled leather face. 'The dancer bird.'

I gaped. 'Erosa?'

Some youths looked their astonishment at Tinker, then guffawed. I drew Tinker away as the crowd surged.

'She wouldn't come till I told her it was you asking.'

My head began splitting. 'Where's Mortimer?'

He slurped, beer trickling down his old greatcoat. 'How the bleeding hell do I know?'

'I'm going in to see her, Tinker.'

'She said to go to the stage door after. I'll just have a pint out here. They've rigged up screens all over Blackpool.'

'Who is she? Does she know us?'

The crowd moved. Tinker was carried off in the mob. I heard him shout a name but wasn't sure. If it was Lydia, I'd give her a damned good hiding and yank her off home.

'She's here!' Blokes shoved round to the side entrance. I knew the performers' entrance from seeing great old stars there – Josef Locke, Arthur Askey, Jimmy James even.

The throng became a mass of charging people, blokes and girls screaming in the pandemonium. Police sirens wailed. All to see a girl wriggle on a pole? They're ten a penny in Soho, cheaper in holiday camps.

A bloke pushed me. He was limping with a crutch. I said sorry.

'It's OK.' He smiled and said, 'Massive crowd, eh? I'd give a fortune to see her just once more.'

'You've seen her, then?'

'Erosa? She turned down a TV contract. Lucky you've got a ticket,' he said. 'Especially not having to buy it.'

'Aye, well.' Hang on, I thought.

He stuck out his hand. 'Ted Moon, murderer. Nice to meet you, Lovejoy.'

'Er.' What now? Here was the killer Laura was hunting so madly, and he simply introduces himself.

'The girl I'm supposed to have slain will join us. I'd forgotten how Blackpool takes a performing genius to its heart.'

The crowd was starting to thin. I looked about. The mob around the stage entrance alone remained, bulbs flashing and people pushing to see.

'Pity about Tansy,' Ted Moon said. I searched his expression for deception. None. 'Broke my heart.'

I needed no lesson on heartbreak. 'How much do you know?'

'Everything, Lovejoy,' he said. Rockets shot up into the night sky, bursting in golden rain as flares descended.

'You'd better tell me.'

'You won't like it, Lovejoy. It's not just that weirdo at the cricket.'

'Tell me who did Tansy first.'

'The people paying Erosa. They're here.'

I swung round and stared at the building in its multicoloured illuminations. 'In there?'

'They paid for it.'

'In there,' I said dully. On me so soon? 'All of them?'

He looked his surprise. 'You really have no idea, have you?'

'Who are they?' I said, my voice thick. 'Names, Ted.'

'The rest are just tiddlers, pilot fish before the Great White Sharks. Me and the girl had to take it on the lam. It's been hard. She kept her business going as a front, with Laura stalking us.'

'Harder for Paltry, old Smethie and Tansy.'

'Rotten cook, Tansy,' he said sadly. 'She loved those deadbeats.'

'They were *her* deadbeats,' I said, anger beginning. 'So they were mine too.'

He held up a placatory hand. 'Lovejoy, I'm on your side.'

'I don't even know if that's true.'

He smiled with kindness. 'If you really are as dim as you seem, you'll be glad to see there's one who stands out.'

A huge limo slowly forced its way in. Out stepped Fionuella. She came across, to whistles from the pavement drinkers.

'Ted, darling. And Lovejoy.'

She shook my hand. Mere acquaintances now? Her eyes warned me to silence. She linked Moon's arm and handed his crutches to the limo driver.

'Shall we go?' Moon moved perfectly naturally.

'Three minders should be enough for us.' She smiled at me. 'I'm the murdered girl, Lovejoy. Will you give my mum a ring?'

'Er, who is your—?' They'd gone.

Humbly I followed, to see Miss Erosa Sexotica.

Chapter Twenty-Eight

bludge (n & v): funding burglary of antiques on commission (trade slang)

Sex is here to stay. And mesmerise, baffle, madden. And drive us to passion, murder, jealousies and despair. Religions say sex is the root of all evils. Others, as old soldiers say, tell the truth.

In that crowded hall, maybe 1,500 people were crammed in a high state of expectation. All were laughing, joking. Refined people – with money to burn, I mean – were on a rimmed balcony. A few daring customers tried to light cigarettes but were quickly blanked by friends with, 'Erosa dun't like smokes, see?' Miss Erosa must be dynamite, to persuade even before she'd begun.

Ba-ba-boom music played, strobes hurting the eyes. Some people were already tanked up and singing. The air was festive, the sort you see in villages where Old English music trills and everybody's at the cider and cake. This was not sedate folklore.

The walls showed giant scenes of copulation. As the images flicked and scrolled, aficionados recognised porno girls and studs, roars greeting the more famous. Not the

natural frolic-on-the-greensward, more reminiscent of
expensive gigs where some rock band – I almost put skiffle
group – played to huge audiences. It worried me, because
they were all thinking: We'd better get the best or else.
Threat was not far away. I hoped to God this Erosa lass
was good or the building would be lucky to survive.

More than that, the great Erosa Sexotica was coming
out of retirement. I was scared. If she failed, there'd be hell
to pay. It would be tough on Mortimer, but I had survival
priorities here, namely me. You've got to be truly naff to
fail in Blackpool. But if this amiable mob once rounded
on you, you were finished. The two artistes I'd seen die
in Blackpool's exalted summer season still try to revive
their careers, but booking agents won't even throw them
a crust. I wanted Erosa Sexotica to do a decent (indecent?
whatever) show.

Familiar faces looked down, four from Donna da
Silfa's group. All were avid. One in particular was glaring.
If Erosa did her stuff, Hugo would eat her raw. It was
that sort of look. I almost shivered. Perhaps this is why
collectors of, wait for it, sexiana (I'm not making the
word up) pay over the top for antiques portraying sex. I
was once asked to paint a sex scene of Joan Crawford with
Marilyn Monroe, who were transitory lovers, cruel gossip
has it, Joan more than Marilyn. A lady offered me a year's
income. I declined because it made me feel uncomfortable.
She said in wonderment, 'But you paint ghosts, Lovejoy,'
and got mad.

On the other hand, I was present when two sexiana
collectors fought over a fake panel listing the mysterious
Latin word *muto*. It was written on ordinary children's

sketching paper, lovely lettering depicting the word in Lucilius, Horace, Martial and other Latin poets. I'd thought what pillocks collectors were, battling for Latin scribbles of words for male genitalia – until the cost soared beyond the price of a new car. Then I marvelled. That the two buyers were women didn't concern me. It was the fortune given for a modern scrawl copied from ancient Pompeii graffiti. Yet I'm the softest touch in East Anglia. I once spent my last groat just to let a caged sparrow go, and went hungry for two days, glad it was at liberty. And you know what? The little bastard flew off without a backward glance. It was overseas. Worst of all, a local geezer told me the vendors caught them again to sell to duckeggs like me.

Two pretty dancers emerged to a roar which quickly turned to groans, as neither was Miss Erosa. Their gyrations got my complete attention. They were only crowd-warmers, fluffers to prepare the crowds for the champ. One was an electric dancer, who shimmied on her silver pole with electric lights all over her body. Neither seemed very good, but of course had beautiful bodies so were great. I'd seen better. I scored these second division.

As the excitement built the erotic scenes behind the dancers continued to flicker. Idly, I began to recognise bits from old cinema releases. I kept a look out for Erosa. Wouldn't have been surprised. Antiques dealers now go mad for erotic art, from pipe-smokers' stubbers to genitalia-shaped spittoons, however badly they're made. Playing cards of Hollywood stars – most often fakes – get snapped up. Every schoolboy owns a set.

My attention wandered back to the performers.

The two pole dancers were ending their routine, the

crowd thumping into action and moshing starting, that great leaping up and down en masse. The mob looked like a tin of maggots. It was mayhem. Two other girls replaced the pole artistes, to slow hand-clapping. The new ones depended on fake copulation involving slithering in cream, but the crowd had seen it all before.

The scenes on the backdrops were the same olds: corny cartoon jokes and dull pseudo-scientific data. So we all learnt, as if we cared, that the most photographed sex-throbette was called Betty (snapped in 55,000 trade exposures), that geneticists claimed red pubic hair would be extinct in fifty years ('Go it, Ginger!' shrieked the film clip), and sperm travels at 0.001 miles per hour.

New black drapes were set up during an interlude. Half a dozen sexthrobs stood posing, muscles and veins bulging, to the boredom of all except a few, with women muscle-husslers showing how they too developed biceps, so there. It was becoming a yawn.

The audience was now catcalling the girls. Nobbins were thrown, bouncers crossing the stage to collect the dosh. (Tip: the bouncers keep the money, even in boxing.) People emerged to clean the stage. The poles vanished into the ceiling. The muscly blokes and birds faded and the stage stilled. Then, strangely, as if by common understanding, the crowd hushed.

Imperceptibly a stirring began, with the same epicentres of riot and the occasional glass thrown needing bouncers to wade in and forcibly remove some foci of discord. On the whole it was fairly genial and the crowd settled down. The show's big moment seemed to be on us. I'd come all this way, yet was no nearer to finding who had killed my friends. I hadn't even a decent clue, except for Gentry's remark about Paltry.

Hang on, I thought, stilling my remaining neurones. Something was starting. People in the crowd were calling friends, swarming back from the bars to keep their places near the stage.

And the music changed. Instead of the thump, thump, thump, a distant fanfare was audible. The music eased, to something subtle, maybe Vivaldi. I tried to distinguish words in the cacophony. Clapping started in a strange rhythm I'd never heard before, out of kilter. People outside began bawling 'Erosa! Erosa!' I looked at nearby faces. I even asked the folk next to me, 'What is it?' The stage darkened, cones of multicoloured lights swirling around one pole as it slowly descended. A deafening fanfare blared – Copeland's 'Fanfare for the Common Man'. Women looked in a world of their own, blokes refusing offered drinks from pals.

Everyone's eyes were fixed on the stage. The pole settled, everybody eyeing it as if it were the Grail. Faces had become mesmeric pale patches lit by the strafing illumination in the eerie lighting. I heard a woman whisper, 'It's the same pole from Germany, when she won the...' And the news spread, 'She insists on the same...' God Almighty, a frigging *pole*?

The place descended into gloom. I'd only once felt something similar, at a witches' thing in East Anglia, but I'd never seen a crowd switch off like this, as if we were connected. I glanced up and saw Hugo Hahn gaping down, mouth open, white knuckles on the rail. He was transfixed.

No sign of Ted Moon or Fionuella. Had he met me to make sure I came? My one consolation was I could easily escape if this Erosa lass disappointed.

Smoke drifted from the wings, clouds forming a grey layer. A man stepped into a cone of purple light. He was dressed as Dracula, long cape and dark sideburns, fangs and a widow's peak. He intoned, 'Ladies and gentlemen. For one night only, the immortal, the supreme world champion pole dancer, the greatest... Miss Erosa Sexotica!'

He vanished in a puff of smoke. I stared. How do they *do* that? Unbelievable. Oddest thing, there was no applause, just total silence. Black-garbed figures lined the space and their arms started moving in rhythm like cilia you see in the sea. For one irreverent moment I wondered at the sheer cost of the production. The audience seemed numb. I realised I couldn't remember how long it was since the announcement. Two minutes maybe? Five? I didn't care.

The forty or so dancers stirred mist up from the vapour sea. Really quite beautiful. Then the whole crowd gave a groan. I looked around in astonishment, feeling uneasy, intruding in something I'd no right to. To regain control, I tried making myself think of daft events. A master forger was gaoled because he spelt Scotland with a 'k', Skotland. Blackpool exports Blackpool air in bottles. Scientists realised Planet Earth was slowing down, so they invented Leap Seconds. The World Walking-The-Plank Championship takes place in Kent. Keeping control got harder. The World Worm-charming Championship is in Cheshire...

A girl's vague form became visible above the dancers.

Merely an image projected on some screen?

The crowd was transfixed. Her features gradually took on solidity. Nothing alluring, but definitely a girl, the eyes luminous. Angrily, I told myself it was only a faded photo on a black rag, for God's sake, so why were we all behaving as if it was a vision? Then I thought, Don't I recognise those eyes? My treacherous mind gave in when somebody called, 'There!' and others joined in, 'She's there!' and the pointing became a riot, the noise a crescendo. Stupidly I asked somebody, 'What?' but nobody answered.

She came so slowly she could have been a patch of shadow, moving with a sinuous motion down to the stage ocean.

And the applause began, and a mad baying mixed with a curious wailing. It was as Bedlam must have sounded in ancient days. A woman near me was weeping. I thought, This is lunacy, yet got caught up watching that dark figure slowly slither inchwise with a grace that became hypnotic, a reasonable exchange for free will. I went along, like OK, it's a bargain.

The figure dipped herself into the opacity of the mist, withdrew then stirred the fog with a movement that would have raised the dead with its suggestion of the erotic. I heard people actually sigh. I was captured by Erosa.

Even now I can't imagine how she did it, with a few slight movements evoking a bealing roar. I found myself saying the silly name in time, 'Erosa! Erosa!' like a fool. I swear I almost heard her splash into the sea, even though it was only vapour from a bottle in the wings of a tatty stage. Her hands made slow swimming movements, imperceptibly bringing her to the surface of the undulating sea. *She almost turned into a bird.* What the hell am I seeing here? I tried to think, wondering if I'd been slipped a Mickey Finn. A tart in a cape waggles a bit, and I actually *see* her transform into a flying creature trying to fly out of a deep tide?

What the fuck was going on? My mind tried not to see an egret struggling in a restless sea, but pity took hold. I've always been a pillock, so I should have just let the poor thing get on with it. A bird is only a bird, right? I heard myself groaning with the rest then cheering as it rose into the air above the waves. I can see her now, becoming that soaring bird, and the crowd going mad with relief as she flew up.

Daniella was light years in the past now, she had become sublime in a way I'd never seen. It was impossible not to surrender. I'm ashamed to say we all became obscene and piteous, the lot of us. Sometimes her movements were so minimal she almost seemed in tableau, but that's only saying the opposite. The lovely creature became sacramental. One part of my consciousness remembered I was merely one of a crowd mesmerised by a simple dancer. Putting it in words sounds daft now. There, though, it was magic, transcendental alchemy practised by the witchcraft of a woman who understood what is divine. Daniella became transfigured.

I was soaked in sweat as she finally rose from her orgasm and her winged form was freed from the degradation. I felt I had seen martyrdom. She was the most magic person I'd ever seen.

As the music quietened and the fog sea enveloped her, the weeping began. I'm not ashamed to say I choked a bit. The lovely bird sank into the rising tide. We saw she was going to die. People actually called, 'Oh, no,' as the goddess clung to her silver pillar. No good. Exhausted, she looked back at us, but her strength had gone.

We fell silent as the bird died and the engulfing ocean took her in. She was gone. The silence seemed leaden. Words seem stupid, but everybody who was there wouldn't think so. In her dance, Daniella had become the goddess every man longs for. Whatever the cost, those moments of dance were cheap at the price.

The sea fog slowly dispersed, the place quiet as stone. When the lights gradually came back on to show the stage in full, she had evaporated with the mist. The stage was bare. People actually stood on tiptoe to look. The glittering silver pole slowly ascended to the dark tabs above. In total silence we turned away. Throats were cleared, people somnolent and almost creeping from the auditorium as if leaving a sickroom.

Christ, I thought, seeing the clock in astonishment, nearly two hours? Couldn't be. Surely it had lasted no more than ten minutes, fifteen at the outside? A faint music began as we left, some pavane. I glanced at the balcony, but the Faces had gone. I neither knew nor cared where to. I had seen her, and now wanted to find her and ask what she knew.

Maybe I already knew deep down. She was the one excuse that would draw them all here. If she could provide even one answer, as Mortimer had implied, maybe there *was* some kind of salvation. Daniella seemed good at salvation.

Chapter Twenty-Nine

card(er): record thefts/sales of antiques

The crowds drifted along the pavement. The women left blotting eyes and fumbling for mirrors, the blokes quietly heading for bars along the promenade. The lot of us seemed still to be dreaming.

OK, I thought. I'd obeyed everybody. I'd gone to Sunderland – all those cars. Lincoln – all those flowers. I'd visited old Smethie, and helped Death's rich harvest. I'd watched the World Suprema Sex Dancer. Was I any nearer? The only thing I'd learnt after getting three friends murdered was that I was due at Somnell House.

Reassembling my splintered mind, I stood by the stage door. No Mortimer, no Daniella. The muted press hung about. I couldn't understand the difference between Daniella and the lustrous dancer who conveyed such sexual passion. Every women has her own beauty, sure. Young or old, loveliness is there.

Yet I'd only seen Daniella as genuinely off-her-trolley. Hell, I couldn't even remember what daftness she was hooked on – recovering Isaac Newton's thoughts from space, was it, or Molly Malone's Dublin cockles? Beyond sense, anyway. She always sat facing the corner among Tansy's colony of crazies in Mehala Bay. How on earth could I be expected to know? I felt done out of my pie and my pudding, as we said when I was little. I might have been in ecstasy for months.

Imagine having Miss Erosa waiting in my cottage ready for… I moaned. Nobody nearby even looked. We were all thinking the same.

Mortimer seemed to have vanished, like Fionuella and Ted Moon, Laura's oppo, Ellen, Donna da Silfa. Seeing the sun-dog hadn't changed my luck. No contacts of any kind. Without Mortimer, I was like an army without its scout.

Over the next two hours the crowd dispersed. I asked at the stage door, 'Any chance of seeing Miss Erosa?' A bloke said sadly, 'She vanishes once a show is over.'

He and his mates eventually loped off to the famous Captain's Cabin, its crowds spilling out onto the pavement. I crossed to a phone box and tried Lydia's home number. Her mother Mavis – she hates me because we once made smiles – answered. I pretended to be somebody else but she snapped, 'It's you, Lovejoy. Stay away from Lydia and from me.' That's the thanks you get. It was unfair. I tried others, but Lydia and Tinker were nowhere.

In the bright lights of the famous Illuminations, a smartly dressed woman stepped into a car. Was it that pleasant woman Joanna? I knew all roads led to Rome, but Blackpool?

Somebody tapped on the booth. I kept ringing dealers. The tapping continued. A woman was outside in the mottled darkness, evidently too impatient to cross the blinking road to a hotel phone. Eventually I opened the door and said, 'Missus, this is a matter of life—'

Breathlessly, she eeled in and pulled the door to. The place filled with perfume. She wore a voluminous tent.

'Daniella?' asked Hawkeyes of the West.

'It's Mortimer, Lovejoy,' she breathed. 'They've got him.'

As my remaining dendrites synapsed, I said in the light of a passing tram, 'Is that really you?'

'You sent word, Lovejoy. Are you ashamed of me?'

I decided to leave the shame bit. 'Me? Send word?'

'My sister, Etholle.' She was so close I could have... I looked into those eyes, never wanting to look away again. 'You begged me to come.'

Passing blokes saw us in the phone booth and cheered as they saw Daniella fumble for a message.

'I saw your performance, love.' I got out.

'I saw you when I was robing up.'

She wore her drab marquee and a hood. 'What was that about Mortimer?' I didn't want an answer.

'They've got him, Lovejoy. They told me.' She lowered her eyes.

'Who?'

'Mrs da Silfa's people. They have him trapped at Somnell House. They said be there tomorrow.'

'How did they catch him?'

'He's so trusting, such a beautiful nature, Lovejoy.' Her lovely eyes filled. 'It's amazing that he's your son, you being so... His mother must have been an absolute saint, when you are...'

A tatty shiftless prat? It's always me bad, and everybody else St Alban.

'What can we do? They'll be trailing me.'

'They know you'll try to rescue Mortimer.' She gazed at me with adoration. I wished the frigging trams would stop clanging past with their lights showing me her lovely features. I was in enough trouble. 'You'll dare any wicked dangers to rescue him from their evil clutches.'

'Hang on a sec.'

This sounded like a Victorian melodrama, the way she was going on. There was too much risking of Lovejoy in her scenario. I felt safe in the phone booth, with nobody quite knowing who I was. I could go south, and let everybody get on with it. OK, there was this father-son stuff, but hang on. If I stormed Castle Perilous, who would be in the firing line? Me, that's who.

Who wants risks? I had no SAS to charge into Somnell House and confront its armed Faces. What chance would I have? They had guns. This called for heroes, not Lovejoy.

Feebly, I said, 'How about the police, love?'

'Out of the question, Lovejoy. They have diplomatic status.'

'And I'm a convicted felon.'

'Don't take on, darling. Please. You will brave the jaws of danger, Lovejoy. You are, after all, their only divvy.'

Darling now? 'True.' I swallowed. It was so hot, Daniella so close and me trying to concentrate. 'It's just that…' I strove for excuses. 'I can't risk you, darling.'

'Me, Lovejoy? You're thinking of me?'

I went for it. 'I must protect you, Daniella.'

She really wept then, her lovely huge eyes streaming with tears. I could have eaten her.

'You're so sweet, when you could simply walk away.

What a beautiful soul you possess, darling. No.'

'No what?' I wondered if I'd painted myself into a corner.

'I am your secret weapon, darling.'

'Weapon?' Only moments before this creature lifted the world to paradise. She was no weapon.

'Yes, darling.' She smiled through her tears. 'Just think. What does subterfuge need?'

'Money? Guns? Police?' I still hoped I'd be left out of it.

'No, darling. It needs bait.'

Like in fishing? You set traps with bait. I've seen poachers at it on the Stour in Suffolk, using snares to strangle creatures in the owl hours. I gulped.

'Bait? You're the bait?'

'Yes, darling. I'm your Trojan Horse. The earlier we start, the better, don't you think?'

We left the phone box and caught the tram along the seafront to the hotel. She lowered her lovely face into her hood, anonymous again. I sat beside her, my spirits sinking. Daniella was determined to make me a hero. I'd never been one before. Coward always, hero never. Still, I might go missing before the action began. I'm good at never being where I'm needed. My three murdered friends already knew that.

Chapter Thirty

swindlers: 'Those who trade in art' (Picasso)

We alighted. I was scared and hung back.

'You'd better go in first, love.'

'Why, Lovejoy?'

Several blokes gave her a double glance, as if wondering why a bird with such a beautiful face wore such frumpish garb. She swiftly donned horn-rimmed spectacles.

'You'll be safer, Daniella,' I lied, man of steel. 'Suss it out, see if there's anybody we know.' I almost said in case killers lurked in the foyer so I could scarper. 'Some of them followed us.' I went all Sir Galahad. 'I'll make sure they don't come after you. Give me a shout if it's all clear.'

'You're so sweet, Lovejoy.'

All misty at my gallantry, she hurried in. I really wish all women were as trusting. How on earth had I missed her first time round? Nervously, I peered inside to see if Donna's madmen or Gentry's killer pals were around. Daniella emerged and beckoned. I did a Dick Tracy skulk, and stepped boldly in.

'They cleared off,' I reported, steely of eye.

'Thank you, darling.' She hugged my arm. 'My protector.'

On the third floor, I sent Daniella in first, in case marauders were snarling behind the door. Smiling, I locked the door after us. They'd either not known the address of this hotel, or were expecting me to dash off to this Somnell House place where they'd taken Mortimer. I felt brilliant, now with Daniella all to myself. Heaven beckoned, its pearly gates opening…

'Sodding hell, Lovjeoy,' a voice growled. 'I'm farting missel' inside out here.'

From the bathroom? The door was ajar, the light already on.

'Tinker?' Who else but the Beau Brummel of elegance, my grotty barker. 'What are you doing here?'

'Trying to find you.' Rural noises sounded. 'I ate some crud from them whelk stalls. I'm suffering here, son. That gabby bitch who drives the tart you're going to wed sent me here.'

Daniella was already stricken. Now she looked on the point of flight. I made placatory gestures.

'It's all right, love,' I told her. 'Tinker's strange.'

'Are you sure?' she said timidly. 'He sounds ill.'

'Lovejoy? You fetched a bird back?' More noises from inside. I wished he'd closed the bathroom door. 'I shoulda known you'd bring in a bint for a shag. I'll get out of your road in a minute.'

'Shouldn't we help the poor old gentleman, Lovejoy?'

Help him? I could have crucified the old git. 'Give him time.'

'You are so thoughtful, darling.'

We sat on the couch, she compassionate, me burning with rage.

My romance, the me-and-Daniella-against-adversity

togetherness, could have made us lovers in a rush of passion. It was now gone, thanks to Tinker's intestinal travails. From being desperate for any ally, now I could have throttled the boozy old soak. He'd ruined my tryst with the most glorious creature on earth.

Tinker emerged after more groans and flushing waters. So ends romance.

Opening a beer from the minibar, he gravelled out, 'That Daniella? Wotcher, luv. Lovejoy, you lucky bastard. Blokes'd give every frigging groat to have her on her back.' He flopped into an armchair and belched on the first gulp. 'Dunno how you pull them, son. Beg pardon, miss. That motorway grub did for me. Gawd Almighty, I'm reamed.'

'Driver, Tinker?'

He leant over as if imparting the strictest confidence. 'That bint with the lawyer. Doesn't look like she'd give Prince Charming a fuck.'

'Ellen? Drives for Mrs Laura Moon?'

He emitted a belch, three notes, each at a different pitch. 'She's up to somethink.'

'Very perceptive, Tinker. Tell me more.'

'Mortimer sent her. Said two o'clock.'

Mortimer was everywhere yet nowhere. Tinker hauled himself up and ambled to the bar, unscrewed a small whisky bottle with one hand. I stared, never having seen that trick. He slumped on the carpet, his shoes gaping their holes.

'Mortimer sent Ellen Jaynor?' I mulled this over. From his dungeon? 'To do what?'

'Come for you.' Tinker gave a suggestive wink, his idea of subtlety. 'If you and Daniella want a shag, take no notice of me.'

'Why exactly, Tinker?' I saw his expression change to one of amazement and quickly explained, 'Ellen, I mean.'

'She gave me this.' Tinker found a scrap of paper.

'Shall I read it, darling?'

Surprisingly, Daniella needed to find spectacles to read, '*Dear Lovejoy, I fear matters have taken a disagreeable turn. Fatalities were never envisaged. I trust you, and your assistant. I shall find you. Yours, Ellen.*'

You can't help watching a lovely woman. Daniella put her glasses away. I noticed the curls of her hair round her face, the tilt of her head.

'How come Ellen knew Mortimer?'

'Dunno, son.'

Abruptly he keeled over on the carpet, snoring like a train.

'Should we make him more comfortable, Lovejoy?'

'I'll do it.' I got him some cushions and a drape thing. I was famished. The hotel had a restaurant. 'Look, love. We should we get some grub before Ellen shows.'

'You're so good, Lovejoy,' Daniella breathed. 'Tormented by anguish over your kidnapped son, yet you look after this poor old man.'

'Oh, well.' I almost said shucks, but it's only for Yanks.

She came close. 'Lovejoy? Would you think it truly terrible were we to rest now? We could dine later.'

'Er, all right.'

'Honestly?' She searched my eyes. 'It's not too self-indulgent?'

'No, love,' I said firmly, thinking, Dear God don't let doubts intrude now. 'We have a long night ahead.'

'Thank you. You're so sweet, Lovejoy.'

'That's all right, Daniella.' I followed her into the bedroom and gently closed the door. 'We must be sure not to waken Tinker.'

'Lovejoy, you are so right.'

We were the last in the restaurant. True to her usual practice, Daniella seated herself facing the corner. I understood her shyness now. The world's most gorgeous anything must bring tribulations.

I couldn't help staring. Her compliance was a revelation. A man never knows a woman before, during, or even afterwards. He just has to trail along hoping to find some clue, like what she got from loving. To me, reassembling the world after having been with Daniella was beyond understanding.

A lady seated herself next to me. Daniella gave a Gainsborough Lady inclination of her lovely head and glanced at me in inquiry.

'How do, missus. Daniella, may I present Ellen? Ellen, Daniella.'

'How do you do?' Daniella said. 'I'm relieved to find another lady supporting Lovejoy's cause.'

'I shall drive you, Lovejoy.'

'You'll come with us?'

Ellen nodded, her gaze touching the wall clock. We ordered our grub. Daniella, true to womankind, had very little, though Ellen dined pretty well without wine. I finished everything they left. If you're off to storm a remote fortress, you may miss your next meal.

'Look,' I said when we were ready to go. 'I've not much gelt left.'

Ellen's eyebrows went??? I glanced at Daniella.

'Sorry, Ellen, but I've lost track. Ted Moon and his girlfriend found me, but they got away.' I went red, forgetting which lie I'd already told and to whom. 'I haven't reported to Laura. Where is she?'

'Who knows, Lovejoy?'

Fine by me. One fewer killer was a plus. I explained that Daniella was coming along to help, and about Mortimer's abduction. Ellen's expression showed more doubt.

'It's true. Mortimer is in trouble. I'd want more of us, but this is all of us. They want Daniella.'

'And you, Lovejoy.'

'That's it. Me for the antiques, and Daniella because she is, er, special.'

The waiter had sent grub up to Tinker, who was snoring again when we arrived. Fifteen minutes later we left the hotel in Ellen's giant limousine. A shoddy drunk, an exotic dancer, a mistrustful woman and a scrounger.

My hopes rested entirely on Daniella. If necessary, I could swap her for my survival. If all else failed, I'd depend on flight.

'Are you all right, Lovejoy?' Tenderly, Daniella took my hand as Ellen took us out of town. 'You seem upset, darling.'

'Just proud of doing the right thing.' I filled up at my chivalry, but kept an eye on the route, just in case I needed to make a run for it.

No illusions any more. No trust anywhere. I knew from the affair in Lincoln Cathedral I might never get out of this alive, because who else knew what the Faces were going to do, but me?

Chapter Thirty-One

to fubble: in antiques, to bluff and counter-bluff

Ellen drove steadily. I dozed as the town lights receded. The county was anciently called Christ's Croft, from its peace and harvests. To the south was Windmill Land, where there were spectacular windmills draining the marshes. In my mind it was still a land of dark mills and valleys with tall chimneys and crammed terraced dwellings. No longer.

'Lovejoy is so tired,' Daniella explained in a whisper to my mighty cohort.

'Working hard, miss?' Tinker cackled.

'At planning, Tinker,' Daniella said with indignation.

Ellen's gaze showed in her driving mirror, suspicious cow. I don't quite know what a sardonic glance is, but she was good at it. I slumped on Daniella, as women don't need sleep after making smiles. Ellen suspected me of getting up to no good with Daniella, while Daniella wanted to pretend we hadn't.

'Ellen,' Daniella said after an hour, 'would you pull in here, please?'

We had stopped at a tavern on high moors, presumably

the Pennines. A nosh place gleamed with lights, cars in its forecourt.

'Lovejoy,' Daniella said gently as I came to. 'We must rest here.'

'And have a drink,' Tinker croaked. 'Old soldiers have bad throats.'

'Tinker,' Daniella scolded. 'You consumed eight bottles. Count them aloud and *then* try to tell us…' etc, etc.

We entered the hostelry. Entertainment was going on, with music thumping and customers shrieking. Daniella hung back, Ellen with her. I was pleased, an older woman minding the timid younger one. We *were* a team.

Daniella gave Tinker money while we found a table in the foyer. I listened to the stupidity in the entertainment room. One-arm bandits rimmed the walls. You can always tell the addicts, fixed on the spinning numbers. One in fifty players gets hooked, willing to rob and kill for their daftness. Leonardo da Vinci said, 'Nature takes revenge on those who want to perform miracles…and forces them to live in poverty.' Trouble is, every gambler is Darnborough, the 'man who broke the bank at Monte Carlo' of the song. (The bank couldn't afford to pay him, to the yippees of gamblers everywhere.)

Ellen and Daniella exchanged glances. Starving, I tackled my pasties but couldn't help wondering about their eyebrow play. Eventually Daniella went to the loo, closely followed by our driver. I asked Tinker if he thought Ellen could be trusted.

'Her? As a die, son.' He spat into an empty glass. I edged away. Tinker eats, as Bilko – the American character played by Bill Silvers – used to say of rural manners, without a net. 'Somnell House is not far now, across the moss. Picture on the wall, see it?'

Carrying my pasty – you can't be too careful – I went to the old sepia engraving hanging by the bar. A manor house on a rising moor. A 'moss' is a local way of saying morass, a quagmire. It looks like ordinary grass, but walk on it and whole acres undulate like a waterbed. Every year ramblers are found trapped or even drowned. The iron gateway looked straight from an old Hammer Horror black-and-whiter. Well chosen, Donna. Hard place to storm.

'That place still here, mate?' I asked the bartender.

'Oh, aye. A few miles. Foreign folk have it now.'

I nodded ta and rejoined Tinker as the women returned. He was chatting with another old soldier, swapping merry tales of massacres and vying for the worst wounds.

From the riotous party came familiar music. At first I thought it was chance, then coincidence, and finally knew it was the enemy. I nudged Tinker.

'Is that singing who I think it is, Tinker?'

He looked his disgust. 'Aye, frigging poofter. Should be "Any Old Iron", him.' The old music hall ditty is a joke song, all Cockney rhyming slang – iron *hoof* for poof, *green* tie for quean (sic) and so on.

'Sandy?' I asked in disbelief. 'So far from East Anglia?'

Tinker looked his surprise. 'Aye, son. He's on our side, right?'

'Er, right,' I said weakly. 'We should be going.'

Drifting over, I looked in. The riot was in full swing. Sandy was on a stage doing his usual 'Give Me Some Men' song, mincing across the stage wearing a Guards' scarlet jacket, thigh boots and very little else. Women were screaming and laughing, Mel sulking and everybody egging Sandy. He loved it, pouting and trying not to fall over his silver spurs.

'Tinker, outside in ten minutes, OK?' I intended to slip off before Sandy and Mel realised we'd arrived. Sandy was as secret as the weather. And wasn't he one of the Faces' backers?

In the car waiting for Daniella, Tinker stowed his bottles and said, 'What do we do when we get there, Lovejoy?'

'Somnell House? Daniella will tell us.'

'Your tart?' He seemed surprised. I felt a faint frisson of alarm. I'd assumed Daniella was going to lead.

'She's gone to bring Sandy and Mel.'

'Why didn't you tell me?'

'Christ's sake, Lovejoy, she's only a bint, right?'

Ellen joined us and shook her head when I asked after Daniella.

'Oh, Christ,' Tinker groaned. 'It's them bleedin' poofters.'

The passenger door was flung open.

'Lovejoy! You bluebeard!' Sandy was there in his ridiculous garb. 'You can't leave me, with this absolutely *obese* harlot.'

His massive motor was nearby, shimmering to the strains of 'Yeomen of the Guard'. Mel was at the wheel, Daniella in a rear seat.

'She can come with us.'

'The bitch absolutely *refuses*. Mel is in a *searing* temper.'

I got fed up. 'Mel always is, Sandy. Bring her. She knows what we've to do.' Fingers crossed, I thought. With

Daniella along I'd stand some chance.

Tinker slammed the door. 'Sod off, you great jessie.'

'My *poor* car won't *reach* Somnell House labouring under her *lard*, Lovejoy.'

This, of the world champion sex bombette? Daniella was not lard. 'Let's go, Ellen.'

She drove us out without a glance, leaving them to it, Sandy shrieking abuse. It's all put on.

'Bleeding ginger.' Rhyme, ginger beer.

Oddly, I caught Ellen smiling a faint smile. When I looked closely her face was set in its usual marble. I must have misunderstood.

The black night sky showed a pale crack over the high moors. An omen? Into battle with too many hangers-on, though. I decided to scarper as soon as I'd sprung Mortimer. Alone, escape is easy. It's friends that slow you down.

Chapter Thirty-Two

whiffler: auctioneer's labourer

There was something wrong. It scared me. Sometimes, when everything seemed fine, a gremlin in the mind whispers life is off kilter. I glanced at Ellen's features in the gloaming. She was the source of my vibes.

We drove along a wagon road. I always dread huge transporters coming the other way. She was a better driver than I'd ever be. Her wedding finger showed a paler band of a gold ring's presence.

Over pitch black moorland we drove, stones scuffy under the wheels. Tinker's discarded bottles clanked on the car floor. Ellen, though. They say, don't they, we've all met in some previous existence and here we are again. Like, a lady falls for Handsome Jack at a party, when really they were lovers in ancient Rome. I don't believe it. Reincarnation is phoney. People who claim to have experienced it were always Cleopatra or Sir Walter Raleigh, never humble Jane, the starving slave, or poor Simple Simon, press-ganged to die at fourteen in an unknown battle. See? We only make up glamorous bits. Still, I may have met her years ago, and who remembers?

Her smile got me worried, though. *I'd seen it before.*

Glancing back, I saw Sandy's glitzy car following us across the moor. Ellen was taking her time. Occasionally, in that floating sea of darkness, I glimpsed the glowing lights of Somnell House through the trees.

All the lights suddenly dowsed. I exclaimed in surprise. Ellen tut-tutted, mildly annoyed. I looked through the rear window. Sandy's garish motor had vanished, its music silenced. I told Ellen. She nodded.

We came up to a hugely ornate gate. I said, 'Stop here, love. I'll sneak over the wall…'

She kept going and the gate swung open. I yelped, 'They'll see us.' Her tranquil smile was full of certainty.

A stone plaque on the gate read *Somnell House*. A man was in the shadows. Others stood along the drive leading to the balustrade's discreet lighting, old oil lamps glowing on the façade. It might have looked charming. More flunkeys were there, servants in Victorian dress wearing trailing lace tails to their caps. The men were done out in satin breeches with frock coats. A stage set from some feeble period drama? Some catering firms do sham historical pageants, where tourists dine as in Tudor courts. Like this?

No secrecy at Somnell House. The plan must have changed, but from what to what I didn't know. My one bright hope was all these witnesses.

I swallowed, and actually said, 'This isn't as secret as I thought, Ellen.'

She drew up before the imposing front steps.

'I mean,' I said, worried now, 'Daniella told me we'd be storming the place.' I sounded pathetic, my relief so transparent. I saw her expression of contempt. It's all very well for women. They don't do the scrapping. Shouting, sure, I thought indignantly, they're all terrif at that. As far as I was concerned, this film set convinced me I'd swapped an arena for a gavotte. No fighting. A good deal. 'I imagined all sorts,' I told her with a nervous laugh.

We got out. Tinker snored as if it was his job.

'Leave him,' I said. 'He'll come round in an hour.'

A flunkey ushered me up the steps. Doors opened and I passed through into a bright porch. Chandeliers with lustrous drops, ladies in evening dress gliding about. A great double staircase swept upwards, elegant portraits on the rising walls. Gentlemen in Victorian attire strolled about. A special evening. I scented grub, so a serious repast was due. My belly rumbled, as ever when I'd not eaten for days. Then the vibrations hit me.

They came from every point of the compass, ahead, above, each side. I almost fell. I actually stumbled and almost retched. My vision swam and I felt sick. I'd never been so struck. Superb antiques did it, sure, but the massive mansion must have been crammed. I froze. Donna da Silfa swept forward.

'Lovejoy, darling!' I fumbled for her hand. She directed my clammy palm. Even that tingled from her antique Berlin lace gloves, rare Opus Anglicanum lace, a split stitch tethering each thread where turns made it impossible to hold otherwise.

Reeling, I clung to her for stability. Her dress was a Marie Antoinette – I recognised it from having seen a show – long bodice, low neck, tight sleeves with prominent ruffles, and a hooped skirt with smaller ruffles, all in a ferocious red. Her hair carried two tremblant aigrettes – meaning waggly jewellery on sprung metal so they quivered. An aigrette is a beautiful feminine trick, because, however slight a lady's gestures, gems in her coiffure draw every admiring eye. Rare rubies, of course, though I felt the enormous padparadscha was a bit over the top. Genuine, though, their diagnostic red, yellow, pink showing they were maybe from Sri Lanka during the Raj.

'On time!'

'Er, ta, Donna.' I said it without a stammer.

'You know Hugo Hahn.'

'Aye. Wotcher,' I said. He shook my hand like wringing wet socks. My knuckles cracked. I thought, He owns the greatest fortune in antiques, yet he's so juvenile he crushes some scruff's hand? Until then I'd assumed I'd be the only duckegg there.

So he and Donna were lovers? You can always tell.

'Ready are you?' he said in that twangy accent. 'I'll be with you,' he said in a threatening manner, 'all the way.'

'Keep your hair on.'

'Now, darling,' Donna gushed. A woman approached. I noticed the original Early Georgian green velvet dress was trimmed with genuine none-so-pretties – correct term – those fancy decorative tapes used in the American Colonies (sorry, but they really were colonies back then). She wore a small Confederate flag on her right shoulder. 'You're absolutely sure, Lovejoy?'

''Course.' Antiques was why I was brought here, of course.

'This is Saffron. She will be with you every step of the way.'

'How day do, Mistah Lovejoy?'

'Very well, ta, miss.'

'No misunderstanding, Lovejoy?' Donna cut in. Guests closed round, smiling. My unease returned.

'No.' For one instant I was tempted to ask if I could see Mortimer, then I realised I'd been had. Ellen had conned me. Mortimer couldn't be here. I was simply here as a divvy, working for enclaves of Europeans and Causacians left stranded by history. Simple.

'And you know exactly why you're here?'

'Certainly.'

For just one fleeting moment I thought I glimpsed disappointment in Donna da Silfa's eyes. Mirage, trick of the light. She smiled at Saffron.

Had she sighed? 'Send for the attendants, Saffron.'

'Yes, Miz da Silfa.'

The girl glided off. Donna eyed me. 'You don't want to change first?'

'No, I'm happy like this.' I thought I'd better explain I hadn't brought my antiques detection pack. Though I rarely use its ten little implements now. I only keep it for old time's sake. Too elementary for my giant brain, you see.

'He's insane,' Hahn said.

If he'd been small and old I'd have clouted him. I determined to do my divvying and be off, as Mortimer was out of it. I'd strike over the moors to that inn, then home to East Anglia. Tinker would have to take his chances.

We all moved towards the interior doors. I heard the strains of an orchestra. I didn't like the way the other guests clustered round me. I could hardly take a step without somebody's satin slipper under my foot.

'Ready?' Donna called.

Smiling indulgently, I was like, why all this ceremony? It wasn't knighthood time at the Palace. The two massive carved leaves of the oaken door swung open.

The ballroom was done out as if for... Dear God. I would have legged it but for the crowd. All were attired in antique costume. I'd hated their smiles. Now I truly could have massacred the lot.

The sickening, tasteless decoration outdid the most junky load of tat I'd ever seen. Every uselessly wrong TV *Antiques Roadshow* was on display. Somebody must have thrown this Ye Olde Tyme theme together for a wedding...

Wedding, meaning a union of two? I broke into a sweat. A hundred guests, in every real or imagined garb quivered in their glitz. They started to clap. Some were already sozzled and one started to sing 'Happy Birthday', laughing. Complexions varied from mahogany to white. And all was sheer affluence. Among the tatty décor, a score of masterpieces hung on the far wall. I was startled by Monet's 1908 Venice painting, *Rio della Salute*. I'd thought I was the only forger who'd faked that 'whereabouts unknown' Impressionist – except this was no fake. It hung between a Turner Yorkshire watercolour and a De Wint.

A hand pulled me forward. A long red carpet led to a...a *priest*? Flowers, with Laura there looking radiant in a wedding dress. I thought, Who on earth...? Then the true horror struck. To get wed. I couldn't even remember when I'd got married, though I remembered when my wife eloped with some South African, bless him. I tried to halt, but Mel – it *was* Mel – dragged me forward. My ghastly rictus began. I even tried to bow to the grinning faces all about, until I caught myself.

Mad thoughts tumbled through my mind. Was I still divorced? Or was divorce like a library ticket that expires after two years? Could I faint? I could pretend my malaria was back.

And among the press of guests I saw Mortimer. He inclined his head towards the priest, at an altar. I filled with rage at his frigging stupid cool smile, like, aren't we all having a great time as Dimwit Lovejoy is made a fool of as usual. Cold as ice, I thought, All right, lad, from hereon you're on your own in life. Lovejoy disowns you, you little bastard.

And Camille, Fiffo's wife-as-was, straight from her dodgy Brum. My brain asked, What the hell? And gave up.

Iron hands gripped me. I must have made a movement to scarper. I told myself, so be it. Everyone had lost any allegiance I ever had towards the frigging world. Devil take the hindmost, and the hindmost won't be me.

The priest was in full fig and everybody about me in gorgeous apparel. Even Mortimer, the slimy toad, was dressed in foppery, as was the corrupt killer Gentry with his sidekick murderer. And Sandy, for God's sake, beside Laura. He's come as Little Bo Peep, with more frills than the parson preached about. He had invented his own stupid dress, even to the high heels with LEDs, light-emitting diodes, shining through mad silks. I thought, This isn't happening.

Laura met me as I was shoved to the altar. For all

my hatred, she looked gorgeous in a plain silk dress of pastel blue with ancient lace. Only the ring finger was prominently undressed.

'Darling!' she whispered. I had suffered from being 'darling'. She bussed me. Sandy burst into tears, wailing for us to wait, wait, while he did his cosmetics.

I wanted the floor to open. I looked at the priest in hopes he'd see my anguish and call the police, SAS, anybody.

All right, I was contracted to do this, though I'd forgotten the bad bits until now. These people had done for old Smethie, Paltry, and my friend Tansy. OK, the agreement with Laura might be legally binding. But surely the deaths, and my robbery at Eastwold, made me a felon? Maybe I could have myself certified insane and land up safe in some loony bin. I'd helped some mentals three years before. They could sign a few papers and certify me.

'Don't worry, Lovejoy. It will be all over tomorrow.'

Tomorrow! My spirits lifted. For some reason, this mad woman really did want a phoney wedding, knowing she would instantly dissolve the marriage. She'd promised. I could wed content. I would soon be freed.

Bussing her back, I whispered, 'You sure?'

'Yes, darling.' She smiled with brilliance, as if I'd tenderly asked after last-minute bridal nerves, a gentility I'm not renowned for.

And I saw Mortimer, now very close, giving that look which is a silent roll-in-the-aisles guffaw. The little sod was enjoying this. I swore to strangle the swine.

'My wedding presents, darling,' Laura was saying, 'just for you.'

A line of four peruked footmen slowly paraded by while the parson observed them. I almost collapsed from the slamming of the antiques they carried. For a moment I thought I recognised one of the men, but put it down to dizziness. I'd been making that mistake a lot lately, seeing familiar faces where there were only strangers.

The first bore a Barr, Flight, Barr bough-pot (think a porcelain piece for holding small flowers) with its late Worcester gilded edges – best you'll ever see. Such precise decoration of feathers couldn't be more detailed. I reeled and had to be caught, Mel cursing. The next two footmen carried a Minton vase in Parian ware (my first love) and a wood block for an engraving that looked, from a quick glance, like a Thomas Berwick of maybe 1789. I glanced at Laura, thinking how lovely she had suddenly become, so tender-hearted to give me such treasures. I said a hoarse thanks and her face lit up.

Then the last servant went by, with a blue-green glass flask that had a trailed ornament round the rim. It resembled a second century Roman – except it didn't emit a single vibration. The fake monstrosity was carried past. Anybody can make these, from genuine old glass fragments. The non-divvy is then easily taken in because they give the correct lab results. I shot Laura a cold glance, wondering at the bitch's nerve, tricking her husband-to-be with a useless dud anybody could knock up.

I went right off the evil cow. She kept smiling and the guests burst into applause. I looked directly at Mortimer in a mute plea. He was glancing around the hall. Laura whispered, 'Well done, Lovejoy!' That steady vibrant glow still stifled me. The antiques were everywhere still.

'Dearly beloved,' the padre began, reading from his book, 'we are gathered here in the sight of God to...'

We were married, Laura and I, before a rapturous throng which did not include Tinker, Ellen Jaynor, Fionuella or Ted Moon, or, I noticed sometime during the service, Mortimer, because the rat had now absconded. So much for his abduction in a dungeon.

The mob, however, definitely included Daniella, now on the arm of Hugo Hahn. She gazed up at him throughout. I even noticed Veronica there, blotting away her tears. No sense in life anywhere.

Sandy wept copiously and Mel snuffled a bit, the pillocks. I should have been the one sobbing, though.

Chapter Thirty-Three

lone bone: stealing antiques by charming an owner (trade slang)

Weddings? I hate confetti.

Not because priests keep on about it: 'Confetti makes the churchwardens cross,' like anybody gives a tinker's. Confetti indicates hysteria. The reason is obvious. Confetti disguises the boredom. This wedding was no exception. At first.

A banquet buffet was laid in the dining hall. The top table was reserved for Laura and Donna da Silfa's big six. Plus me. Sandy threw confetti from a maid's gilded basket. Everybody was junketing. Those smiles got to me.

Today's only difference was, this wedding was mine. I'd already given, one marriage being the moral limit per life. And here I was, a digamist, being applauded like I'd won. Sandy was in tears ('So-o-o beautiful') and Mel in a state because he was toastmaster, and everybody smiling like they were enjoying some stupendous joke. The mirth was aimed *at* me. And throngs crammed in. So many, though, and all Laura's pals? She looked over the moon, really desirable, but that's women and weddings. I only wanted news of my impending divorce, please. We noshed, said how the wedding had 'gone off', like some monstrous firework.

After a bit, something else felt wrong. Numbers dwindled. Mortimer, fascist turncoat, had already evaporated, though he always did that. Daniella, too, had done a flit, to Hugo Hahn's clear annoyance. And among the uniformed serfs I'd noticed Leg-Breaker, who'd driven me to the Beeches Hospital. Now he too had gone. Maybe I'd imagined things, the stress of all this happiness.

Another problem. Usually, wedding guests fall on the nosh. This lot merely picked at the grub. I reasoned, feeling more uneasy, that it was due to different cultural backgrounds, different languages – Portuguese, German, and something like Tagalog, French without that Parisian tongue-rolling. Maybe they were moving on somewhere else after? I was spooking myself.

People nibbled their way with indifference, just politeness. Laura was all smarm, trying to put her hand in mine. I smiled back with a cardboard face, feeling held by staples. People nodded in our (I hated that *our*) direction as the speeches were signalled. The gathering quickly moved into clusters, reminding me of overseas boozers where squaddies and matelots used to gather, troopers with their own regiments. These guests all knew their own, though they were in mufti and on the same side.

Hugo Hahn rose to toast the health of everybody present, significantly not the bride and groom. They were horrible words.

'Ladies and gentlemen,' he began. 'Serious celebrations, before the real *toast* of the evening.'

For some reason everybody went into paroxysms of laughter. People fell about, some even shaking hands. I kept smiling. Such merriment.

'We must thank Lovejoy here for coming *hotfoot* to perform his final labours.'

More rolling in the aisles, people clasping hands boxer style.

'You know the drill,' Hahn went on, as Laura squeezed my hand. I turned to look at her, but she shone with what seemed to be pure love and I was moved. Except I'm always taken in. Females know the game because they set up the rules. I don't. Then a thought came. Who were the divorce lawyers? Would they come in soon and say, 'Let's get down to business, sir. Here's your millions. Sign and you'll be rich and single...'

Hahn droned on. For the life of me I couldn't get his witticisms. The guests could. One or two oldies were slipped in there, straight off pub graffiti, like, 'What food puts a woman off sex? *Wedding* cake!' Har-de-har.

'Now the serving staff are gone, I take this *final* chance of addressing us *all* together...' pausing for laughs '...and I thank you all for seeing the bride and groom *off*.'

Nudges and winks everywhere. All I could see was teeth.

'Then Lovejoy will divvy our – your! – antiques brought to Somnell House from our ancient cultures. His divvying guarantees their authenticity. The six of us you elected will supervise. It will be recorded on film for international investors.'

Hahn raised his glass. He drank our health. Laura bussed me to applause.

'Once the divvying is done, we shall celebrate as never before. No longer mere Faces, the "forgotten white tribes" the world pities. The world will be ours!'

The crowd went wild, pressing forward and shaking my hand. It was a riot. I would divvy their antiques, and the antiques world would join the spending frenzy. Yet I couldn't help wondering why I was here. This could all have been done elsewhere. Every London auction house had antiques experts from front to back door. Was it a tax thing? Laura hadn't asked about her ex-husband, either. Why, in fact, was I essential?

Thoughts of Tansy kept coming. And old Smethie, and Paltry. Amid the celebrations, a daft news item came to mind: a Tennessee prisoner broke out and stole some hamburgers, then returned and gave the food to his pals. True story. In clink he was a hero. Moral: a story depends on who the listeners are.

People filed past congratulating me. I said ta. One old man told me, 'God is love.' I said ta. A slender gaucho spoke in Spanish. I told him ta. A lady gave me a kiss that was more than perfunctory. I told her a breathless ta. I told everybody ta. For what? A ranchified chap who looked sun-pruned told me in some Germanic accent, 'Payment in full, hey?' I said ta. He seemed in tears.

The parade went on, and people began to drift. I hate to drink before work. I honestly think wine is for slurping at home. Swilling is one-and-a-half glasses a night. Tea's for quaffing in public. It's a pity women expect wine when they're out. I always think they want it to show other women that her bloke is giving it large.

One other thing was getting to me. At least a dozen

mobiles will interrupt any ceremony, anywhere. During tender musicals, even sermons, for God's sake, off go the jangling summonses and *Peter Pan* is ruined again.

Here, though? Not a single jingle.

For the first time, concern made me look at Hugo Hahn. Everyone shook his hand before they strolled to the exits. Note, *all* of them. Like he had pulled off something momentous, led them across quagmires to freedom. He was the hero. I was an incidental.

Nobody had expressed fervent thanks to me. The thanks were all for big Hugo Hahn. I was the one saying ta. They only said their God-bless and payment-is-due. And most looked away as they left. No eye contact.

Now, these people were carriage trade. I was once in Guadeloupe, then St Lucia, and more polite people you'll never meet. Honest, it's all through the Caribbean. Sri Lanka, same thing. I'd never been to Poland, but the Poles in East Anglia have meticulous manners. Namibia I didn't know, but South Africans are the only ones in international sports who *always* say thanks to the umpires and referees.

Something was wrong, and I was it.

All life is a mess, I urged my frantic mind, so keep calm. Life's mess is simply made up of hundreds of small errors. Sooner or later it becomes a final landslide, and over you go to perdition. I kept a brave face, stoically said ta and returned Laura's hand squeeze.

The last of the guests left and we were alone, Donna da Silfa's big six, Laura and me. I scoffed on, ploughing through the grub in case I didn't get the chance later.

Sounds of the departing guests diminished. Distant slamming of car doors made me wonder where Ellen had got to. I wanted to ask Laura when I might expect her legal eagles. She was busy reminiscing with Donna da Silfa while I asked after those ancient playing cards they'd been using when we'd all first met up. Does the ex-bridegroom get to keep the wedding presents after a divorce? I didn't think so. What better antiques than antique cards?

The man seated next to me was the glitzy bloke, with those gold teeth that had impressed me. They'd been the valuable Goodall issue (the cards, not his teeth) for Queen Victoria's jubilee. Elegant in his Confederate uniform, he sported a Dundreary moustache.

'Those playing cards. Still got them?'

'Always, sir.' He tapped his coat pocket. 'You aren't suggesting a hand at this late juncture?'

'No, er, Major. How much?'

He drew them from his pocket. Military uniforms are handsome, but useless for galloping in. I felt queasy. Genuine.

'I keep them with me, sir. Family loyalty.'

'No chance of a sale, then?'

'Hardly, sir. Handed down, like faith in the Confederacy.'

'OK. You don't mind my asking?'

'Hardly, sir. You're an antiques dealer, after all.'

I realised all talk had ceased during this exchange. Hugo was staring along the table, Donna da Silfa also earwigging, as if they were scared Francisco Polk would let something slip. The tension eased, and they talked happily on.

'Laura?' I said quietly. 'The lawyers?'

'Do the divvying, Lovejoy, then we settle up. It's in the old library.'

'I can divvy forty an hour.'

'Fine, darling. Go at your own pace. Then we'll be done.'

That sounded a bit final, but was what we'd agreed.

'Promise?' I asked. She looked gorgeous. I'd not noticed her much until now. Stress again, maybe.

'Promise, Lovejoy.' She glanced at Hugo. 'I keep my promises.'

'Lovejoy?' Donna da Silfa rose and the men stood together. Like I said, politeness rules among expatriates. 'The place is now entirely yours. The staff are here if you need anything.'

'Come through, please.' Delius flicked his giant cigar and wheezed forward.

They accompanied me into a drawing room off the main hall. The darkened room's walls were covered with greyish velvet, as repellent as it sounds. In the centre was a chair, with a whist-drive table. I felt aggrieved.

'You could at least have got me an antique.'

'Mortimer left you the pen and ink set.' Laura pointed. 'He said it was the only one you always trust, Lovejoy.'

'Fine,' I said. I showed no trace of the dismay I felt, clapping my eyes on what Mortimer had left. *That* inkwell? *That* pen? The little sod's final jeer.

'We'll give you ten minutes, Lovejoy. The staff have instructions to start bringing in the antiques any time after that. All right?'

'Fine.' I stared at the inkwell and pen.

'Pad of paper to make notes,' Laura told me.

'Fine.' *That* inkwell, *that* pen. I felt ill.

'Nothing else you'll want?' from Hahn.

'Fine.' Iller and iller.

'The staff shall carry the antiques in one at a time through the far door. As you give each antique the nod, it will be carried out through this near door. Tell them if you want them to come faster or slower.' Delius said that.

'Fine.' I was sickened.

'Then we shall leave you.' Donna da Silfa led the way out. A carafe of water and a glass, both modern, were on the baize table. I badly wanted a swig, but thought of poison. 'Bye, Lovejoy.'

'Fine.' It was all I could say.

Laura came and kissed me. 'This is more than a promise, Lovejoy, darling. It's my moment. And yours, for everything you've done and are. You're wonderful.'

'Fine.'

'We'll be waiting in the main library. Just send the staff for anything.'

'Fine.'

I managed to keep saying it. I'll never know how. I couldn't take my eyes off the inkwell and the pen.

'By doing this for us, Lovejoy,' she said, cupping my face in her hands, 'you are rescuing whole races of people. We honour you for it.'

Saying fine was pathetic. 'I understand.'

For one instant a cloud passed before her eyes. They say that if you can fake sincerity you can fake anything. In that instant I was faking for my life. I smiled.

Hugo Hahn paused in the doorway, then, reassured by my tone and Laura's behaviour, moved out. Laura went too, turning at the door to give me a ripple of her fingers.

A footman came in, gave me a nod and withdrew, closing the door.

Alone and waiting. Everything was fine, just like I said. The inkwell was there, with the glass pen and the notepaper. Mortimer had sent those in deliberately for me to use. What had Laura said? Mortimer said they were my favourites that I always trust?

Voices receded. Feet clacked on marble flooring. Some door nearby opened and closed.

Silence descended in the room like a cloak.

I stared at the inkwell.

Now, there are inkwells and inkwells. Some are valuable, some not.

This thing was the brass head of a cat eating a brass mouse. Horrible. I'd seen it before. It was the only antique I'd ever thrown away, literally chucked out when Lydia wanted me to divvy it. I'd raged at her, demanding who the hell wanted to be faced with a tortured mouse murdered by a hunter? You lifted the mouse to reveal an ink reservoir in the cat's gaping maw. Fine nineteenth-century German workmanship, sure, but who on earth wanted to see that bloody thing?

I'd lobbed it out into my wilderness of overgrown garden, and told Mortimer and the weeping Lydia never to let me see the sickening thing again. I'd told Mortimer: 'If I see that thing again, I'll run a frigging mile.'

There was a cheap glass pen beside it. No message on the writing paper. The Faces would have checked.

Listening hard, I looked round the room. No cameras. I was stuck, with Donna's team and Laura supposedly waiting in the library with lawyers, and sundry serfs poised to bring in all those precious antiques.

Quietly, I went to the door. Locked. The other door, also locked. Well, security is essential, right? No windows beyond the black drapes, which were there simply for effect. Solid walls. Putting my ear to the door, I strove to hear a single sound. Nothing. Could I smell smoke?

The glass pen was just that. You get them in any shop. It's a modern glass stem with one end twisted. You dip it in the ink, and the ink dribbles down the grooves. Simple. The monstrous brass cat-head inkwell was only for ink.

No weapon, nothing to batter a door down with. The table and chair were light modern constructions, so useless. No windows to climb out of. Nobody within earshot. Was the whole place now empty except for me?

Nothing on the walls. I felt panic begin. Could I get out through the hall? I tried to recall the layout of the place, but couldn't. I'd been too anxious to take stock.

Ten minutes, they'd said. Did they need that length of time to get away, be elsewhere in some tavern perhaps? Maybe the Faces had called the police, to collar me here alone?

Then I noticed: not a single vibe any longer. There wasn't a single antique left in the entire building, just space. And me.

Solid flooring, parquet blocks. The ceiling? A single flex. I felt trapped. Laura had got me here, with Donna da Silfa and her team setting me up. How could Mortimer and Lydia land me in this? My frightened imagination ran riot. Me trying to steal some great haul of antiques, maybe getting into some dispute with friends, foes, anybody, and coming to grief, a rumble over the missing antiques. And

Lovejoy alone in a great empty building.

Good plan, I thought. Except bad, because I was in it.

Then, thank God for mercy, I heard feet clumping, staff moving in the great hall where the wedding reception had been. I almost fainted from relief. I wiped my sweating brow and sat still to wait. Everything was going right at last. How stupid I'd been to mistrust them. After all, I was the one essential.

Chapter Thirty-Four

prog (v): to hunt (crim. slang)

There came a faint racket of people talking, 'Mind that trestle,' with 'I'll go in first, OK?' and 'Is that pot thing second?' showing the usual level of perception of the vannies. Except...

Maybe I was wrong. Everything had seemed authentic, the wedding business, Laura's all-loving gaze. They'd said ten minutes, hadn't they?

Another minute passed. I tried the door handle. Still locked. I didn't make a fuss, crossed to try the opposite door. Same. Doubtless some natural mistake. They'd be along any sec, no worries. What floor was I on? Still no windows.

The Faces were, I remembered, cold-blooded killers, and had left me here with hired staff, presumably bringing the antiques in from storage. It felt like hide-and-seek. 'Coming, ready or not,' we shouted before starting.

In myself, I felt around for the divvy feeling. Nil. It hadn't come back. Not one single chime. Hadn't it stifled me as I'd arrived? Was I sloshed and couldn't sense the vibes? No. I was sober as a judge. At gatherings, I hardly ever touch a drop. I always pretend, and leave drinks untouched. Often I finish up the only sober bloke. It's the only sensible way. Fine, stand your round if you have the dosh, but boozing all blinking night is the road to rusty ruin. I've seen it happen. My great-great-something Grampa Turner of Preston had practically founded the teetotal movement, family legend says. He'd have been proud of me – maybe.

Mental fingers drumming, my breathing going just that bit faster, I was on edge. Either the antiques began coming, the way Laura said, or it was time to get the hell out. If I went out, I could always come back in saying I'd only wanted a breath of air, couldn't I? And appear the same smooth Lovejoy. Ten minutes? I'd already spent that long daydreaming. Bad thought: maybe the place was due to fill with Blackpool's finest any second. Or, God Almighty, explode?

My mouth dried all of a sudden. I almost whimpered. If the mob of serfs outside in the main hall was real, I'd look a prat. But better a living prat that a dead sprat. I shouted. No one answered. I knocked. The noises stayed constant. Seriously wrong?

Sweating, I looked for tools. I needed tools. The glass pen was easy. I held it in my jacket, snapped it into four, edges sharper than any knife. The chair was an el cheapo with a false wicker seat. Shakily, I wrapped the heavy brass inkwell in severed wicker strands I cut with the glass, and swung it at the door's middle oak panel. I'm not the strongest geezer on earth, so hefted it like an olympic hammer thrower chucking that heavy ball. The inkwell thudded against the panel.

No change in the noises, people still clumping and calling instructions about bringing antiques in the right order. Nobody exclaimed, 'What the hell was that?' They just kept on listing antiques, saying 'You go eighth, Bert.' It began to sound oddly made up, a panto crowd. Nobody shouted, did I want to be let out?

I swung my brass missile again. The panel splintered. I warmed to the work, knotting more cane strips when the first lot snapped. The panel gave on the seventh swing. My hands got cut from clawing at the wood. It took fourteen smashes to get one panel out. By then I was a gibbering wreck. I shoved an arm through and felt. No key. They weren't daft. I peered through. Nobody in the hall, just a couple of music centres with red LEDs glowing. The crowd sounds came from them. They'd planned well, which meant the place would go up in ten minutes – Christ, how long?

The main struts of the door were too thick. Now into frank terror, I stripped my top off and wriggled through the space I'd made. By the time I was out among the wedding debris, my back felt tarry with blood from scraping through the scagged opening. I didn't care. I had splinters, but I was free – sort of.

I'd had the presence of mind to bring my tied weight for a weapon, just in case, and my shirt. No jacket, though. I went from that building like a ferret, through the main foyer, and now I really did scent smoke. Not a single motor in the drive. The swine had gone and left me. No Ellen, no Mortimer to watch his faithful and caring dad get crisped, no Tinker, no Donna da Silfa, no Lydia. No friends. Trembling with self-pity, I huddled in the shrubbery and watched the huge building. It began to burn.

Odd to see your own funeral pyre. After a few moments I became fascinated, almost detached, thinking, Good heavens, look at the way those flames are licking the roof. It was a spectacle, the blaze evolving from a plume of smelly smoke to a real inferno. Within minutes, I was speculating whether I'd have set the fire exactly as my murderers had.

It actually started where the wedding feast had been. That, I thought bitterly, was to prove to the fire brigades that good old Lovejoy had been carousing and somehow set the place alight as he, poor soul, slept in a drunken stupor in a side room. Lovejoy, never changing the habits of a lifetime.

The conflagration climbed up that grand staircase. I worked it out, watching the show. A wise incendiarist would lay secondary starts halfway up the stairs, so the evidence would be consumed as the ceilings fell in. They actually erupted where the stage was. I saw the kitchens go up last.

The whole building whoofed into a frank blaze. Eventually fire brigade sirens sounded across the moors. From Blackpool?

Hating everybody, I kept griping about friends who hadn't come to help. I'm really good at sulking, keep it up for hours once I get going. You're always on your own in life. You're alone, so get on with it.

Morosely, in the shelter of the Somnell House shrubbery, I observed the Keystone Kops start chopping their way in, smashing windows and spraying water from the ornamental ponds. My gran used to say there were different kinds of temper. Her special concern was cold temper, meaning somebody who would stop at nothing to punish a wrongdoer. 'Never have a cold temper,' she told me, '*because you never come out.*' She made me promise. I did, of course.

Circumstances change things. I found myself telling the night air that, as sparks gusted aloft and firemen shouted and slices of the manor house tumbled into the fiery maw. Sorry, Gran, but tonight it's cold temper, but whose fault is that?

Right, I thought. They wanted me dead. If it hadn't been for the manky writing implements they'd carelessly left me, I'd have been done for, trapped in that locked room, fondly waiting to divvy those precious antiques. They'd intended me to die. Why they wanted me wed *and* dead, though, was anybody's guess.

It came on to rain. I stayed long enough to see that no other soul started screaming from the upper windows. Somnell House lit the moors for miles around. Nobody seemed to need rescuing. In a truly ugly mood, I buttoned my bloodied shirt and set off on the long walk to the inn. I followed the roads Ellen had driven. The firelight was enough to see by. Marker constables were stationed along the route, so not even I could get lost. They held flashlights. One ploddite had the gall to accost me.

'Out walking on this foul night, sir?'

Like, no, Constable, I'm playing golf. 'Yeah.'

'Do you know anything of the fire at Somnell House?'

'No.'

He shone his light at me and seemed taken aback by my appearance. 'Had a fall, sir?'

'Yes. Trying to get out of the bloody way of your stupid motors. You police should obey the fucking road rules.' Like I said, an ugly mood.

'There's no need for that, sir. Doing our duty.'

'That old one?'

'Did you see the fire start, sir?'

'No. Have you seen my dog? Your stupid cars knocked it over.'

'Not seen any dog, sir.' He flashed his light to signal another police car racing up to do nothing.

'Can you take down its details?' I kept on. 'It's a brown Labrador with facial markings.' I couldn't recognise a Labrador if its name was written on it.

'Sorry, sir. Not just now.' He wanted rid of me.

I'd had to save myself from getting crisped and now had to trudge miles to where the Faces were celebrating, having pulled off the biggest antiques heist since Christie's and Sotheby's lost their criminal-conspiracy bosses in the law courts. I lectured the constable I'd report him for lacking sympathy. In a rage I mentioned the Dog Society, hoping there was such a thing, and the Animal Lovers' Welfare Agency (ditto), and left fuming. The idle sod stood there shaking his head. No pity for my poor dog, heartless bastard. Rain came on heavier, a real moorland downpour. I thought of him becoming drenched to the bone. Serve him right for running over my faithful dog.

Like a drowned rat, I plodded off the hillside to the inn.

There in the car park I split my remaining usable thumbnail hot-wiring a miserable old Fiat. (Tip: VWs are said to be easiest.) By then I was apoplectic. As I drove away, my bloody shirt sticking me to the seat, I planned a furious complaint to Fiat about their junky vehicles.

Some days nothing goes right. Within a few furlongs of the Golden Mile, the petrol gave out. I coasted to a stop. The famous Tower was visible in criss-cross searchlights by the sea. Luckily I found a man's jacket on the back seat, one pocket full of condoms. Bad planning, mate, I thought, finding a few notes. I looked like nothing on earth, but at least my back had stopped blotting everything with blood. Whimpering from pain, I plodded into town.

Nobody could see I'd been in a mess unless they stared hard. I went slowly. You can't get lost in Blackpool. You simply head for the Tower. The Faces would finish up there, at the one venue where a couple of hundred strangers wouldn't raise a squeak of comment. Tourism is what Blackpool is for.

It was also the place for working things out, like who were killers and who not. I approached the Golden Mile.

There used to be a zoo in the Tower. I think it's gone now. Lifts take you to the Tower's very top. You can hire a plane to fly round it on a good day. There is a giant ballroom for international dances. It is a palace of entertainment.

Among the evening crowds as they milled on the promenade, I thought, Now what? I had assumed that, saving myself as I had – thanks to nobody – answers would simply come. Maybe I imagined I'd simply stroll among those avaricious and astonished killers, lighting a cheroot one-handed like Bing Crosby always did in the *Road* pictures, 'Thought you'd got rid of me, hey?' then signal Inspector Lestrade to arrest the lot.

In reality I stood there like a lemon. Buffeted by crowds,

I stood on the corner. A limousine drew up. I ducked my head.

A man alighted with a gorgeous lady in full evening apparel, all glitzy. Slender and lovely, she was far more glammed than when she married me. I shuffled off among a mob of football supporters chanting some result or other. I looked back. Laura was successfully concealing her grief at the death of today's husband, viz. me. The gent wore spats, would you believe, and a Ronald Coleman tash, hair slicked 1930s style. Wait long enough, fashions come back.

Uniformed minions ushered them through. If winter comes, etc, or something. There would be others. In a moment, I recognised two of Donna's big six, including the mighty Hugo, who'd made that oh-so-amusing speech, toasting – as in *toast*, get it? – me in those witty puns. Everybody got the jokes except me. They were all posh and glamorous.

One strange thing. I went to a pub on the Golden Mile, certain none of that elegant crowd would drop in there. I went to the loo, then got mineral water and some pasties. I believe in the Duke of Wellington's dictum. In war, pass water at every opportunity. I presumed he meant have a swig and a nosh too. They'd tried to burn me to death. That's what war is. I thought of Laura's escort.

Tall, elegant, suave, with a political decoration in his lapel. I cast about in my mind, and remembered where I'd seen him. My weary mind needed time to rally its neurones. Once I'd got it, I went on a recollection spree. The saloon noise receded, and for a moment I was back at one of the most famous London antiques sales of all time.

Not every collector is famous. Some were only famous for their secrecy. Like Nathan Wildenstein, a humble necktie salesman. He did well, young Nathan, bought the Hôtel de Wailly in Paris. All along, Wildenstein was fascinated by art. He bought and sold. I'm not making aspersions about that elegant Polish countess he knew, honestly I'm not. Their business, and I'm no gossip. But by selling a supposed van Dyck to her, Nathan made his number.

Buying cheap eighteenth-century French paintings, slickly selling them on for a multiple, he made serious money. From your simple want-a-tie-guv trader, Nathan became the buyer-in-chief of Old Masters in Paris.

The Wildenstein Collection grew. Nathan kept some items for himself, and annoyed rival art dealers by never showing his private collection. Nathan died in 1934 or so. His possessions included sculptures, rare André-Charles Boulle furniture. Also, a massive antiquarian library of a quarter of a million tomes, plus virtually everything else of European importance. His place became the Wildenstein Institute. Sadly, the new millennium dawned with the inevitable lawsuits. Judges hit the fan and the mightiest sale on earth began.

I'd been in the street near Christie's on the day of that giant mega-sale. They wouldn't let me in. I saw the buyers arrive for the viewing, and two women I'd once bought antiques for. I recognised a Yank lady who owned a theatre in New England. She refused my calls (jealous of her friend I knew). And, that soggy day in London town, I saw a movie backer I once bought Edwardian jewellery for.

The man who went in the Tower ballroom with Laura

was that same bloke. You see his name on picture credits, Nateo Dunknaister. Once, it had been 'Call me Nat, Lovejoy.' No longer. I wasn't jealous, sipping my mineral water, feeling like a train wreck and wincing from the splinters in my torn back. But somebody would have to suffer. Who had to face poor Tansy's ghost when she came asking if I'd caught her killer? Me, that's who. And poor Paltry's spirit? And poor old Smethie's ghost?

'OK, mate, keep your hair on,' the bloke standing next to me said. 'I only asked the score.'

'Sorry, wack,' I said. I must have been glaring.

'I am sorry, sir,' a familiar female voice said to the annoyed Liverpudlian. 'My brother forgets to take his tablets. I apologise. Would you allow me to offer you a pint?'

Dully I watched as the bloke was mollified. Nice folk in Blackpool. He told the woman it was OK, and best get him (i.e. me, like I was an imbecile) home quick. She drew me outside into the cold night air. The pavement crowds had thinned. Time for the second house in the main shows?

'You could have got me one, Lovejoy,' Tinker groused. 'I'm frigging parched.'

'Where the frigging hell were you, you idle old bastard?'

'That will do, Lovejoy.' She held me in a firm grasp. I looked at her with curiosity. 'Come along.'

'How come you are the boss?'

She said, exasperated, 'You're so slow, Lovejoy. Can you still not see the obvious?'

'That bird who got topped by the sea marshes,' Tinker said helpfully.

My head swam, because Ellen Jaynor wasn't topped in any sea marsh. Nobody was. I wanted a lie down. Wanting order, I said, 'Shut up, Tinker.'

'We must take urgent steps, Lovejoy. You must decide how to bring the miscreants to justice.'

'Look,' I began.

She propelled me to the pavement. 'Into the car, please. Front seat, where I can keep an eye on you.'

Her limo was pristine. I seethed with anger. She'd managed to clean her sodding motor while I burnt to death. Another great ally.

'Got a drink, missus?' Tinker asked. 'My chest's bad in night air.'

'When I say, Tinker,' Ellen said with asperity, 'and not a minute sooner. In, both of you.'

'But I got wounds. It's always me that suffers.'

'I shan't tell you again. We're all so sorry, Lovejoy.'

I almost filled up at her kind words. The car moved along the promenade.

Chapter Thirty-Five

ken: store of stolen antiques (ancient slang)

We drove to what folk now call a trailer park, copying the American name for tin caravans, tin homes on tin wheels. They stood in miniature streets with lights and tubs of flowers. The tidiest place I ever did see. I could hear the occasional television set in the darkness.

'Here?' I was incredulous. They had these places near Great Yarmouth on the east coast, but this wasn't for holidayers. This was a town and looked planted.

'Make no noise,' Ellen warned me. 'People go to bed early.'

'Where are we?' Shouldn't I have been in the Tower planning revenge?

'The Fylde, Lovejoy. The others are inside.' She spoke in that laconic way. It really narked. 'You're our one hope, Lovejoy.'

The night breeze felt chilly. Ellen shivered. Tinker hawked, coughing with his usual piledriver noise. So much for sound sleep in Moss House Caravan Park.

'Others who?' Weren't we secret, us battlers against the dark powers?

'You'll see. In.'

The caravan was astonishing. Like a shoe-box on the outside, within it simply went on and on, one room after another. You could believe you were in a dinky hotel. Kitchen, sitting room, bedrooms, loo and bath, you could take to such a home. The group looked at me.

'I see you all made it,' I told them in my frostiest voice.

'You should have been here before now, Lovejoy,' said Mortimer. He didn't even stand. What happened to respect? I thought, God, just listen to myself. I sounded ninety. 'Whose jacket is that?'

'I couldn't stop to pack,' I said with sarcasm, 'after you left me to die.'

Determined to be nasty, I vowed to make the treacherous little punk suffer. Instead, he calmly sat next to the gorgeous Donna da Silfa.

'I left you obvious means of escape.'

'Don't sulk, Lovejoy. Mortimer thought it all out.'

'Can somebody tell me what Mrs da Silfa is doing here?' I asked.

Everybody looked at each other. Mortimer said, 'A possible ally.'

'And I,' said Leg-Breaker, sitting there as if he owned the place, 'am on Mr Hennell's staff. Ex-SAS, seeing you still haven't got it.'

'I changed sides, Lovejoy.' Donna gazed at me with defiance.

'From which to what?' I sat facing them. 'Members of Parliament change sides and say *they're* honest.'

'How can you be so insolent, after...' She dried up, checked with Mortimer.

'After you forced me to wed a murderess?'

'Any chance of a drink?' Tinker went and groped in the fridge. 'There's not much.' He coughed over whatever sterile produce it held. He opened a bottle by clicking it on the edge of a table. If I tried that, the neck would snap and send beer everywhere.

'Is your loyalty anything to do with the gold price?' I asked Donna. I turned to Dr Giles Castell and his randy wife Penny. She was smiling. 'And is *your* greed what you two got me arrested for?'

'Now, Lovejoy,' Penny Castell purred. 'The roads we travelled do not matter. The fact is we are here to save the day.'

'Whose day?' I waited. 'Nobody's answered me about the gold price.'

I reminded them of a few facts. Gold is the pulse of the world's economy. Every year, India buys a third of all the world's mined gold, and its banks hold over 23,000 tons of the pricey stuff. Worldwide, stock markets scrabble after Ghana's gold as South Africa's seams decline and new finds elsewhere come in. As I spoke, I saw Donna da Silfa's eyes flash. She remembered that an English king's-head sovereign – the most desirable – had been less than 800 rupees in Madras when she was younger, but one now would cost an arm and a leg. They joke in Kerala that you can't see that lovely ancient city because of the gold merchants' adverts. Three-quarters of the world's gold has already been dug up. Not much left.

'Gold,' I ended, 'is a mania. It will buy anything.' I could have mentioned peerages but didn't because I'm kind deep down. 'And you love it, Donna. We talked of it.'

'You're becoming fanciful, Lovejoy,' Dr Castell boomed. 'We must block their wicked schemes.'

'Can I smoke this?' Tinker lit a monster cigar he'd looted.

'He'll be here soon. Dr Castell can explain, seeing as he knows Daniella.' That was Donna da Silfa.

Does he now? I thought. 'Who?'

'You'll see, Lovejoy.'

'Who?' I looked around. Mortimer looked exasperated, like I ought to have worked things out, the arrogant little sod.

'Time you got me some smokes, Lovejoy,' Tinker said, alternately glugging and fuming the air with carcinogens. 'When you get paid.'

'I'll wait outside.' I choked on the smoke. 'Give me a shout when the gang's all here.'

'Please wait, Lovejoy,' Mortimer said. And he sounded truly sad, like he had the very worst news. The others looked at the floor, and stayed silent.

'We shall have to tell him,' Ellen said.

'Not me, please,' Donna da Silfa said, tears filling her eyes.

'Well, I can't.' Ellen looked at Mortimer, who shook his head.

'You poor bugger, Lovejoy,' Tinker said. His eyes are always rheumy but just for a nanosec I wondered if even he was near to skryking.

'Tell me what?' I asked.

'Tell him, Giles,' Penny said.

'Please, no, Penny. You.'

'How can I, Giles, after...?' She halted.

'What?' I said again.

This was probably the first time Giles – or any man, come to that – had ever denied Penny Castell.

'You poor sod,' Tinker said.

In a temper I flung outside. I'd had enough. Let them get on with their stupid glances and innuendoes.

The open air was marginally more breathable. I stood in the gloaming among those tin dwellings. Greed had to be the single determinant. Hadn't I just proved so, with my gold prattle? What else was strong enough to bring those antiques-rich Faces from their rock pools, and turn them into a murderous team?

If any crooks wanted to make a fortune, they could clean out America's Folger Library, the world's biggest Shakespeare hoard. Every stolen thing is saleable, whatever the Antiques Fraud Squad pretends. More difficult would be Virginia's National Firearms Museum – you're talking untold wealth in antiques there. A third would be Washington's International Spy Museum. It doesn't sound likely, but it all depends what you like... *What was I thinking?* Here I was, night-dreaming, when I was seriously up against it. Whatever Mortimer said, I hadn't a clue what was happening on my own patch.

One thing clung to my mind.

It's called ransom.

Not long back, two Turner paintings were nicked, clean as a whistle, from London's mighty Tate during a loan exhibition to Germany. Art experts everywhere sobbed into their champagne. Curators were edgy, reputations plunged, and the criminal world rocked with laughter. I well remember how we (correction: *they*) threw a party in the George. Fabulous works of artistic genius vanished forever, sob-sob, right? Well, no. Not quite.

Because the paintings (*Light and Colour* was one, *Shade and Darkness* the other) suddenly reappeared *in the Tate Gallery*. Miraculous? Yes, produced by handing over millions to a Continental lawyer who incurred certain 'expenses' and had 'information leading to the recovery of', as euphemism has it. Now, I've nothing against Frankfurt lawyers. And don't believe the rumours about Balkan mafia. The Tate hierarchy waffled their usual blandeur. They'd 'paid in a number of directions'. Cynics said a reward would be necessary. Darker mutters mentioned ransom, a term hotly denied. One does not pay ransom to criminals, old chap, what?

Listening for the latecomer's car, I watched a bank of lights on the wine-dark sea (sorry, I pinched that phrase from schoolboy Homer). It joined smaller dots. Presumably little boats, ferrying friends to an ocean-going yacht anchored offshore. All right for some, I thought bitterly.

It's true. Art movements are dishonest. The famous Waverley Report yaks on about export controls. Like, say you have bought the fabled Clive of India Flask – an exalted item everybody knows is worth millions. You intend to take it to your hot native clime, and ask the UK Government for an export licence. Instantly, politicians grumble about the nation's treasures being lost. Museums begin begging for money to match the market price. You let the various museums scratch around for some months – then blithely announce you've no intention of taking the item overseas at all.

To the criminal mind, this scheme offers massive chances for deception. Not accusing anybody, but in East Anglia there's a woman in a faded university who collects data on such possibilities. She lives in Royston, near where that old mill…

My mind went, Hang on. Why wasn't I back in the warm fug listening to their dud explanations? I *never* do things according to reason. I only ever go by instinct, possibly wild and random, then think, Good heavens, how come I worked that out?

The sea lights separated. I stamped a bit like you do when you are frozen. The smaller vessels, two lights only, must still be ferrying friends out to the splendid ocean-going yacht party. Plenty of friends when you're loaded. Like that English noble multimillionaire. Sir Benjamin of Maunsel, still youngish as I scrawl, looked into his family history and learnt that his umpteenth great-grannie had been a close lady friend of King George the Fourth. An earlier grannie had cavorted with King Charlie Two. An interesting snippet thrown up by history. Except the snippet hit the headlines, and suddenly 20,000 heirs came zooming in. (If your ancestors are called Slade, good luck.)

And I thought of Hugo Hahn's speech at the wedding nosh. And tried to guess who we might be waiting for.

The jokes in his woody speech kept echoing in my skull. I'd been daft as a brush all along, missing the obvious. *Toast*, he'd said, and *last*, and everybody had laughed. His speech, in fact, was all farewell.

The night breeze freshened. I shivered in my stolen jacket. The original owner would be even colder, poor chap.

Float, Hugo Hahn had quipped, in that terrible historical phrase: 'floating the idea of the final solution'. No wonder I was shivering, because finally I knew what they were doing. 'How' problems could remain unsolved. Forget the worrying bits, like how did Dr Castell and Penny know the Faces. That College? I felt a twinge of sorrow, or was it only pity? I've seen a gillion scams tried, and one way or another they crashed. Or they ended in ugly deaths in alleyways. That is their fate.

Tasker, best of friends and worst of enemies, warns, 'The only foolproof scam *is the next.*' Like politics, that art of making a dog's dinner of perfection.

It was Hugo Hahn, so he'd have to kill me. And the beautiful Donna was his double-agent envoy. Daniella, Veronica, Ellen, Laura, I didn't know what to think. Mortimer was innocent, surely? I badly needed help. What were they so reluctant to tell me in the caravan? The trouble was, waiting for Morgyn the Mighty to stride over the horizon is comic-book stuff. I'd have to go on my own. I could honestly say that I wasn't thinking that I could snaffle those delicious antiques, no. It didn't enter my mind. OK, I could have phoned friends if I'd had a mobile thing, and I might have called out Tinker and maybe Mortimer on some pretence. But they'd hold me back.

Of course, I didn't march off and get a taxi to the police. To arrest diplomats? Instead, I slunk like a night-stealer down to the sea.

The beach, maybe four furlongs from North Pier, was all activity with hardly any lights. High tide, of course, making loading easier. Eight or nine vannies were unloading two giant pantechnicons by the glim of hand torches. I heard one call, 'Last-but-one load, wack.' One of the giant lorries closed its rear doors and was driven off.

Two small craft nosed to the shingle, their painters looped over staves driven into the shore, the men plodding back to help carry loads from the last wagon. I walked down to the boats. Both engines still muttered in neutral. I shoved one off and boarded the other. A good hundred yards off the beach, I heard the first shouts and looked back. One bloke ran helplessly into the waves after me. The rest stood there gaping. I towed the other boat. Nobody could follow because I'd nicked both boats.

The engine was the familiar kind I knew from Mersea Island. I aimed steadily at the great yacht thing, so brightly lit out on the dark sea. What, a mile off?

The beach seemed static, the vannies baffled at my theft of the boats. No spare boats, so I felt momentarily safe. Unless they got a power boat from somewhere, I'd at least have time to get close to the big vessel and see what the hell. Easy to steer with a tiller – point this way or that, the craft moved in the opposite direction. Simple.

Slowly puttering towards the looming yacht, I was aghast at the size of the damned thing. She was the *Maeonia*. God, she swelled into a giant as I butted my way to stand off from her to seaward. She was lit all over, portholes and gangway visible, and a set of chained steps with a miniature gantry ready to haul up furniture and other heavy antiques.

My breath was rapid but not from the cold. They would have left an armed guard on board. And I could guess who that was. The big boss, the leader of the pack.

I cut the engine of my towed craft and cast it adrift. If it was Hahn, I had some daft idea I might be able to jump overboard and swim for it, with any luck. My own boat I tied to the bottom of the gangway, its engine still on the go in neutral, and climbed up on deck.

Chapter Thirty-Six

'raj': the boss of a group of antiques criminals

For the first time in my life I felt in control, at the nearness of a world's worth of antiques. The yacht must be bulging. An unbattened hatch showed light slits from its edges. They must be confident. Chimes made me shiver, gorge rising and my left temple throbbing.

That's when I heard the first human sound. It was me. I'd tried to nudge some wood thing aside. For a frightened second I almost ran for it, but halted. Criminals in mid-heist would leave a sentinel aboard. Armed? Sure. And he'd be my favourite speechmaker. I heard his voice exclaim, 'Listen to the noisy sods.'

And a female voice, husky with love, said, 'Never mind them, darling. Come back here.' And I thought another thought, except this one was even more stupid. I actually recognised her voice, until I corrected myself. It couldn't be, never in a million years. One thing about my stupidity, it never gives up.

The man was furious. 'Christ knows what they're doing. If it's my Ashanti carvings I'll machette the bastards!'

'You've your own work to finish, darling.'

The voice was sweet, charming, graceful. I'd heard it so many times, though not exactly in these circumstances. The man was tough. I'd seen that among the traffic in Head Street, and when he'd glared down at Erosa. The blighter had haunted, hunted me. And now...

'That's it, darling,' the female voice purred, 'right there.' I'm so thick. I moved quietly forward, then reminded myself that the loaders wouldn't tiptoe. I clumped along the deck, giving a guttural grunt, trying to sound like seven or eight vannies heaving antiques.

Passion in the cabin started again as I reached the curtained portholes. Curtains. Even then, trembling from the divvy malaise, I was still foolishly half-smiling at the sounds of lust. I couldn't see her face, but her body I'd known well. At least so I'd assumed, the way you assume you know love. Her modulated voice urged the man on, in a growling quality I'd only heard once. Back then, I'd felt rather proud, a beast raising my own Miss Ice Maiden from her usual primness to passion.

This bloke seemed be doing all right, beyond the concealing porthole curtain. Of course, that was the sort of demure move she would make, make sure the sacking was over my cottage window in case somebody came a-peering. I hadn't been lucky often, no, just a few times. Each was beautiful, in the relish of the moment. She was superb. Was. Past tense, if she was the one I imagined.

Then I caught myself. It couldn't be. Some human events are beyond possibility. No question. Making sounds like that? Calling for him to do this, that, hurt her and gagging in the height of rut? Never. Then something she grunted *was* her. It was her ultimate phrase, only gasped *in extremis.* Couldn't be anyone else. The evidence of senses is horrible stuff. I retched on the deck outside their porthole, spewing what grub hadn't got down far enough. A right mess.

Moments when your world ends come pretty often to me. I've always found that. The ground goes from under your feet, and you might as well float off in space. And not from happiness. Not horror either. A woman I knew once told me, 'When I found my feller sleeping with my best friend, I almost smiled.' I'd asked her why. And she smiled at me along the pillow and murmured, 'Because it was suddenly all so simple.' And she told me, 'I ran her over in my car.' The best friend, treacherous to the last, hadn't been helpful enough to die. Doctors worked frantically, and saved her. The principle is the same, though. Think of the very worst that could happen, and the vilest punishment whispers, 'Why not top her? She deserves it.' Logic never fails.

Without knowing quite why, I looked over the side. The sea seemed hell of a way down. I glanced round the deck. No smaller craft nearby. On shore, to my amazement, the dark scene now seemed mad, like some old jerky film. I guessed the plod had arrived, from the swirling blue lamps and headlights trained onto the beach where blokes struggled. Who had called them? I could hear brawling sounds, reminding me of distant midges by the Stour. Ambulances were nosing through the gathering crowds up on the promenade. Where do people lurk until mayhem brings watchers out?

Down in the cabin passion stormed on. I felt giddy listening. Time had gone or not gone. It could have been an hour or a few seconds. I wiped my sicky mouth on my sleeve. How long since I'd come aboard?

They say the woman becomes worse than the man, when sexual craziness gives utter release. What was the old saying? 'A woman in a parlour an angel, in a kitchen a fiend, and in bed a monster.' As here. I felt so tired. I honestly wasn't bitter. Maybe I'd known deep down she was never mine in the first place. Dunno. I just felt weary, like when you recognise the mufty con, the scally, or the drop-drop con, and know you've been had. Tricked into complicity by her seeming innocence, even her love. Love, was it?

My head was pulsing from the antiques in the hold, the inaudible vibes shaking me as if I were the clapper in some psychic bell. I gathered myself. I didn't have long. Soon I'd need to make a run for it, or be caught here with the two lovebirds. Their cries and grunts were reaching delirium. Detumescence soon, and they'd be free to have a cigarette – though she hated smokers, wouldn't even touch tobacciana at Gimbert's auction.

They would come up to see the last of the loading. A killer guarding his valuable sea-going yacht, his wondrous woman, and his priceless haul of antiques, would have to be armed.

And Lovejoy would be done for. Unless I scarpered? I could leave in my trusty little craft bobbing by the gangway. But…?

I almost started down as the couple below reached finality. And I thought, No. I wasn't standing by my gun, nothing brave. And I'm not one for vengeance. Vengeance is a failure of reason. We should think of charity, find a way where all would come right.

I'm not the most moral bloke on earth. I'll never make Archbishop of Canterbury. But all these certifiably genuine antiques? And the people who'd killed Tansy – Christ, I thought, aghast, who *had* killed Tansy? Surely it couldn't have been…?

No, a thousand times no. I even started humming that daft old music hall song as I went to get the thing I'd fallen over. It was a roundish bat. Long as a cricket bat, but heavier at the far end. Baseball, like bouncers carry in nightclubs? I stumbled over two more, picked up a second, and went down into the cabin. I listened at the door. The lovers were swearing undying love and lust. I decided to trap them in their love-nest by shoving a baseball bat through the handle. I honestly intended nothing vicious, and I mean that most sincerely. 'Course, it was natural to feel sad, to put it no more strongly. And didn't the 'holy' (he wasn't) Pope Innocent the Third famously say that it was no sin to kill somebody over a game of chess? He did. Look it up. He wasn't joking. This wasn't chess.

Then I noticed the extra door. A storm door? It would just fit. As they settled from their climax, I slotted it in place. OK, it would trap them inside, as it was for keeping the sea out in a hurricane. They were sealed.

Betrayers inside, innocent people outside. I could leave. They couldn't.

For a second I stayed there, as their passion descended through the superstrata to sea level, so to speak. I'd never felt such sick hate. Love does it.

See how often I use the word love? 'Love' is today's code word for every noble and beautiful sentiment. Yet it now only means want. Read the glossies in any shopping mall. Simply replace the word love for want, and you have it. I knew that now. 'I don't love him/her any longer' means 'I don't *want* him/her any longer.' Or even more bluntly, 'I've had a better offer,' and off they go. And remember, they've sworn undying fidelity, and written the altar promise down. Meaning, of course, until they become bored/ disinterested etc, or find somebody younger/richer. Sorry, but I didn't invent cynicism. It's just how people behave. Half of marriages end in divorce in five years. You can get those odds spinning a coin, heads or tails. Gamblers call it luck.

On deck, I examined the controls. Still no chasing craft full of enemies. The riot ashore was diminishing. I was still safe. The switches were elementary, if I could believe the labels. *Anchor Aft* meant, I hoped, the chain in the water at the rear. *Forward Anchor* meant same at the front. *Lift* could only mean to hawk it up from the seabed. Now I'd fastened Hugo Hahn and his – *his*, note – eager lady in, they could share their undying love in their watertight cabin. Whatever I did with this grand sailing machine was now up to me. I wasn't really upset. I don't get that concerned most of the time.

The on switch was a simple button. An electric-sounding roar told me I'd done it. I'd been thinking of those old piston-engined steamships that they show on late-night TV. This engine meant serious business. I levered the anchor, hoping it would work. Clatters, a sudden release in the ship's gentle rocking and she pulled free, slewing seaward. I suppose I ought to have put some headlights on, but you can't think of everything. Anyhow, she had lights on her mast. I was surprised when I looked up. I'd expected to see square-rigged canvas sails like in Errol Flynn pirate pictures, instead of a stumpy little stick with wires. Maybe I lived too much in films. Once I've seen some oldie, I can run it through my mind over and over. Fiction, though. Like love.

Not hurrying, I headed out to sea, the speed lever only halfway along its groove. I was in no hurry. Was there some law about how fast you could go?

That woman downstairs, though. I mean, how do you tell the difference between a lie and truth? You go by feel. At least I do. You listen to how a woman says things, and guess. The lie-detector test is unreliable. Or you can do that MRI scan of the brain. (A liar's MRI lights up fourteen brain areas. The truthsayer's brain ignites a paltry seven.) The real way is to wait and see. I'd waited, and I saw. The hard way.

The cold breeze stung my eyes. Not sorrow, because I don't feel that emotion much. Women are women, and there's plenty written about them and truth, right? One way to look at it is to see it as an aberration, and then forgive. Sociologists claim sixty per cent of wives forgive erring husbands, but only thirty per cent of blokes pardon wives. And employers nowadays are urged to forgive workers who abscond from work and 'pull a sickie' on National Sickie Day – it's 6th February. Liverpool's our major sickie capital. Glasgow holds the world record in scamming Social Services Benefit money. Statistics are nonsense. Nothing alters. We all know it's just counting numbers. Life is fable against feelings.

In Lancashire they used to say, *Old flame, new foe.* Was

the old saw reliable? I faced the sea, steering my stolen ship. Now she was moving, it seemed to have grown. Doing its thing, I suppose, glad it was no longer tethered in the swark.

The shore had somehow swung. I was headed slightly towards the washing-lines of promenade lights. I turned the wheel, making for the tip of North Pier. Easy as driving a car. I looked round for something to hold the wheel in place. I let go of it and picked up two of the bale hooks. They looked strong enough to do the job, but I was sorely narked. If those vannies had used these great hooks to haul any of the antiques aboard and damaged any, I'd...

The shore had gone quiet. Somebody was starting an outboard motor, the kind that powered the two small craft. They'd sussed that this big vessel was the focus of the goings-on. As long as it was only the uniformed plod and not the coastguard, I was OK for a while. This ship could really move. It was slicing through the dark waters with engines in mid-yawn. The speedo was marked up to over forty knots, whatever they were, and the digital display showed I was doing a mere six. I was still trying to lodge the wheel by a bale hook when somebody said, 'Can I help?'

Like a fool, I said, 'No, ta. I can manage...' and stopped.

Behind me stood Hugo Hahn. God, but he looked tall.

'Think I was trapped in the cabin, friend?'

He laughed, all tan and teeth, sinewy the way blokes should be and never are because we're idle and eat the wrong grub.

'No,' I said, eager to placate my way out. 'I was worried water would come in and—'

'You barricaded the wrong cabin, hey?'

Typical of me to do right wrong. I'm pathetic. He reached, took a hook off me with such a swift motion I didn't even notice. I'm so stupid I almost offered him my second hook. He shook his head in disbelief.

His laughter was all Hollywood, a belly roar that cowboys in Indiana use to show their contempt for greenhorns.

'So this is the great Lovejoy in action, hey?' I wished he'd stop saying 'hey'. It really annoyed me. He glanced behind and beckoned, his gun held so casually. He didn't need to point it to threaten. He knew weapons. I didn't.

She came up the cabin steps looking demure as ever, except now she wore the look of the loved woman, her eyes puffy but exactly as I remembered her. They had betrayed all antiques, murdered my friend Tansy, sad Paltry, and poor old Smethie, who'd tried so hard to warn me, and Hahn could do almost anything, now he had all the antiques in the hold. Buy a Greek island, any political appointment, simply on the nod from a bent prime minister. International auctioneers in Bond Street, Park Lane, Manhattan, Switzerland or Austria would climb over themselves to serve him. In my daftness, I'd been the instrument of his success.

He was smiling. 'The penny finally dropped, Lovejoy, hey?'

'Some, not all.'

'Watch him, Hugo.' She stood close to her man.

'This lettuce?' He did his Hollywood laugh. I was reminded of Burt Lancaster in his circus performer days. 'With one bound he leaps free?'

'Be careful, darling. He can be dangerous.'

'You seriously think I need to be, woman? With this dolt?'

'So what was it?' I asked her, coming right out with it. 'Remember when I said there's only three kinds of love? Which sort was mine?'

'There's only one kind of love,' Hahn said, interested despite himself. He still kept a weather eye on the sea, and had already clocked the two distant craft hurrying in our wake. He was a born killer made in the mould.

'No, Hugo,' I said. 'Ask her. She knows all three.' I looked directly at her. No watery eyes now. 'Which was yours, in the end?'

'Love is love, Lovejoy,' she said, all defiance.

'Three kinds?' Hahn said, so I explained.

'There's larder love, Hugo – security, money, possessions. It's a dog's love for its master. The word *cynic* meant dog-like. It's what moves a woman to leave one bloke for another, like catching a luxury express instead of some beat-up old trundler.'

'Stop him talking, Hugo,' she said. She was wrapped in a dressing gown, her hair mussier than I'd ever seen it.

'Why shut me up when I don't matter any more?' I was talking for my life. 'Hugo has a right to know where he stands. Didn't you just promise him perfect sexual ecstasy for ever? I heard.'

'Shut him up, darling.'

'Let him talk, woman.'

'The second kind of love is passion, Hugo.' I kept my eyes on the face I'd loved with the same delirium I'd once believed only antiques could bring. 'It is eagerness to vent, learn, take on human desire at its uttermost.'

'Third?' said the killer.

'Third is in the spirit, Hugo. It doesn't depend on greed or passion. It transcends, and is unconditional. I felt it once. I'm not sure any more.'

'Hugo, darling, you see what I had to put up with?'

'Interesting,' her man said.

'Most blokes hope a woman has the last kind, when it's only greed or passion disguised.'

'You're right, bitch,' Hugo told her. 'He is a fool.' I knew now I was to be eliminated. He held the bat. 'Get below. Dress. Be back here in five minutes.'

'Yes, darling.'

And she really did simper at the command in his voice. Whatever power existed in their relationship was his, and she was his to rule. She wanted it. For a fleeting instant I was envious, but her betrayal of everything – antiques, friends – was beyond me. OK, I was angry. She'd only once said those words to me, the same words that she'd cried out to him.

Stumbling forward, steadying myself on the rail, I saw the sea below going faster. The ship was not so steady as it felt the sea drift. He was strolling easily behind, called something cheery to Lydia.

'Yes, darling,' she answered. Had she ever said that to me in that way?

Reaching where I'd been sick, I stepped over the ghastly patch. (Why do carrots never dissolve? Can't the stomach handle the bloody things?) Knowing what was coming, I felt unsteady. The sickening realisation that Lydia of all people had betrayed me to join the vilest of killers, was the end. The trace memory of the woman standing near Tansy the instant before she fell to her death in Lincoln Cathedral, returned. He told me to stop. I clung one-handed to the railing and turned to be killed.

If I'd been a hero I'd have tried to leap over the side, hoping to swim and somehow survive, though I'm a rotten swimmer.

He slipped on the patch of vomit and cursed. I shoved forward, clumsily grabbed for the baseball bat. He let go to clutch the rail, his gun in his other hand. Gibbering with fright, I swung the bat, letting go of the railing to do it. I hadn't the sense to try for the thin end, so only flailed with the wrong end. He raised his gun hand to shield himself. I felt myself start to fall but thought, What the hell, reversed the stick and swung it. It clapped him on the temple. The bastard was still smiling, like he was about to say, 'What does this oaf think he's up to?' All in an instant blood spouted from his head, a splash dotting my eye, then he slid down to the deck and lodged halfway over the side. His chest stopped any further movement.

Head down to the sea, he hung there. Hell, but we seemed to be going faster.

I dropped the bat thing over the side – did they float? Wood should. With luck it would bob over to Eire, maybe plant itself and like Joseph of Arimathea's Christmas-flowering hawthorn Cretaegus at mystic Glastonbury. I clambered to my feet. I'd not intended to kill him. Fear, probably, or trying to get away. And it was nothing to do with losing Lydia. I'm not that kind of person. I mean that.

Wearily, I went to the bridge. No Lydia. She must be

tarting herself up. I judged the ship's position, and turned
the wheel so the vessel dragged her head round. At a rough
estimate, she was now some three miles out on the Irish
Sea. Four boats were scurrying after me with that odd
bouncy grace little vessels have. Police? Time to get clear.
I could come alongside North Pier if I got the speed right
before Blackpool's finest caught me. I increased the ship's
speed by a knot or two – more guesswork – then lodged the
wheel with the hook, and went down the steps and knocked.

'Coming, darling!' she trilled. Well, I'd always had little
or nothing, and she was onto a winner with hero Hugo
Hahn. Once. In life.

Clambering back up to the bridge, I saw we seemed
to be speeding. Had I misjudged the lever? Trembling, I
was too tired to muck about. In any case, I wouldn't know
what I was doing. We were batting – sorry – along at a
fair old pace towards the great North Pier. It didn't look so
pleasant now, but I could slow down to get off.

'Is Lovejoy gone?' she asked, bright as a button, coming
up.

She looked dazzling. Had she ever dressed up like that
for me? Yes, several times. Beside her I must have looked a
tramp. Why had she never been ashamed of me? Or had
she just kept quiet?

Her expression changed. She recoiled, staring. I realised
I must be splattered with blood. Like a fool I raised a
blood soaked hand to smooth my hair, with my usual
success.

'Hugo,' she managed. Then with alarm, 'Hugo?'

'He had to go,' I said, sorry for her. 'He took the boat I
came in.'

Blood seemed to drain away from her face like berry juice from a tapped flask.

'Lovejoy?' she said, making sure.

'What did you think he was going to do, Lydia?' Hard to keep bitterness out. 'Talk crops and weather? Invite me to be there, advise international buyers? I've already done that for him.'

'No.' Her voice was flat.

'He wanted to kill me.'

'Yes.'

'He had a gun.'

'That's blood,' she said.

'I know.' I didn't say it was Hugo's. I have a sensitive side.

'What happened?'

'I persuaded him not to kill me.' Her eyes were on my scraped knuckles. 'I said I mistook the antiques, and that the genuine ones were those left ashore.'

'That can't be true. They were all burnt...'

'In Somnell House?' By now well into lies, I didn't care. For once let her do the guessing. I was fed up doing it all the time. Everybody leaves me to work out which are the true lies.

'Hugo wouldn't leave me.'

'Well, he has, love.' True, true.

'Did you do something to him?'

'Me? To the only man who could be what you want?' It was the precious phrase she'd used. *You are the only man who can be what I want.* I'd once been awarded that.

'He will come back for me.'

'Yes. He said so, Lydia.' My kindly side, still there.

'I knew it! He wouldn't leave without me.'

Not strictly true. Uneasily, I glanced along the port side behind her, as if Hahn was going to come climbing back like in those double-ending Hollywood frighteners. In her voice was the contempt of a lifetime for the likes of me.

'Did you always think that about me, Lydia?'

'Of course. I finally saw you as the utter worm you will always be.'

She stood by the cabin gangway, above the steps that had taken her down to bliss with Hugo.

In that moment I saw how near we were to the pier. It was rising steadily from the dark sea and beginning to move at the bow of the ship with an alarming speed. What, a mile? Less? They measured distances in cables, nautical miles and such. Who knew what they meant?

'Why did Hugo kill Tansy, Lydia?'

She blazed into a cold temper – she never did do hot. 'You need to ask, Lovejoy? You preferred that tart, so she had to go. Hugo explained it and it all became clear. I too could have a destiny. *Me.* I have a right to own, to love, to progress. To have ambition.'

Hugo had done a good job in changing her. Or maybe it had simply been there in Miss Prim all the time, a murderous Lydia lurking latent within, waiting for the mighty Hugo Hahn to come along? I stared, appalled.

'*You* killed Tansy?'

'I had to. It was my commitment to Hugo.'

Well, poor Hugo was committed now. I told myself I'd never had any intention of hurting him, not the way I finished up doing. I must have gone berserk. I'd been driven by fear, not anger, nor hate. I mean that most sincerely. I felt sorry.

'And Paltry?'

'Hugo had special advisors. Paltry overheard Hugo telling me his ideas. Hugo's friends did it.'

'Old Mr Smethirst?'

'Hugo's syndicate bought that private hospital. He has bought a Mediterranean island for me, my wedding gift.'

She smiled tears at the beauty of their future together. Charming, truly romantic and full of gaiety. (And love. Mustn't forget love.)

'And me?' I asked it without bitterness, because I love (sic) a sweet ending. Truly.

The pier's black line was rising hugely from the sea. We were near and closing. I could hear the sloshing sea and faint shouts.

'You, Lovejoy? Hugo has definite plans for you. We should say goodbye.' She smiled with certainty at thoughts of my doom.

She pointed out to sea. Three chasing craft were closing in on us, the fourth racing for shore. One was hooting, searchlights wagging about the sky.

'Hugo's people, Lovejoy. He will leave you somewhere, I shouldn't doubt. I shan't mind where.'

'Alive or dead, you mean?' Two furlongs now at a guess, and lessening.

'You expect me to plead for you, Lovejoy?' Her luscious lip curled. 'I wouldn't lend a finger if you were in hell.'

'Goodbye, Lydia.'

She looked her surprise and almost laughed.

'Yes, Lovejoy. Goodbye.'

'And farewell, love.'

She was still surprised as the bow struck the pier

uprights and careered sideways in an ugly twisting movement that flung Lydia on her back down the gangway steps. She struck her head on the first of the cabin doors. I heard the horrid crack. I was carried by the ship's impetus and thumped into the side of the bridge, my head and shoulder ramming the control panel. Something short-circuited with a blue flash and shed sparks. The ship started a horrid whining, engines coughing as she tried to shake free of the tangle of metal, pier and bow caught together. She worried the metal struts like an attack dog does a felon.

Dizzily, I crawled to the hatch and made the side gangway. Down I slid, headfirst. The small craft was still there and afloat, its engine still muttering. I pulled the painter clear, got in and shoved off. People were yelling and sirens doing their whoop-whoop as I pushed the tiller and slowly sloshed clear to seaward. The *Maeonia* didn't seem to be sinking.

'Hey, you!' some geezer bawled over some electric Tannoy thing.

My boat was caught in a searchlight, a coastguard vessel standing some furlongs off.

'You! Pull clear this instant!'

'I'm trying! I'm trying!' I bawled back. 'Can I help? I was night fishing near the pier when that bloody great thing came crashing—'

'Pull away eastwards. That is an order!'

'OK, mate,' I called, then added feebly, 'Aye aye, sir,' trying for maritime yak. Where the hell was east? I chugged away, anywhere, from the scene.

The sea spray made my eyes sting so they ran sea tears

all the way to the sandy shore. How long was it, five minutes? No, more.

At the main beach, I nudged onto the sands and climbed out into the shallows.

Shivering at the cold – probably it was only the cold – I walked unseen into the night sea and sat down gasping for breath as the water soaked me. I let myself flop about as if I were half-drowned, rolling over and over. I stayed there for maybe half an hour until I heard the hullabaloo lessen. By then I hoped the blood and the rest of the gunge had washed off me, or that it was at least mixed up with enough of the sea's contaminants to raise doubt in the most dedicated forensic pathologists. Crawling eventually to the dry sand, I dropped my stolen jacket into the sea and stood trembling. Then I walked up onto the beach.

Not once did I look back at the rescue ships and police boats clustering round the good ship *Maeonia* and the pier. I was just glad no flames had started. The antiques would be safe. They were sure to have packed them well. Great planners, after all.

Love is never needing to trust, I suppose.

Chapter Thirty-Seven

slanting: thievery (Aus. slang)

Cold as an eskimo's tool, I woke on a promenade bench. A bloke was sitting nearby, shouting into a mobile, demanding his taxi. The people I least admire are reporters. Worse scavengers than me. The giant Pleasure Beach, with its spectacular Big Wheel and Big Dipper, and the wahwahs hurtling about had roused me. The newshound yelled he was 'working against the odds'. He snapped his phone shut.

'Hard night?' he asked, not caring.

'You wouldn't believe it.'

'Couldn't have been like mine.' He spoke with the usual proud grievance. People who do sod all always want worship.

'Bad? Good?' Despite my exhaustion I felt interested. How would the local rags print my calamity? Was he airwave or muck – meaning a broadcaster or merely newspapers?

'Brill.' He felt compelled to talk. 'Good for news. An ocean-goer got stolen, some maniac slammed it into the old North Pier. Didn't sink. The plod's gone berserk. Two dead aboard. Fucking *Marie Celeste*.'

'Nobody was dead on the *Marie Celeste*.'

He eyed me curiously. 'Right. I tried to get to it. The plod blocked it. Couldn't even hire a fucking boat. Like D-Day out there. Coastguard, fire engines. Nobody knows what the frigging hell's going on.'

'Whose boat?' Two dead, he'd just told me. Hugo and... I wasn't going to be the one who told Mavis.

'Some old-money syndicate. Antiques cargo.'

One of the open-topped trams, Art Deco in coloured livery, came slewing along the promenade doing its whoop-whoop. 'One of the boats, so early?' I said. A boat, in local parlance, is an open-topped promenade tram.

He gave the tourist tram a glance. 'Sightseers love destruction.'

'Who got topped?'

'A bloke, battered to death. Then a bird on a gangway. Police spokesmen are prats.'

'So you got the story.' I felt wobbly and wanted to scarper.

'Some Fraud Squad goon is up from the Smoke. The bastard never heard of press freedom.'

'Who is the goon?'

He looked. 'Do you know something I don't? Tight-arse called Kine. Bela Lugosi from a Hammer Horror.'

'What more do you need?' I was drawn in.

'Something's going on. I'd get a frigging knighthood if I could dig it out. Big noon meeting in the Free Trade Hall.'

'Manchester?' Twenty miles off.

'It's their ploy to keep us from that fucking ship.' A taxi drew up. He rose, paused. 'Sure you don't know anything?'

'Me?' I thought, God, they're double-shrewd in Blackpool.

'You haven't even looked at the scene. A bit odd. And you look like you've spent time in the water. Know why I sat here?' When I didn't answer, he said, 'I wondered what the hell a bloke was doing with no jacket, his shirt caked with sea salt, no shoes, hands a mess, kipping on a prom bench.'

'Dozing, that's all.'

'You have nothing to do with anything, right?'

'That's it.' As he walked to the car I called, 'Mate? What's your name?'

He stood looking back.

'Frendolce, Jass Frendolce.' He came back and gave me a card. 'If you hear anything...Why exactly *are* you in such a state?'

'My friends chucked me overboard.' I stuck to lies, the way reporters do. 'Somebody's wedding.'

He was unconvinced. 'Gelt in it, if you can help.'

'My friend Liza might be in touch.' I squinted up at him. 'Mate?'

'Yes?' He stopped.

'Lend us a note?' He gave the cadaverous grin of the cynic and made to walk off. I called, 'Best investment you never made, Jass.'

Pause. 'How much do you need?'

'Socks, sandals, breakfast and enough to telephone East Anglia. And the train fare.'

'Where to?' He scrutinised me, wary.

'Manchester Free Trade Hall.' I shrugged. 'If you can't, that's OK. Don't get yourself in trouble.'

He gave me a couple of notes. 'Got a name yourself?'

'You'll hear it from Liza.'

'Ring me, OK?'

He left. Caffs started opening. Getting on for eight o'clock, I crossed and had a mega-nosh.

New socks and plastic sandals later, wearing a scarf with a *Kiss Me Quick* legend, cheese rolls in reserve, I rang Liza, gave her a potted summary, then caught the bus to Manchester. I slept all the way, warmer than I'd been all week.

Manchester isn't easy on strangers, though I was no stranger. I hung back to be last off the bus, and won a bloke's hat off the rack. It felt as itchy as sandpaper. Warm, though.

The Free Trade Hall was once the epicentre of the world, when Lancashire textiles ruled. It's a walk from the bus station, where new trams – are they not really trains? – run along streets. I remember seeing old news photos of Mahatma Ghandi on that very spot. He was told the drop in exports of Manchester's cotton dhotis was purely temporary. I'll bet he thought, Yeah, right.

Strolling in the lovely city's centre, I lurked, like any criminal suspecting things were not quite right. I had a pal on Dartmoor doing time, who said that hesitation spells failure. He'll be free in four years, extra delaying time. Still, I lurked. There's truly nothing like Manchester's grand old buildings. Spectacularly beautiful, they were created in the conviction that life was brilliant, as long as *Manchesterturm* was mankind's sole faith and people worked for pennies. Half a century of meaningless conflicts that politicians swear are not really wars at all, have cured us all of that, and of the religions that go along with it.

Finally, they started coming in their limousines, none

with police, so they must still have been in the clear. And it was still legal to sell antiques. The plod must have been too busy with the *Maeonia* to pay the Faces any attention. Especially, I thought with bitterness, if most were diplomats. I found a newspaper and folded it.

Counting, I got to forty-seven witnesses, gave them an hour, then entered. Lovely central walkway straight out of Dickens, walls and ceilings embellished with the industrial skills I love. Is that what Empire was?

Signs *To The Conference Room* led me upstairs. Uniformed ploddites loitered with comatose vigilance. I followed the signs. The room was at the end of a corridor. I heard a babble of voices, as if the meeting was starting. A ploddite said, 'You all right?' No politeness for the likes of me in plastic sandals.

'In here, is it?'

He nodded. I stepped inside a room vacant except for Mr Kine. He looked up from his *Guardian*.

'I always read at least one newspaper, Lovejoy, to get my bearings.'

'It used to be the *Manchester Guardian*.' I realised I'd been had all along. 'Is it true they once banned Jews?'

'History does things to the mind.' He snapped, 'Somebody turn that bloody racket off.' It silenced. 'Too little history leads to mistakes.'

Nowhere to sit. 'I'd kill for scrambled eggs on toast.'

He raised is eyebrows in admonition. I went red and said, 'Sorry.'

'If you'd learnt anything at school, you'd have known the Maeonians conquered the ancient city of Lydia. Name of Hahn's ship, the *Maeonia*?'

'Your point being?'

'The conquest of Lydia gave the king of the Maeonians the art of minting money, weaving, dyeing, inventions. Including', he said with a smile from midwinter, 'the Lydian mode of music, his particular love. I believe Beethoven composed an oddity, *In The Lydian Mode*. Was it Opus 132 in A?'

'What is this to do with me?'

'Didn't you know? It's in all the papers. The good ship *Maeonia* got wrecked on Blackpool's North Pier. Dreadful. Know anything about it?'

'No.'

'Your apprentice, Miss Lydia, was dead on board. Hugo Hahn was battered to death. Your fingerprints were on everything.'

'I remember Hugo. Best man at my wedding.'

'In Somnell House.' He eyed me, so affable he should have been in rep theatre. 'Which you, Lovejoy, burnt down. Tragic. All those antiques inside.'

'Believe that, you'll believe anything.'

He sighed, so weary after his monstrous ten-minute day when he could have been at Goodwood Races quaffing champers.

'Let's stop this, Lovejoy. He stole your Lydia.'

'She was never my Lydia.'

'Shut it. You pirated the entire ship and killed him. Two birds with one stone, eh, Lovejoy?'

'Look—'

'He caught you at it. You took the chance to do her in too. Close?'

'Not even near.'

'Revenge plus unlimited profit. Does life get any sweeter for a bum like you, Lovejoy?'

You have to be patient. 'Mr Kine, you should leave your snooker club more often. You ploddites get delusions.'

'Then explain what happened. I'm willing to listen.'

'Got your recording box? Then here it is: I remember nothing of the past three days, from some accident. If you find out what I did, please let me know.'

'I have witnesses.'

'Can't recall a thing.'

He stood and gave me the arrest patter. I listened politely. It is the most absurd prattle ever, and I include Parliament. Formidable competition.

'You do not have to say anything. But it may harm your defence if you do not mention now something you later rely on in court. Anything you do say may be given in evidence.'

Could anything be sillier? If things weren't dire, I'd have laughed. 'May' only means 'maybe not', so it's heads or tails. And the bit about evidence is preposterous, because the prosecution – namely, the plod – don't have to disclose all their evidence, *even if they know it proves your innocence*. Laws are only for the law-abiding. There's none for the rest. Law is therefore a swizz.

'Can I go now, Mr Kine?'

'To the London nick, Lovejoy. With me.'

'I get car sick, Mr Kine. Can I go by train, please?'

His first hesitation. 'Very well.'

'I won't run, I promise. Can I borrow a coat? And some grub?'

'You'll be looked after, Lovejoy.'

'Ta, sir.' The kindest words I'd received in a twelve-month. Our policemen are wonderful.

This thought recurred because my arrest was phoney. They have to serve you with a written notice, giving the name of the officer concerned and other crud. It's their silly Code C under the Act. I could wander off any time.

We caught the train at twenty minutes past twelve with two plain-clothes men. Mr Kine sat in a first class carriage, me opposite and the two suited goons between me and the aisle. I was served with a good meal, and wanted to sleep the sleep of the just. Do I keep saying that?

Mr Kine kept up a desultory chat, asking things – Mortimer, Tinker, and what really happened at Somnell House to cause that terrible fire. Lucky old me, I couldn't remember. I said I'd help his inquiries, and meant it most sincerely. The two guard plods seethed. It's a sad reflection on humanity. I thought of telling Mr Kine to send them on one of those anger management courses. I asked them politely to wake me up if the ticket inspectors came by so I could explain why I didn't have a legit ticket. Mr Kine finally told me to shut it.

Euston, the train was on time. I was in the police nick before nightfall. Travelling in a Black Maria feels strange, like a great city is out there and inside it is almost silent. Mr Kine and his two nerks were replaced by uniformed ploddites. I thought of everyone except Lydia. My cell mattress was lumpy. A former inhabitant had tried to scrawl William Blake's lines about *Tyger tyger burning bright/In the forest of the night*, but had petered out. It reminded me that lately an old folio of Blake's watercolours, found in a Glasgow bookshop for a bawbee, was under the hammer in New York, expected price over 18 million zlotniks. 'Cost a jam butty,' the trade always grieves. Maybe I'd be lucky one day.

Sleep's always easy in clink. Being so safe, you see.

After breakfast they told me my lawyer was coming to discuss bail. I told the screw I needed no lawyer, being innocent, and I hadn't any money to bribe one.

'Shut it, Lovejoy,' the turnkey ordered. 'LF Volkenheid, Inns of Court, is appointed.'

'Who'll pay? I'm broke.'

'Friend guaranteed lawyer fees.' He chuckled, a witticism coming. 'Surprised you've got a friend.' Harf-harf. He cautioned me, and took me down to the interview room.

Four minutes later in walked Laura, radiant as ever. Stunned, I shook the hand she offered.

'Volkenheid,' she announced to uniformed plods. 'Can I have a moment alone with my client, please?'

'Right, lady.' They were clearly influenced by a beautiful woman.

'Please be on hand, in case he proves troublesome.'

'Certainly.'

'Lovejoy?' She sat facing me as they left. Slowly I sat in the other chair, a tacky table between us. 'I am your lawyer.'

'How come?'

'Your expenses will be paid in full. They are a present from your biggest fan.' She opened her briefcase – the only item nicks fail to search. She brought out a sheaf of papers. I relaxed.

'Fan? Who?'

'Time for you to perform the only action I require.'

She puzzled me. I'd never seen her so jubilant, like somebody opting for madness.

'Look, Laura. I've no intention of spending my life going in and out of court to please you lawyers.'

'You must accept, Lovejoy. I intend to apply to have you out on remand today.'

'Sorry, Laura. I won't trust anyone or anything except antiques from now on. So long.' She gestured me down.

'You entered into a contract with me, Lovejoy.'

'To marry you? And divvy a load of antiques so you and Hero Hugo could abscond? Stealing the dreams and wealth of all your pals?'

'Please do not be silly. That's hysteria.'

'Leaving me to burn to death in Somnell House?'

'Stop it.' No joy now, just a pale face with thin lips.

'Killing my friend Tansy, you murdering cow?'

'That was Lydia,' she said dully. 'You saw her.'

'I couldn't be sure, but she told me on the yacht.'

She suddenly went like a pricked balloon, deflated and listless. 'It's astonishing how far a woman will go once she convinces herself. After Hugo first took her that night, she became utterly transported. Having', she went on with spite, 'found a real man to commit himself to her.'

'Was she wrong?'

'Hugo treated tarts like her as a joke. We used to laugh after he'd rogered some up-tight bitch. He'd go on about them, the things he made them do. They went delirious with sex.'

'He fell for her? Was she wrong?'

'I thought so, until I heard her and Hugo talking.' She took an age to go on. 'Then I knew he was going to leave with her. Can you imagine?' Well, yes, I could. 'She was younger, almost pretty, and she knew antiques. Maybe she told him lies, said she too could be a divvy. I don't know.'

'The Castells reneged on you, Laura?' I was guessing now.

'Spineless. Penny and Donna went to Eastwold as girls. When they heard Gentry's lot killed Paltry, they chickened out.'

'Your plan was hopeless from the beginning.'

'Lydia went along with it all. Daniella got the Eastwold College list of past pupils, and told Tansy. Tansy's mistake was to tell Lydia. They went to warn you at Lincoln. Lydia knew, oh yes, she knew.'

'But poor Smethie did no wrong.'

'That was Paltry's fault. He was hustling in the George bar, overheard bits when I stayed there with Hugo.' She barked a hyena's laugh. 'He tried to blackmail Hugo. Paltry told Smethie Hugo's idea. It brought on the old man's attack. You know the rest.'

'So some were honest,' I said.

She almost smiled but habit was stronger. 'Smethirst was an Anglo-Dutch burgher of Ceylon, Sri Lanka. He was the only honest one.'

'Mmmh.'

'Smethie's daughter always hated Hugo, wouldn't have anything to do with her traditions, her origins. Despicable.'

'Two honest, then. Miss Farnacott and Mr Smethirst?'

'And Mortimer.'

'That's good, then.' I'd been waiting for that. The rest could get lost.

'Won't you accept my offer of bail? I guarantee your release. Mr Kine left absurd procedural holes in your arrest.'

'No, ta. My releases never work, Laura.'

She sighed. 'Then it shall have to be here. Still, it will be worth it. After all, I've lost everything.'

Out of her briefcase she hauled a heavy handgun, the sort you buy for 200 zlotniks down Streatham – or anywhere else these days, I suppose.

The thing mesmerised me. I stared at it. A genuine shooter? I'd no idea where the safety catch was, or if the damned thing even had one.

'What are you on about?'

'Haven't I made myself clear?' She had kept her gloves on since she came in. Lawyers don't do that, not visiting clients in clink.

Nobody was recording this, lawyer-client confidentiality being a myth you have to pretend. I almost screamed. Where were the fucking plod?

'There's obviously something you haven't heard, Laura.' My voice quavered. New lies make it do that, especially when I never know what they're going to be. 'So I'll accept your offer.'

'Stop lying, Lovejoy. You were jealous of Hugo's influence over Lydia. You heard of the *Maeonia* shipment and determined to wreak revenge.'

I thought, People don't 'wreak revenge' except in old Farnol books, any more than they say 'swashbuckling'. She was off her head. I judged the distance to the door. What would the screws out there do if I yelled for help? Laugh their silly heads off, that's what.

Gloves don't leave fingerprints. My hands could, if I were shot. She'd make sure of that. Wasn't it Chekhov who said that if you write a play with a gun in it, it has to be fired or you're a cheat? My breath felt hot.

'People don't say "wreak revenge" any more,' I actually said.

'Ah, but they act as if they did, Lovejoy.'

She was almost hugging herself, a little girl keeping an enormous secret from teacher. Desperately, I thought, This lunatic is my frigging wife, for God's sake. My mind went funny.

But maybe the plod were listening? I said, 'What's the idea of the gun?'

'The charge will be laid against you in an hour, Lovejoy. You boarded the *Maeonia* to kill him and Lydia, to make off with the antiques.'

'That's rubbish.'

She looked dynamite, so attractive now she was into madness. Conviction adds radiance to women. They take on a lustrous quality. We men can't do it.

'How will you do it?' I asked Laura.

'I'll wrestle with you, Lovejoy.' Amused, she went on, 'Screaming, of course. This gun will go off. The headline? Brave little woman struggled with a multiple killer.'

'Then you'll miss out, Laura.'

'Miss out?' Her features grew ugly. 'Haven't I lost everything?'

'Who else have you killed?' I thought back. 'The girl your husband, Ted Moon, was supposed to have topped?'

'Fionuella? She set her cap at Ted. He was always weak.'

The last tile in the wall. I invented new lies, fables, untruths, thinking how to stop her fondling that gun. Her addiction was Hugo Hahn, so I invented –

'What about Hugo, Laura?' I said it with what I hoped passed for assurance. 'His trial is next week.'

'Hugo?' Uncertainty showed in her eyes.

'Look. I don't want Hugo blaming me, with his flaming temper. Don't muck me about. You were in on it with him. He told me so last night.'

'Hugo's dead, Lovejoy. You murdered him.' But hope hung on.

'He's in Gonerstone,' I managed. Having to make names up always tires me, because I forget them. 'On the inter-prison phone link. I promised I'd give his lawyer Mr Smethirst's recorded explanation. As long as Hugo promised he'd get me sprung.'

'Hugo? Alive?' Tears flowed from aghast eyes. It looked weird.

''Course.' Impatience now, me acting away. 'Will he keep his promise?'

'Alive?' She shone, blinding me. I'm always impressed by the power of a well-told lie. She seemed as if levitated. 'It was…?'

'Don't come it, Laura. You knew. I just want out.'

'What's the evidence?' Her gaze raked my face for truths.

'You and your maniac Faces can get on with whatever you want. They're all diplomats. OK, I'm sorry about Lydia. She tried to fight Hugo and fell. Lawyers can prove it was accidental.'

'He's safe?' Rivulets ran down her cheeks. It would have been beautiful, except I remembered this loon had a gun. Did she know how to use it?

'Don't deny it. You and Hugo set it up.'

'Prove it, Lovejoy.' She fiddled with the damned thing. If I'd been a hero I'd have bounded across.

'Promise you'll get me off? In exchange for the recording?'

'What is this recording?'

'The chip thing Mr Smethirst did.'

'What does it say?'

'God knows. About the Faces and civilisations, the day before he died.'

Before he was killed by your killers, you bitch. I was begging in my usual whine.

'Where is it?'

'Don't blame me if it's a bit damaged. I sent it by post…' I let cunning show. God, I'd have been a brilliant actor. 'How will I know you'll not just take off with Hugo and leave me rotting?'

'I promise, Lovejoy.'

'And pay me the fee? And dis-wed us? No more Somnell House stuff?'

'That was a mistake. Those others…'

I stood and casually walked round the table. 'Swear it?'

'On anything you want, Lovejoy. And thank you. I almost—'

She had blossomed, was exhilarated, about to rescue her man Hugo even though he was a murdering bastard who'd betrayed his pack for greed. Like the rest of us, really.

Cocky now I was free of her threat, I extended my hand

as if to shake, and like an idiot said, 'On Hugo's life?'

'I swear it on Hugo's...'

Her eyes stopped smiling. Abruptly, they hardened in horror as my lies struck home. I screeched, grabbing for the gun. It went off with a deafening bark. Something shoved me in the right hip and spun me across the floor.

The table went over and people came milling in. I couldn't hear anything for a woolly thudding, like somebody's heart trying to thump hard. *Whose heart?*

Shouting? Was that shouting? Boots, scores of boots. I had a view along the floor. It hadn't been cleaned for a generation, I saw with detachment. Lydia would play hell with them for that.

Thinking of Lydia and how she would shed tears for me when she learnt that I'd gone, I thought, Oh well, at least Laura would spend the rest of her life in clink. The world began to vanish.

Chapter Thirty-Eight

to dup: to open, as in robbery (ancient street slang)

Hospitals are the pits. They leave you in a bigger mess than when you go in.

They took their time mending the hole Laura's weapon made in my pelvic bone. I now stood wonky, listing. The surgeons had done their stuff then drifted back to the golf course before another ten minutes' work was due. A tired house surgeon about eight years old came daily, but I soon proved too uninteresting to hold his attention. He too stopped coming.

It took a fortnight for Mr Kine to call, though a uniformed ploddite often drank coffee in the corridor to demonstrate eternal police vigilance.

'Better?' Kine had the nerve to say, plonking himself down.

'Managed to get through the security screen?' I felt sour, having tried three times to escape, each time captured by bad-tempered nurses.

'I have influence. I'm considering letting you go.'

'Not fixing up to have me shot by some other maniac?'

'Now, Lovejoy, don't start all that.'

'I didn't,' I said, nasty. 'Your madwoman gunned me down.'

He was unfazed. 'Why hold grudges, Lovejoy? It's a sad way to be. It was your criminal wife shot you, not the police.'

'You keep fitting me up with false charges, I'll tell the judge.'

'It might not come to trial, Lovejoy, if you'll sign.'

Sign what? I didn't say.

'A simple statement, then you can hop it.' He smiled. 'Well, limp.'

'No.'

'I have statements from Dr and Mrs Castell, Laura Moon, Ted and his Fionuella, and that dancer lady, Daniella. Oh, and your son, Mortimer.'

'All as reliable as ever, I trust?' I wanted Lydia to help me here.

'They paint a credible picture of events. Your apprentice, Lydia, is, ah, unavailable. You already know that.'

'And the Faces?' Emotion is a pig.

'The usual. Diplomatic immunity, skipped the country. Your affair with Donna da Silfa hasn't gone unnoticed by your lady friends. I failed to keep your reputation unsullied.'

He gave a bark of a laugh. He had nothing legal on me, and knew it.

'I'm leaving hospital tomorrow, Mr Kine. For a holiday.'

'Ah, no. Sorry. I can't allow that.'

'I've hired a lawyer. Phoned while your policeman was on his three-hour lunch break. I'm suing the police.'

'You're making this up, Lovejoy.'

'Wait, then. My two solicitors will be here in an hour.'

He'd had to suffer police procedure meetings, and not emerged unscathed. He was in serious trouble, having got everything wrong. I almost felt fond of Laura. Her obsession with Hugo Hahn put me in quite a good light. Playground stuff, but it was my ball now.

'I'll have to vet them, Lovejoy. You're in police detention.'

'Arrest?'

'As far as you're concerned, yes.'

I was interested, never having seen him lose his rag before. He looked ready for a scrap. Well, playgrounds after all.

'Go and finish your tea.'

He left in a silent rage. I'd guessed his position exactly. I was in the clear.

For a while I limped about doing a lot of groaning. Three weeks since my accident, and physiotherapists had done their worst. I was good for a slow yard. While the corridor plod chatted the nurses up, I nicked a mobile from the nurses' desk and tottered to the loo, where I rang the music school.

'Miss Farnacott? Lovejoy.' I spoke with cheery innocence.

'It is not convenient right now,' she said in that get-lost voice.

'It's about the murders you paid me to do.'

Lo-o-o-ong pause, then, 'I'm in conference. Ring later, please.'

'I'll be with police lawyers. It's now or never.'

'A moment, please.'

The mobile's battery was running out. I blame nurses,

those high wages and nothing to do all day, and still they can't bother to charge their phones. It's sloppy. Nurses don't get organised.

'Lovejoy? What are you ringing me for?'

'That Hennell,' I reminded her. 'He's my lawyer. I want paying, please.'

'Paying?' No ice now.

'I have your father's last recorded testimony. And your offer of payment for the desperate work I did for you.'

'I don't remember.' Her voice was appalled.

'The recorder does.'

I gave her the address of the hospital and told her Hennell could be through the front door in five hours if he got his skates on. She rang off in a temper. I told the nurses I needed my clothes to meet my lawyer.

Then I returned the phone to the desk, saying I'd found it in the sluice, earned their eternal thanks, and slept.

That afternoon I dressed with painstaking care, got the plod to help me to Radiography, and limped through Casualty Out-Patients among exhausted football rioters being sewn up. I sat by the hospital entrance. I collared Hennell by yelling 'Terminal!' a few times before the penny dropped and he came over. Two uniformed plods emerged and started yakking into their mobiles.

'Lovejoy.' Still sweating. His suit looked battened down ready for a Biscay storm. 'You survived, then.'

'Ta for the protection.' I wasn't going to let him off. 'Your success rate is down, Mr Hennell.' In a flash of insight, I added, 'Tasker will be pleased.'

He blanched. 'Lovejoy, there's a small problem.'

I cheered up. 'Yours, I take it?'

'You see, I like Tasker. But he is not given to kindly analysis. We may need to amend some facts.'

The day was suddenly much, much brighter. When people start saying *we*, they're trying to wheedle. I said, 'I once saw Tasker wrap a man round a lamppost. His limbs broke. Nasty business. Did it all himself.'

He ahemed and blotted his face.

'Also, Mr Hennell, I want this Laura marriage sorted.'

'It's done. Marriage under duress is not valid. I've seen the Marriage Records. It was never registered. I'll just see Mr Kine, then we can go.'

'We? All I need is the fare. I want to be back in my own cottage.'

'Ah,' he said.

Half an hour later I was seated in a grand limo on the way to East Anglia. Leg-Break drove, he who'd taken me to visit Smethie. He stayed quiet, but sneered a lot.

There was something different about the fairground. I climbed out making audible creaks to get upright.

The electric was back on. I heard a generator's comforting thrum, and saw two or three blokes heaving on guy ropes. Over the far side two lorries were dumping gravel, workmen laying paving slabs.

'Lovejoy.' Pete came to shake my hand. 'Welcome to the restoration.'

'Doing OK, then?'

He indicated the farmhouse. Lights there too, and the horse in the paddock looked decidedly smarter, its lads grooming it. A saloon car stood by. 'We're opening up in a three-week.'

'Great,' I said lamely.

'Thanks, Lovejoy. We start in Mehala Bay.'

I'd come to say I couldn't help, and here was Pete with his fair a going concern.

'Lovejoy!'

'Donna?' I smiled. Events were moving fast. 'I thought you...'

'No, silly.' She spoke with a woman's complicity so I knew she meant shut up. 'I came a few days early.'

'Good idea. Those trains.'

She took my arm and walked with me, her maid hovering nearby. Donna wore garish wellingtons.

'Pete is charming,' she said quietly. 'We see eye to eye, you understand.'

'Of course.'

'My proceeds from the sale can easily cope with Pete's fairground. It has all worked out.'

Hennell and Pete weren't close enough to overhear.

'What about the others?'

'My antiques are selling separately, Lovejoy.' And she trilled her little-girl laugh. 'No, Lovejoy. I don't need a dealer. A distinguished London firm in Bond Street is coping.'

'Sotheby's have had trouble with the law. And did Christie's behave themselves over the Princess Margaret sale? Why not me?'

She wouldn't listen, stubborn bitch, then made me promise eternal silence about her lustful smiles. I swore lifelong honesty, and meant it most sincerely.

We made our goodbyes and I left in Mr Hennell's grand limo. Not half as posh as Donna da Silfa's, but life is one long hardship.

That evening I reached… 'Hang on,' I told the driver's array of neck boils. 'This isn't my cottage.'

'No. Out.' He opened the door. I cranked out and stood.

'You made it, Lovejoy.'

She ushered me inside the small bungalow. I vaguely knew the area, on the outskirts of Sudbury. I felt like a visiting vicar, she still smart and brisk with something new about her. She offered me a seat. I sank into it, looking round. Thank God they'd taken my tubes out a fortnight before.

'What is this, Miss Farnacott?' I waited for calamity to strike. It had done a lot of that lately, mostly from women.

'You must be hungry after your journey, Lovejoy.'

And then I saw. She was friendly. Because I'd killed her dad's killer?

'Killing Hahn wasn't my fault,' I said. I almost added it was more luck than anything, but that didn't sound promising.

'Of course not.' She coloured. Her newness was a gentle air of submission. To whom and for what? 'Your meal will be up shortly.'

'Why?' I rummaged in my mind for explanations. This lady held a high position with lots of pull. Also, exactly whose bungalow was this?

'I have reassessed, Lovejoy, since I learnt everything. Your actions were commendable. I could not have found better.'

Did she mean me? 'Than me?'

'Correct. I mistrusted you, yet you sacrificed friends and wealth to achieve vengeance. That is true worth.'

Me, an avenging angel in unrelenting pursuit of killers?

'Sorry, love. You're mistaken. I'd no idea what was going on.'

'I quite understand, Lovejoy.' She became conspiratorial. 'Caution is everything. I bought this for you. Here.'

Bought? 'I live in—'

'No, Lovejoy. Your cottage was purchased by a lady with a vile temper. You live here now.' Anxiously, she glanced about. 'I furnished it in haste. Please do shop around. I'm rather good at décor. You'll live rent-free, of course.'

'What's the catch?'

'No catch.' She smiled. 'Freshen up, and I'll feed you. I shall appreciate having a man around.'

She showed me to a bedroom and ran a bath. New clothes were laid out on the bed. 'I guessed your sizes, Lovejoy, but you can buy new tomorrow.'

'Sorry, love. I'm broke.'

Her high colour returned fleetingly. She avoided my eyes. 'Cost is irrelevant, Lovejoy. Expenses are taken care of.'

'I can't pay off any debts, Miss Farnacott.'

'Jonetta, please. Owing each other is a thing of the past, Lovejoy, now we've settled in. Shall we say twenty minutes?'

She hurried into the kitchen. Was I a kept man? There were dangers, though. Rural as the bungalow was – I could see trees, a river, cows being boring – Tasker could zoom in and I'd be a goner. Time to scarper. I heard her humming and clattering in the kitchen and nipped round to the french windows in the living room. The garden led to…

'Lovejoy.'

Tasker stood there, still as a hunting heron. In the bushes two larger shadows loomed, his goons. I swear I heard them cracking knuckles. I thought, Rocco? Another piece clicked into place. That volume he surprised me by reading, the day I left prison. He was Tasker's serf. Then, I thought sadly, weren't we all?

'Tasker,' I croaked. 'I was just coming to ring you.'

'I apologise, Lovejoy.'

'Eh?' I felt the blood drain from my face. I'd once heard him say that before tying some bloke to a carthorse... 'Look, Tasker—'

'Let me finish.' He only ever speaks in a sibilant whisper but his meaning is never in doubt. 'I'm sorry you had to do it all on your own, but with the Fraud Squad around I had to risk somebody, and it couldn't be me, right?'

'Certainly not, Tasker,' I agreed.

'Losing Lydia must be a sad blow. In payment, you get the Antiques Arcade. The boys fixed Sandy and Mel. Fire that idjeet girl. She makes rotten tea. The Arcade's yours from today.'

'I've not a sou, Tasker.'

'You own it, Lovejoy. Make it pay.'

'About the tea auction, Tasker.' I didn't want any wrong memories troubling his sleep.

'You did well, Lovejoy. Good guess that it was a set-up to show your divvying talent. And your lad Mortimer didn't let on. You bred a winner there, Lovejoy.'

'Oh, well,' I said weakly. 'Stab in the dark.'

'Well done. See you.'

'Thanks, Tasker,' I called anxiously, making sure he knew I was a total ingrate devoid of moral strength.

He went round the side of the bungalow and I heard a car start. Gone. I sweated with relief.

Jonetta helped me to bathe, then fed me. Later that night she helped me to rest properly for the first time in ages. She was beautiful and full of kindness.

Next morning she went off to the music academy and her infant prodigies, insisting I stay in bed until she came back about five. I promised.

As soon as she'd gone, I dressed and got a lift to town from a passing dog-handler. In the library I got the Antiques Fraud Squad's number and rang from the main entrance. I asked for Joanna, on a psychic whim. She came on and said, 'Lovejoy? I'm so glad you called. You did well.'

'People keep telling me that. I still don't know why.'

'Clever old you! You stopped the Faces' antiques scam.'

'I rang to ask after a friend in Brum.'

'Fiffo? He's on my staff now, as technical advisor.'

'Oh, right. And Ted and Fionuella?'

'We lost interest in Fionuella as soon as we discovered she was still alive. That story – feared dead from an unknown assailant – was estuary gossip.'

'Of course, I knew that,' I lied, joining the winners.

'They've gone to live with Ellen Jaynor, Fionuella's mother. She runs the Yorkshire Foundation for Arts.'

'I heard,' I fibbed coolly. 'Wish them well, eh?'

She laughed. 'Anything else you want cleared up, Lovejoy? Now you're chained in Jonetta Farnacott's little nook?'

That hurt. A man has his pride.

'Just visiting, while I get back on my feet. Then back to speed-dating any old scrubber.'

She hated that. 'I shall look out for you, Lovejoy, for

when our paths cross. Oh, some messages. A lady called Chloe says please call. Lear has an urgent message.'

Dear God. Who from? 'Er, right.'

'About Veronica, your agent.'

'Eh?' I only knew one Veronica, and she…

'She's been involved in disturbances. A brawl with Penny Castell, who left an invitation. Then actual fisticuffs with Colleen, who is suing you for two forged ghost paintings.'

Who could remember lies after the sort of month I'd had? Colleen always wanted promises kept. Joanna's crack set me thinking. I could do a stunning ghost painting, pour my heart out as a tribute to Tansy, showing her all saintly and beautiful in lovely Mehala Bay. Time the Great Healer? Time heals nothing, just cools lies.

'Ugly to see women fight, Lovejoy. That Veronica is a virago.'

'Is that it?'

'And Daniella, your favourite sex pole therapist.'

'What the hell for?'

'Daniella's the one who bought your cottage. Veronica had barricaded Daniella out and the police were called. Your past sins are starting to annoy us, Lovejoy. Straighten things out, soon. Have a pleasant stay.'

'Joanna,' I barked just in time to prevent her ringing off. 'Look. Could I ask a favour? In the interests of, er, cooperation?'

'Go on,' she purred, enjoying herself. I shouldn't have made that crack about speed-dating scrubbers.

'Could you say you don't know where I am? Just for a few days?'

'Judging from the pleasant slumber you enjoyed with Jonetta Farnacott, you are fully recovered, Lovejoy. So, no.'

Gulp. The swine were watching me. Well, in for a penny. I wheedled, 'I'll help you with the antiques frauds, Joanna.'

'Until all these combative women flit from your rafters, you mean?'

It took me three goes to say it. 'Yes.'

'Say "yes, please, Joanna".'

Four goes this time, and a long swallow.

'Yes, please, Joanna.'

'Good,' she purred. 'Want a lift back to Jonetta's?'

'No, ta. I know the way.'

She laughed and said, 'Welcome home, Lovejoy.'

Historical Note

The 'Faces in the Pool' Lovejoy meets in this tale of antiques mayhem are no mere myth. They are features of history.

Called by modern chroniclers the 'Last Colonials', they were displaced from their homelands centuries ago yet remain the most staunchly independent of all ethnic groups.

The Germans of Jamaica, the Yiddish of Soviet Birobidzan, the Welsh of Uruguay, clusters of Old Confederates who took refuge in Brazil from America's Civil War, the Poles sent by Napoleon to Haiti, or the resolute Basters of the 'Free Republic of Rehoboth' in Namibia, the myriad remnants survive in almost every corner of the world. They live uniquely independent lives.

In his years working and living overseas, the author encountered many such admirable peoples, and his memories of them are the inspiration for this story. If his tale offends any, he is sorry; if it pleases, he is glad.

The words of the modern historian Riccardo Orizio say it well: 'But all of us, beneath our apparent normality, belong to a lost tribe.' However bizarre the origins and opinions of the Lost White Tribes, Lovejoy admired every single one he met.

Jonathan Gash